The Valentine Retreat

Valentine's Vendetta, 1

LAURA R. LEESON

CHAMPAGNE BOOK GROUP

Best wishes
Laura
aka Rachel x

The Valentine Retreat

Published by Champagne Book Group
2373 NE Evergreen Avenue, Albany OR 97321 U.S.A.

~ ~ ~

First Edition 2021

pISBN: 978-1-77155-438-1

Cover Art by Melody Pond

www.champagnebooks.com

Version_1

For "Miniseries" Tanya, with my deepest thanks.
You bring the tea, and I'll bring the biscuits. x

Dear Reader:

Thank you for choosing *The Valentine Retreat*. I hope you have as much fun with Megan, Jim, and Anthony Valentine as I did when I had them rampaging through my head.

As with many novels, this one started with a "what if…?" moment. If I remember correctly, I was choosing breakfast cereal in the supermarket at the time. Clearly the mundanity of my task had allowed my mind to wander and thoughts to run riot. And once they got going, those thoughts gained speed and traction, like a runaway train.

Back then, I didn't carry around a notebook. Instead, I drove home like a crazy woman to write stuff down. Now I take a notebook everywhere in case inspiration strikes.

I had such fun writing this novel, and there was still so much to explore with these characters that I couldn't say goodbye to them at its conclusion. As a result, *The Valentine Retreat* is the first in a trilogy. Find out what I have planned for Megan, Jim and Anthony Valentine when they return in *Valentine's Revenge*.

Laura

Chapter One
Saturday Evening

The knock on the door was firm. Even though Megan was expecting it, she wanted to ignore it. She didn't have to do this, did she? Taking a deep breath and holding the air in her lungs, she tightened the cord of the silky robe encasing her body, a tiny act of defiance. There was nothing stopping her from staying where she was and refusing to answer the door if she wanted to.

Why had she agreed to this? Why wasn't she in the bar with Jolie or, better still, at home in her apartment on the other side of town? What was she trying to prove?

Megan knew exactly what she was trying to prove, to herself more than to anyone else. That she had ridden out the storm without drowning. That even after everything she had been through, she was inching her way back to a normal existence. She was determined to be a regular person again. Whatever that meant.

She let the breath out slowly as there came another knock. This time three harder raps. Annoyance, perhaps. The irritation of being ignored, of being made to wait. Her heart rate spiked, even though logic told her there was nothing to worry about. This time the knocking was backed up by a single word. "Megan?"

"Just a moment." She didn't need a moment, not really.

It was simply another act of defiance. Almost imperceptible in its minuteness, but there, nonetheless. Enough time to run a hand through her hair, or put down a glass, or straighten herself in a chair. Not that Megan wanted to do any of those things. She wanted that final moment all to herself. She held out a hand, noticing the quiver in her fingers, taking hold of them with her other hand to steady them. The moment was gone. There were no further excuses.

"Come in," she said, gripping one hand more tightly in the other. "It's open."

The door handle swiveled, and a man entered the room. "Hi, I'm Jim," he said with a corporate smile. A set of brilliantly white towels embossed with the hotel logo was draped over one arm. "How are you this evening?"

"Fine." The word didn't really come close to describing how she was feeling, but it wasn't like he really wanted to know.

And she certainly didn't want him to know. It was none of his business. Sometimes exchanging nothing more than pleasantries was the only way Megan got herself from one day to the next.

She tried to swallow, but her mouth was too dry. This wasn't William. She had to hang onto that fact. It might be the first time she'd been alone in a room with a man since William, but this wasn't him. This was someone totally different, something totally different. She was in control.

Who was she kidding? She hadn't felt in control of anything for such a long time.

"How are you enjoying the city?" He busied himself organizing one of the towels on the creamy leather of the treatment couch.

The dark curls covering the crown of his head were razored into oblivion at the nape of his neck, his shoulders pulling taut the pale blue fabric of his shirt as he tucked in the edge of the towel. He shifted, knocking the rest of the pile onto the lacquered wooden floor.

"Oh, goddamn it." He failed to catch the words before they escaped, his gaze flicking in her direction. "My apologies. I'll go get a fresh set."

"No, it's fine." It occurred to Megan that this guy was lucky William wasn't in the room.

He didn't tolerate incompetence however accidental it might be. She forced herself to relax her shoulders, aware of how they had jacked themselves tight at the thought of him.

"If you're sure?" Jim looked relieved, stacking the pile out of harm's way. "Whenever you're ready," he said, gesturing toward the couch. "Would you like me to take your robe?"

She shook her head, unable to stop frowning. Turning away from him, she hoped he'd take the hint. She fixed her gaze on the city outside, the lights bright against the dark sky. When he did the same, she slipped the robe onto a chair and climbed onto the treatment couch, pulling another of the towels to cover everything from mid-spine to the backs of her knees. Pressing her face into the u-shaped cradle, she concentrated on keeping her shaky fingers still and her breathing regular.

~ * ~

As Jim poured a little of the massage oil onto his fingertips, he realized he should first have asked the client if she wanted him to use it. He could always wipe the oil off again, he supposed, but he'd messed around enough already. Knocking the towels onto the floor, then asking her for her robe? Anybody would think he didn't know what he was doing.

Not that he had expected to end up working as a masseur. A course completed a number of years ago, primarily with the aim of impressing the girl he had been dating at the time, had sealed him this job.

Pressing his thighs against the edge of the couch, he took a breath and let his fingers find their way to her skin. He began softly but soon had to increase the intensity of his movements. Her shoulders were tight, almost as rigid as his own.

Jim needed this job, no question, but he found The Valentine Retreat a difficult environment to inhabit. The place screamed opulence. Absolutely everything was available from room service, for a price. One look at the in-house restaurant menu was enough to tell him it wasn't the kind of place he'd frequent. He'd never had much time for meals with a bigger price tag than portion size. And twenty-five dollars a pop for a Long Island Iced Tea in the bar? The joke wasn't on the hotel, that was for sure.

If he was being honest, he was a fish out of water in these surroundings. He far preferred the atmosphere in the little diner he'd found a couple of blocks away. All he had to do was to walk inside the Tick Tock to feel his shoulders dropping a good couple of inches, to stop them feeling as if they were welded to his spine. A decent cup of coffee in there, and he was almost himself again.

He worked on unknotting her shoulders, his thumbs pushing in from either side, moving toward her neck. She shifted under his touch, the strands of burnt gold in her ponytail slipping further to one side. He pulled his hands away, concerned she was uncomfortable, that he might be hurting her.

"Your neck is a bit tight," he said. That was the understatement of the year. "Are you happy for me to carry on?" His voice sounded unnecessarily loud and brash in the quiet calm of the room as he waited for her reply.

Megan eased out a breath before she answered. "Yes."

~ * ~

In truth, although his fingers seemed to be finding every painful knot and kink in her back, it was a good pain. The sensation lingered in the heat left behind by his fingers, her rigid muscles giving in to the pressure and gradually releasing themselves.

She let out another long breath, settling herself again as his thumbs resumed their circular patterns against her skin. The Valentine Retreat wouldn't have been her first choice for a vacation spot. It was far too much like the kind of place she would have stayed with William. For him, the trip would have been about business—it always was—whilst she would try to fill the days with lonely sightseeing and shopping. And the nights?

Her shoulders jacked up again, the masseur's fingers hard against the muscles he'd only just managed to unknot.

Megan forced herself to focus her thoughts on something else. She would have preferred a weekend cabin in the Rockies, or a stay on a dude ranch, or a pop-up tent on a camp site. No, scrap that last one, camping was pushing it.

Too many childhood memories of damp Cornish campsites with her parents being overly enthusiastic about a brief glimpse of the sun and having a face full of stinking feathers whilst a seagull pinched her ice cream. Camping on the West Coast was bound to be warmer than Cornwall, granted, but she still struck it from the list.

Her cheeks warmed against the soft leather of the treatment couch. She was overthinking things, as usual. Best to simply go with the flow and try to enjoy the luxury one last time. It was unlikely she would stay somewhere like this again. The days of charter jets and extravagant hotels as standard fare had been left behind when she left William.

It seemed ironic that barely six months later she was back in the kind of place he would love. The kind of place where staff, ever fearful of losing their jobs, fell over themselves to make sure the guests were provided with every last whim. Where the disparity between the "haves" and the "have nots" was like something out of a novel about an Edwardian stately home.

She saw it in the masseur's eyes when he dropped the towels. The innate worry that she would complain to management about his clumsiness.

Little did the staff know that the innate worry wasn't reserved for them. There was always the possibility of another job, but some things were much harder to replace.

She wouldn't be complaining about anything this evening. There was nothing to complain about; quite the opposite. She pulled in another deep breath, aware of how heavy her arms had become. She hadn't been this relaxed in a long time.

Perhaps Jolie had been right and taking advantage of what the hotel had to offer on their girls' trip was a good idea. As Megan's body yielded the last of its tensions to the masseur's hands, she decided he had been a good idea too.

~ * ~

Was it possible she'd fallen asleep? Although Jim wasn't sure his skills were all that impressive, he had managed to get rid of a lot of the tension held in her frame, and her breathing was relaxed and rhythmical.

He withdrew his hands, reaching for a towel on which he could wipe the remnants of oil from his fingers. She wasn't moving. Her whole body seemed to have sunk into the leather of the treatment couch.

He unfolded another towel and eased it over her shoulders. This was her own suite of rooms, she could stay put for as long as she liked. He checked his watch. No such luxury for him. With a full schedule this evening, it was time for him to hustle to the next appointment.

Turning to leave, he caught sight of the lights of the city, all the tiny boxes of life on the other side of the plate glass window. Jim sometimes found himself speculating what was happening in those boxes, whether the lives taking place in them were more straightforward than his own.

An insistent ringtone broke the quiet in the room and made him start. The client jolted from the treatment couch. She slid back into her robe, eyeing him as she rummaged in a bag. From across the room, he saw her shoulders tighten again under their silky wrapper as she looked at her cellphone. She dropped it back into her bag without answering, the sharp pinch reasserting itself on her face.

"Sorry about that," she said. "I'll let you get on?"

"Sure," he said. "Was everything to your satisfaction?"

"Absolutely." She fastened the cord around the robe and smiled. A muted, half-hearted smile. Or perhaps it was simply a smile she used for strangers. A polite shape for her face to adopt without the need for any depth of feeling.

He gathered the towels, leaving a card printed with his details in their place. "In case you'd like another one." He headed for the door. "Or call reception. They'll be happy to book you in."

~ * ~

"Thank you," Megan said. His clumsy fumbling with the towels reminded her of the action of a tumble-dryer.

Then he was gone, the suite door closing softly behind him. In another time and place, a distant place she used to inhabit, she would have talked to him. It would have interested her to have found out more about him. Megan wasn't sure she'd ever get back to that place. It seemed as if every time she took a step in the right direction, something brought her crashing back down.

Her phone rang again. No need to check who was calling, she already knew. No matter how much she wanted to ignore him, she was going to have to pick up.

Perching on the edge of the scroll-ended sofa nearest the window and fixing her gaze on the view, she pressed the phone to her ear.

"Hello William," she said. "What do you want?"

Chapter Two
Sunday Morning

Across the street from The Valentine Retreat, Andy Mossbury glanced at his wristwatch. The heat from the morning sun was already noticeable; sweat was prickling in his arm pits. Not even half-eight, and he'd been sitting in his ubiquitous Ford for nigh on twelve hours already. He had a go at stretching his back out, cursing himself for not having chosen a vehicle with more comfortable seats.

Andy rubbed at the ache in his lumber spine. Being a PI came with a raft of drawbacks, but pulling an all-nighter was, without doubt, one of the biggest.

The long lens camera lay ready on the passenger seat, placed on the only patch of fabric not covered with cellophane wrappers and fast food cartons. He reached for the polystyrene cup lodged between the dash and the windshield, holding it up to his lips and tipping before he remembered it was empty. Shaking the container wouldn't magically make more coffee appear, but he took the lid off, just to make sure.

Sighing and huffing a laugh, he dropped the cup into the passenger footwell. The lid followed a second later, arcing through the stale air before it came to rest on top of yesterday's newspaper. He cracked a window, letting in some fresh air. It was a close run thing, deciding what he needed most: another coffee or a visit to the rest room. Or maybe he needed both with equal desperation.

He had an empty fizzy drink bottle somewhere in the car for all-night stakeouts like this one. But it was too late to use that on the side of a busy downtown street with the heat of the sun already beginning to make its mark. His instructions about staying in position had been exacting. They always were when they came from William Wiseman's office.

Andy prided himself on being the go-to private investigator for Mr. Wiseman, or more accurately, for Mr. Wiseman's assistant. Mr.

William J. Wiseman didn't trouble himself with anything as menial as a PI. Instructions were always received through Don Onesta's office.

His work generally consisted of tailing Mr. Wiseman's business contacts and obtaining photos of the people they were meeting with. Times, places, that sort of thing. Swimming with the sharks, Andy called it. Some of the people Mr. Wiseman did business with were…well, Andy didn't like to question things too hard. He shuffled in his seat, trying to stretch his legs. In his opinion, those people weren't exactly working for the greater good.

But the job was lucrative, there was no denying that. Mr. Wiseman paid handsomely, especially if the information he was provided gave him the inside edge on some business deal or other. Andy didn't much care what happened to the photos or the notes he handed over. Those sharks could handle themselves.

However, about eighteen months prior, Don Onesta had asked him to start tailing his boss's wife, Megan. Andy didn't know the ins and outs of it. He had enough trouble of his own with a son creating merry hell at home and a wife blaming him for not being around enough to be of any help. He didn't realize at first that Megan had filed for divorce. He had assumed that Mr. Wiseman suspected her of having a wandering eye.

Within two days, Andy was bored. She didn't work, so she filled her time like most rich women did: having her hair and nails done at the same time, same place every week; going to the gym; shopping and meeting with friends at expensive restaurants which charged a fortune for a half empty plate of salad leaves. She didn't hop into cabs and hightail it to a discreet apartment block to meet a string of lovers. She didn't have a secret penchant for strip clubs or blue cinemas. There was no sign of her trawling the streets for cocaine. In short, there was nothing to report.

The sole oddity in her regular-as-clockwork life was an unexpected cab ride to a chocolatier on Santa Monica. The break with routine had Andy ditching his car in the closest parking space, puffing his way back along the street in time to find her ordering bars of handmade dark chocolate stacked with pretzels.

He frowned as he pretended to admire the chocolate fountain display. He hadn't seen Megan consume anything that wasn't low calorie. Was she a secret chocoholic? Perhaps the guy behind the counter was the reason she was there. He was certainly giving her his full attention. Well, who wouldn't? Andy had to admit his boss's wife was a total knock-out.

He eavesdropped as she gave and checked information for the

chocolate's recipient. It wasn't for her or her husband. It was to be mailed to an address in the UK, for someone called Craig. Andy noted the name and headed back to his car.

Don was totally unimpressed when that was all Andy had to offer him, brushing the name aside with a wave of a manicured hand. But he couldn't provide information about something that wasn't happening, could he? He'd imagined Onesta would be pleased to be able to reassure Mr. Wiseman, to let him know his wife wasn't secretly meeting some man.

When news of the divorce became public knowledge, Andy understood. Don wanted him to find some dirt on the wife, find some way to blame the split on her. When it became clear—however hard the lawyers tried to squash it—that William Wiseman was the unfaithful one, Andy felt a stretch in his loyalty to his employer. It wasn't as if the man had a mistress, like most of the elite seemed to manage to wangle. Turned out he had bedded more women than Andy had eaten hot dinners. He huffed another laugh. The analogy he'd chosen was probably pushing the realms of believability, but suffice to say, the numbers for both events were considerable.

Couple that with the knowledge that Mrs. Wiseman had been playing her end of the marriage contract to the letter? He shifted uncomfortably against the fabric of the car seat. Andy didn't have to like the man to work for him, did he? Scruples were all very well, but they didn't pay the bills.

He hadn't expected to be asked to tail Megan Wiseman again once the divorce was final. Yet here he was, parked outside The Valentine Retreat with his exacting instructions. He was being paid double for this gig. Which made it slightly easier to suppress the scruples all over again. With the money he would earn from this job he would be able to take some time off, take a proper break and sort his life out.

He drummed his fingers against the edges of the steering wheel and yawned. He was tired, stiff, and cranky. Maybe a double espresso would see him through the last hour or two before the daytime guy arrived. He had to wonder why he'd been stiffed with the nightshift.

And his bladder? There was no way he could ignore that a moment longer, especially if he was going to add another cup of liquid to the mix.

He reached into the passenger footwell, feeling around for the empty bottle. If he hunched down and used the newspaper over his lap, maybe he could manage to relieve himself discreetly. It wouldn't take long. Unscrewing the cap from the bottle, he grabbed the newspaper and spread it out, peering underneath to ensure he didn't miss the neck of the bottle.

A few moments later he looked up, debating with himself as he zipped his trousers. Could he get to the street vendor on the corner and back again while keeping the hotel doors in his line of sight? Before he had decided, his attention was taken by a familiar figure skipping down the last of the hotel steps. Megan Wiseman, accompanied by another woman. Andy recognized her too. Undoubtedly one of her friends from the last time he tailed her.

The two women set off along the sidewalk, linking arms as they went. Damn. Caught with his trousers down. Literally. He'd missed his chance to photograph her coming out of the hotel, but he could be on their tail in no time. Sliding the sealed bottle into the footwell, Andy swung open the car door and winced as he stretched his legs and climbed out.

He shoved the newspaper over the camera. He couldn't follow them with that hanging around his neck. Photos taken with his phone would have to do. He locked his car, dodged his way around the slow-moving traffic then joined the flow of people. Keeping Megan in his sight, he hung back far enough to remain anonymous and sauntered after them until they stopped at a deli-café a few blocks away.

He took a seat at one of the tables just inside the door. With a clear line of sight to where the women had chosen to sit, he pulled out his phone, pretending to check messages while clicking a couple of photos of them.

I'll bet they make a great espresso here, he thought.

Chapter Three

"I'll have English breakfast tea, please," Megan said. "No milk." She shrugged off her jacket, slipping it over the back of her chair.

The server switched his attention to Jolie, leaving Megan free to scan the café. An elderly couple sat at the table closest to the window, and near the counter a woman with a tired expression studied the menu card whilst she did her best to ignore the griping baby in the buggy parked beside her. By the door sat a man, alone, his chair set back from the table to accommodate his ample frame and his concentration fixed on his phone.

Something about him was vaguely familiar, but she didn't recognize him. She certainly didn't know him. Her gaze drifted across to the display of pastries on the counter amongst which nestled cinnamon whirls drizzled with icing, finger blocks of tiffin, and a tray of individual fruit tarts.

"Do you want one?" Jolie said, claiming Megan's attention.

"One what?"

"One of those tarts. They look awesome."

Megan shook her head. "No. I'm fine."

"Oh, go on. Keep me company? I'm getting one of those cinnamon buns."

They had been through this process many times before. Megan stared at the counter, her brow furrowing. The waiter fidgeted with the edge of his cuff as he waited.

"Okay. I'll have an apple tart." She had no intention of eating it, but she had danced this jig with Jolie more times than she cared to remember. Watching what she ate was another one of her residual hang-ups from her time with William.

"Good. That's good," Jolie said. "So, how was it?"

"How was what?"

"Duh. The deluxe massage. Was it? Deluxe, I mean." Jolie leant forward, fiddling with the condiments in the center of the table. Her fingers curled around a pretty sugar shaker in the shape of a cupcake.

Megan had to smile. "Deluxe? Was that how it was described?"

"Yeah. Why? Wasn't it any good?"

"No, it was fine. More than fine actually. He was good."

"And in the comfort of your own suite—how cool is that? Such luxury." Jolie grinned.

Megan nodded. She didn't want to pour cold water over Jolie's kindness, but over the last few years, Megan had had more than her fair share of luxury. In her experience, it came with a high price tag, in more ways than one.

Now wasn't the time to be negative. This was Jolie's adventure, and Megan wasn't about to spoil it. An all-expenses paid stay at a swanky hotel. She remembered how Jolie's hand shook as she showed her the email.

"I won," she'd said. "I never win anything, but look, I won. And you're coming with me."

Megan could hardly refuse to accompany her friend. Jolie had been entering competitions for as long as Megan had known her. Back in school it had been magazine competitions to win makeup or concert tickets. Latterly, Jolie had aimed higher, entering draws for cars, apartments, luxury vacations like this one. Megan had always assumed they were stealthy ways to gain personal information and questioned whether anybody actually won. It seemed she had been proved wrong.

"So, while you were being pummeled, I went to the bar." Jolie broke off as the waiter edged a tray onto their table, unloading cakes and drinks.

Megan thanked him, then tipped the lid on her teapot, the waft of steaming leaves filling her nostrils. Sometimes Americans had an odd idea about what constituted a decent cup of tea, but this smelled good, with an unapologetically strong woody edge.

"How was it?"

"Cocktails in the fanciest glasses I've ever seen. The place looks like something out of a Bond film. Megan, there was even a guy playing a piano. Unbelievable. Let's put it this way, I'm glad I brought my best underwear." She grinned.

"Oh my god, Jolie. Why?"

"I think it's the kind of place a couple of good-looking, unattached girls like us need to hang out."

Megan's shoulders dropped. Not this again. Jolie meant well, but she wished her friend would leave it alone.

"Serious eye candy, my friend," Jolie said. Her cheeks colored.

"I met someone."

"That's great." Perhaps if Jolie's attention was distracted by a guy, Megan could skate under her radar.

Sometimes she wished she had the ability to bounce back from a failed relationship as easily as Jolie. Her friend had only split from her long-term boyfriend, Troy, a few months ago. Or perhaps it was simply that she was better at papering over the cracks than she was.

Megan blew on her tea and took a sip. "What's he like?"

"Blond. Smiley. Fun. His name's Chris."

"What does he do?"

Jolie's cheeks colored again. "Why does that matter?"

"It doesn't. I was being interested."

"Feigning interest, you mean." Jolie crossed her arms. "He works for the hotel at the moment. Anyway, it's not all about how much they earn, you know."

"Ouch."

"Sorry, but you know what I mean."

Megan knew exactly what Jolie meant, although hindsight was a wonderful thing. Megan had only met William because she was home from college and happened to be helping Jolie waitressing at a white-tie function he was attending.

When he asked her out on a date, Megan didn't recollect her conversation about it with Jolie including any stark warnings about being impressed by a man with money. Megan remembered it being more along the lines of Jolie being pissed off that William hadn't asked *her* out. She had a distinct memory of Jolie referring to a fairy tale involving a prince and a glass slipper.

"He called again last night," Megan said.

Jolie unfolded her arms and leant forward. "William?"

Megan nodded.

"No way. Really? Why?"

"I don't know. No real reason. Some nonsense about knowing we belong together, about last chances. Wanting to meet to talk, to iron out the issues." Megan shook her head. She wished she hadn't mentioned the call. Her stomach tightened at the thought of his words.

"Issues? Like the fact he shagged half the women in the city before you divorced him?"

"Thanks for reminding me."

"Sorry." Jolie picked up the sugar shaker again. "I don't understand why you don't block his number."

"It's no big deal."

"Yes, Megan. It is."

She sighed. "I know. You're right. But I have to think of Craig. I can't risk William changing his mind on that." Taking a sip of tea gave her a moment to think. "Sooner or later he'll move on. He'll get bored with me and let me go." If only she believed that. Sometimes she thought it would be easier to give in and go back. "At least he's stopped going on about me having the Easter egg."

Jolie dropped the sugar shaker, swearing under her breath as white granules spilled across the table. She swept them into a pile with her hand. "Did he ever find it?"

Megan shook her head. She couldn't believe it when William had given her the egg-shaped pendant. A genuine House of Fabergé white gold and diamond pendant on a long chain to celebrate their first holiday weekend together. She wore it constantly for months, back when things with him were good. More than good. Things were amazing, at the beginning.

By the end, though, she wanted nothing which would remind her of him. Having left everything behind, she couldn't understand why he kept referring to the Easter egg. She had no idea what happened to that necklace.

"Whatever he thinks, I haven't got it," Megan said, pushing the plate to one side, the apple tart still intact on it.

"You're not going to eat that, are you?"

"Nope. I'm not hungry." Thinking about William made her stomach clench. She wondered how long she would feel like that. Was it going to last forever?

"You're never hungry anymore." Jolie frowned. "You can't live on fresh air, Megan."

"Thanks, 'Mum.' Anyway, I had toast in my room before we came out." She hoped Jolie couldn't tell that was a lie. She'd eat something later. Maybe she'd even have lunch today.

"Changing the subject," Jolie said, "you never did say what your massage therapist was like. You just said he did a good job."

"He did do a good job. What does it matter what he was like?"

Jolie gave her a look. "Spill," she said.

"Oh, okay then. Tall. Dark. Clumsy." Megan couldn't stop the corner of her mouth twitching into a smile.

"Ooh," Jolie said. "Three of your favorite things."

"Stop right there, will you?"

"Why? I've said it before, and I'll say it again, the best way for you to get over William is to get under—"

"Oh my god, Jolie. Stop. No. It isn't." She was smiling though. "Come on, let's get out of here." She stood and pulled on her jacket, leaving some money under her mug. Jolie swung her bag over a shoulder, then Megan scanned the table. "Put it back," she said.

Jolie went for a bemused expression, but Megan had seen that look before. She waited, as Jolie bit her lip then reached into her bag. Neither of them said anything as she set the cupcake sugar shaker back onto the table. Then they left the café.

Chapter Four

Sunday Evening

Jolie headed toward the interconnecting door leading into her part of the hotel suite. "You're not going to dip out on me, are you? You did promise."

"Yes. I'm coming to the bar with you," Megan said, checking her watch. It was a quarter past seven. "Give me twenty minutes, and I'll be ready."

Jolie grimaced. "I wanted to curl my hair."

"How long can that take?"

"It always takes ages." She ran her fingers through the natural waves in her fair hair. "But it goes all frizzy otherwise."

Megan wasn't sure she agreed. To her, Jolie's hair had natural bounce and character, not frizz. "Okay. Shall we say eight o'clock?"

Jolie's face relaxed. "Perfect." She pushed at the door leading into her bedroom. "Oh, don't forget…"

"Forget what?"

"To wear your best underwear." Jolie winked and disappeared through the door before Megan could throw something at her.

She settled back against the folds of the generous sofa and picked up a magazine from the pile on the coffee table. There was no need for her to rush to get ready. When Jolie said she needed three-quarters of an hour, it was unlikely they would be getting any change out of an hour, at the very least.

Megan leafed through the pages, ignoring the glossy adverts and articles on jewelry and nail varnish. She half-read an article on the latest blockbuster movie, flicking the pages when she lost interest. Then, there he was, his smile almost as glossy as the paper his image was printed on. An article about LA's most influential men.

The double pages were populated with film stars, sports personalities, and businessmen. One of them was William. The photo was taken from the left side, his favored profile. Shown from his immaculately suited shoulders up, the dark blue of his jacket was offset by a glimpse of a deep ruby-red tie with a herringbone pattern. The beginnings of salt and pepper in his dark hair, and his expression radiated authority. It was the expression William reserved for corporate shots. His public face. It made Megan's mouth go dry. She scanned the words beside his photo.

William J, Wiseman, 38, built his impressive fortune from the ground up. No family handouts for this mega-star of the corporate world. "I had a very happy childhood," Mr. Wiseman confided, "but money was tight. I certainly learned the value of every dollar, and I think it gave me the drive to get where I am today."

When asked what he might have been if he hadn't been a businessman, Mr. Wiseman said, "A collector. I find it hard to let things go."

And the question all Living the Dream *readers want the answer to?*

"Relationships?" Mr. Wiseman's expression took on a wistful quality. "When you have loved and lost," —an obvious reference to his recent divorce from media-shy Brit, Megan— "it's hard to give your heart away again."

Swoon. I think plenty of our readers would like to help him with that. I know I would. Wendy Mackey x

Megan flapped the magazine closed and squeezed her eyes tight. Go for it, Wendy, she thought, if you think you're strong enough. Megan's stomach twisted, and she glanced at his photo again, looking more closely at the tie he was wearing. It looked very much like the one she'd given him for their first anniversary. Not an expensive tie but chosen carefully by her for its beautiful color—the exact red of the roses he regularly bought her back then. He'd loved it, and she'd loved him, back then.

Had its choice for the photoshoot been a conscious one? He had racks of more impressive neckwear. Perhaps he was making a point in case she saw the magazine. Nothing William ever did was by chance; she knew that well enough.

It had taken all her resolve to get through the divorce, to try to negotiate her way through his sea of lawyers and their legalese. To do her best to walk away with the only thing she'd ever wanted: the promise of a secure future for her brother. She believed she'd sacrificed enough to ensure that, but however hard she tried to walk away from William, he seemed able to keep pace. She just wanted him to let her go, once and for all.

Megan rolled the magazine tight and dropped it into a bin on her way into her room.

~ * ~

"I totally lost track of the time," Jolie said as they exited the lift an hour later and headed for the bar. "I'm sorry."

"Why are you sorry?" Megan said. "We're on holiday. Who cares how long anything takes? That's the whole point."

"I suppose."

"You look fabulous, so it was time well spent. You scrub up well, my friend." It wasn't an idle comment.

Jolie did look great. She oozed Californian color and curves and confidence as she led the way across the foyer. A whirlwind of life that sometimes left Megan feeling like she was trailing in her wake.

Jolie hadn't been exaggerating about the bar. Notes from a piano were just audible above the buzz of an already busy room. Something which sounded classical, but when Megan listened more closely, she could make out strains of Barry Manilow. She found herself humming along to it, trying to work out which song it was.

Potted palms whispered secrets to the pillars they stood next to, swaying gently as serving staff brushed past them. Most of the seating was in use, but there were a couple of unoccupied tall stools at one end of the bar. Jolie led the way, sliding her purse onto the smooth coppered surface. As she climbed onto the stool, her wraparound dress shifted, revealing a bronzed thigh. She smiled in the direction of the bartender and left the dress where it hung.

Megan glanced at her skinny black jeans and silky blouse. Perhaps she was underdressed, but she hadn't packed for seduction.

"'Made it Through the Rain'," she said, lodging a hip against the other bar stool.

"Say again?"

"The song he's playing." Megan waved a hand in the direction of the piano. A full Grand, the high polished grain of the lid shining in the room's spot lighting. "It's a Barry Manilow song."

"Oh, please." Jolie rolled her eyes. "You and your eighties music fetish."

"This might have been late seventies, actually."

"Whatever. More importantly, what are you going to have to drink?"

"Aren't we going to wait for your new friend?"

Jolie glanced around. "Might have something to settle the nerves."

"You really like him."

Jolie sucked in a breath. "I do. Crazy really, but sometimes I think you know."

"If you say so." Megan wished she still believed that with the same level of conviction as Jolie. "I'll have a glass of Pinot Grigio."

Her friend ordered for them both. "Before Chris arrives, can I say something, Megan? I know I keep going on about you finding someone new."

"Yes. I had noticed."

"I'm not talking about finding your new Mr. Right, nothing like that. Just someone to have a bit of fun with." Jolie shuffled on the stool. "I think it would put things into perspective a bit."

"Put what into perspective?"

Jolie didn't reply, her attention taken by the approach of a lean blond with a lightning-bright smile and astonishing blue eyes. From the look on Jolie's face, Megan reasoned this had to be Chris. A couple of paces behind him was Megan's masseur from the previous evening, Jim, wearing a nervous smile.

"Good evening, ladies. Can we join you?" Chris addressed them both, but he kept his line of sight purely for Jolie. "I love your dress," he said.

Megan caught a waft of Chris's aftershave—strong but not unpleasant—as she slipped from her seat and faced Jim. "Hello again," she said.

"Hi, Megan." He edged across until he could lean against the bar. "How are you doing?"

"Fine, thanks."

"You didn't want me again, then."

She frowned. "I'm sorry?"

"A massage; you didn't want another one." He held a finger up to the bartender, ordering a beer. "Can I get you a drink?"

"Oh." She smiled. "No. And no." Her glass was still almost full. "Not that I didn't enjoy it, the massage was great, it's just…"

He shook his head. "No need to explain."

"You're not working tonight?"

He frowned slightly and said, "Not enough treatments booked to fill my schedule this evening, so I've got a few hours to myself."

"And you chose to spend them here?"

He shrugged. "There are worse places to be. Are you in town for long?"

~ * ~

Jim settled an elbow against the bar and took hold of his bottle of beer. He was only a couple of weeks into this job and already he found himself doing his best to avoid spending too much time in the hotel bar. This evening a lack of massage appointments had left him at a loose end. So he had little choice but to accompany Chris, grab a beer, and see how things went.

A quick scan of the room cemented what Jim had already decided about the place. It was full of people with too much time and money on their hands. Gaudy jangling gold bracelets studded with gemstones, designer dresses and tailored suits, and the stench of expensive perfumes. There was even a guy playing a piano, for Pete's sake.

But the woman he was talking to, Megan, managed to outclass everyone in a pair of skinny black jeans and a white shirt. The shirt floated over her frame, discreetly hiding the gentle shape of her body. Thinking of that shape made him smile. His mind flitted to his memory of her from the night before, a clear picture of the curve of her hips and the way her ponytail waterfalled the nape of her neck.

She stared at him expectantly, then lifted herself on tiptoes and raised her voice to say, "I said we're here for a few days. Planning to make the most of exploring a few places in this part of the city in the beautiful weather."

Perfect. So now she thought he was deaf, as well as clumsy. "That's great," he said. "Can I ask you something?"

"Sure."

"Are you British? I'm not great with accents, but I think I've nailed it. I did think you might be Australian to begin with." He took a pull of beer.

"No, you're right. I'm British. Did my mentioning the weather give me away?" She shrugged. "I've lived here for quite a while, though. I thought I sounded like a bona fide American. Are you telling me I still sound like a Brit?"

"Yup. Without a doubt. Where do you come from? Is it anywhere I would've heard of? London? Edinburgh?" He was struggling to think of any other geographical locations in the UK. "York?"

She smiled. "No. None of those places. I seriously doubt you've heard of the tiny English village I grew up in."

"Don't be so sure. I'm a bottomless pit of knowledge. Let me have a guess." He trawled his memory for something British and village-sounding. Then he grinned. "St. Mary Mead?"

She laughed, and the light from her smile pushed up into her eyes. Little flecks of gold danced in the green. "Are you messing with me? That's where Miss Marple lives. Agatha Christie's Miss Marple."

"Yeah, sorry. I couldn't resist. Is it even a place?"

She frowned in concentration. "I don't think so… I don't know, to be honest. But I grew up in a place called Handleigh Parvill."

Jim hoped she wouldn't expect him to have a sudden revelation of knowledge about this Handleigh wherever. "Okay, you win. Never heard of it."

"Told you," she said. "It's quite near Stonehenge."

"Oh, okay. Yeah, I've heard of that. A big pile of rocks arranged in a circle, in the middle of nowhere. That's Stonehenge, right?"

She nodded.

"Fountain of knowledge, like I said."

"You said bottomless pit."

It was his turn to smile. "Yeah, that too. How come you wound up living in the States?"

"My dad came for work when I was about fourteen, and we all moved here for a while. But then my brother got into…" She stopped, sipping from her glass. Then she sighed, her smile gone, and said, "Long story short, they ended up going back to the UK. I stayed. I'd met someone by then."

Typical. He should have realized there was no way someone like her would be single. She must have had men fighting one another to be the one bathed in that smile of hers. "So you're married?"

She stared at him. He'd overstepped; he had no reason to ask her such a personal question. Except he realized he really wanted to know the answer.

Chapter Five

"Sorry," Jim said. "It's none of my business."

He ran a finger around the inside of his collar. Megan couldn't help but notice the path his hand took, the almost military severity of the razored lower half of his scalp in stark contrast to the brown curls on top. The smooth skin, already rich and vibrant and made more so from time spent in the Californian sun, wrinkled gently beneath his fingers.

"No. It's fine," she said. "I was married, but things didn't work out. We divorced earlier this year." She shouldn't feel awkward talking about it—there was nothing unusual about getting a divorce. It happened a thousand times a day.

"I'm sorry."

She shrugged. "It happens. We are in LA, after all."

"Yes, but any breakup is difficult, isn't it?"

He was right, but now was not the time to go into details. There was always the danger that William's "celebrity" status would draw too much interest. She'd found that out the hard way too. She decided to change tack. "What about you? Where did you grow up?"

As Jim told her about his family, it occurred to Megan that this man, whom she didn't know better than any of the other strangers in this room, had already apologized to her more than William had in all the time they were married. Being correct was an innate part of William, a God-given right. Even when he was wrong. Nobody questioned William Wiseman. They might advise, suggest, or even try to persuade him toward their point of view. However, there was never any question that the final decision would be anything other than his.

At the start, it hadn't come with the oppression that accompanied it toward the end. When they met, he was already flying high. He was a commanding, experienced presence. She was impressed by him, that was undeniable. But there was far more to it than that. This handsome, accomplished man romanced her relentlessly. He promised her a life of opulence she could barely imagine. And it was everything he promised it would be, to begin with. Jolie hadn't been far from the mark when she'd compared it to a fairy tale, and Megan couldn't believe her luck.

Even when everything went wrong for her brother, William had been like a knight in shining armor. He flew her back to the UK on a private charter. They spent weeks in Handleigh Parvill after the accident, whilst Craig was rehabilitating in hospital.

When it became clear that Craig's recovery had stalled, that he would never manage to live a normal life again, William insisted on providing the best ongoing care money could buy for her brother. He took all the worry away from Megan and her parents. She remembered how grateful the whole family was, how overwhelmed by his generosity.

She spent so many sleepless nights trying to work out when it changed. Trying to work out what had tipped the scales from two people being in love into a very different relationship. A one-sided power struggle. When did she notice him begin to expect her to be grateful, to be compliant with his wishes purely because it was what *he* wanted?

Had it always been there, and she had chosen not to notice? Maybe he had never seen her as anything more than another piece of property. Something he wanted to own and went after until he had secured it. Something to add to his portfolio. Maybe she had been nothing more to him than a naïve and easily manipulated piece of stock.

Megan puffed out her cheeks, bringing herself back into the warmth and color of the room with a quick glance around.

Jim was watching her, the edges of his walnut-brown eyes crinkling as he said, "You look like you're a million miles away. Are you okay?"

"I'm fine."

"Is that a British thing?" he asked. "Being *fine*? Or is it a code word for 'leave me alone, you moron?'"

She smiled at his perceptiveness. "A bit of both." Although, once the words were out, she realized she didn't want him to leave her alone. He was easy to talk to, and amusing, but there was something else. He was treating her as an equal; he was interested in what she had to say. Perhaps not earth-shattering, but definitely refreshing. "But only a bit." She drained her glass.

"Let me get you another?"

She recognized this as the moment to say no. This was when she should make it abundantly clear she wasn't interested, that there was nothing she wanted less than to spend a moment longer in his company. Despite Jolie's best efforts to drag Megan out of her shell, over the last few months she became more convinced than ever that she would spend the rest of her life on her own, living in a mobile home in Connecticut. Sharing her life with a bunch of cats. And she hated cats.

Which was why she frowned at herself when she said, "All right. I'll have a Pinot Grigio. A small one."

The pianist had moved on to a repertoire of show tunes by the time Megan finished her second glass of wine. Whilst she waited to see if Jim could work out the answer to her fiendishly difficult eighties pop quiz question, she pressed her fingers to her cheek, hyper-aware of the muscles in her face.

Jim scratched his forehead, his face a picture of concentration. She was about to tell him the answer, but he held a hand up. "No, don't tell me, I'll work it out in a second."

She was sure he'd never get it. The reference she'd given him about George Michael was far too obscure.

"Was it Aretha Franklin?" he said. "I can't remember the name of the song though."

She smiled. "Yes. How did you get that one?" His eighties music trivia knowledge was almost as comprehensive as her own. Now she knew why her face hurt. She hadn't smiled this much in ages.

He looked triumphant. "Told you I was a fountain of knowledge." He grinned. "Or bottomless pit, whichever way you choose to view it."

"Definitely a fountain of knowledge," she said, slipping her glass onto the bar. She should head back to the suite soon. She'd already stayed far longer than she had intended.

"Okay, I've got one for you," he said, but he never finished the sentence.

A strong waft of aftershave with a heavy floral note took their attention and heralded the arrival of an immaculately dressed man, tall and dark, with a smile that oozed confidence. Jim's expression tightened, and he shifted to give the man his full attention.

"How are you this evening, Jim? Everything good?" He clasped Jim by the shoulder. Without waiting for a reply, he focused on her. "Delighted to meet you. I'm Anthony Valentine. I hope you're enjoying your stay in my hotel." He thrust the hand that had been resting on Jim's shoulder in her direction. She shook it. "May I have the pleasure of your name?"

"Megan. Megan Leadbetter." It was time she got used to using her maiden name again.

"I hope Jim is looking after you to your satisfaction?"

She nodded. "He is."

She wasn't sure why it would be Jim's responsibility to look after her in the bar, but perhaps it was nothing more than an old-fashioned attitude. An outdated piece of chivalry. The guy must be in his late fifties—there was no disputing the deep crows' feet radiating from the corners of his eyes—but his hair was a carefully styled shade of mahogany. The flourish of a purple tie and matching corner of a folded handkerchief visible in a top pocket added to the aura of a painstakingly curated exterior.

He moved on to Chris and Jolie, giving them the same greeting, beaming a smile in Jolie's direction. Mr. Valentine looked as if he was about to walk away, then glanced back at Jim. He held Jim's gaze as he pulled at one of his cufflinked sleeves, then he moved away.

"Interesting guy," Megan said to Jim. "Is he a good boss?"

Jim shoved his glass onto the bar, fussing with the sleeves of his shirt to reveal a red braid on his right wrist as he tilted his head. "Depends on what you call good." His expression took on an unfocussed edge, as though something was distracting his thoughts.

"Are you happy working here?"

He laughed. "I've worked at worse joints than this. It's fine."

"You're as bad as me," she said.

He frowned. "What do you mean?"

"You said it's *fine*." She wondered if he used the word with the same level of unspoken pathos she did.

"Oh, yes. I suppose I did. Does that make me into an honorary Brit?" His face took on the light crinkle of a smile.

"If you like." She smiled back and held his gaze.

It occurred to her that she should look somewhere else, focus on the tune the pianist had moved on to, or on something else in the room. If she didn't, he might get the wrong idea and think she was interested in him. But she was having trouble making her eyes comply. They seemed perfectly happy with their current view.

Jolie bumped arms with her, breaking the spell. "Sorry to interrupt," she said. "Can I have a quick word?"

"What is it?"

Jolie's cheeks were flushed, her speech soft around the edges, and her breath was spiked with alcohol as she leant against Megan's ear. "I'm going to the suite with Chris. Do you mind?"

"No. Why would I?"

"How's it going with what's-his-name?"

Megan would have been surprised if most of the bar hadn't heard Jolie's attempt at a whisper. "His name is Jim. This evening's been—"

"Don't you dare say fine," Jolie said, a fraction too loudly.

"I wasn't going to." Megan tilted her head so she was sure only

Jolie would hear. "It's been fun. He's interesting."

"Coming from you, that is awesome progress," she said, winking. "Just remember, don't do anything I wouldn't do, you hear me?"

"That doesn't leave much off the table." Megan smiled as she said it. Jolie had always been far wilder than she was ever likely to be.

"Remember, the night is young, and so are you," Jolie said, taking hold of Chris's hand and leading him away.

~ * ~

Jim tried not to listen to the conversation, although it was difficult not to hear at least fifty percent of it. He forced himself to stare into the distance and pretended to be fascinated by the pianist's choice of music. Chris and Megan's friend wound their way out of the bar, toward the foyer and the bank of lifts. He pulled in a deep breath and smiled at Megan.

"One for the road?" he said, placing a hand on the bar, willing her to say yes.

"Haven't you got somewhere you would rather be?" she said.

It was true he was still on the hotel's clock, and Jim reasoned he could find other things to do to fill the time. Something in the spa supply room, perhaps, like sorting towels or checking stock levels. But why would he want to do that when he was enjoying the company of a woman like Megan?

"Nope," he said.

"I think it might be polite for me to stay down here for a while longer, if you've got nothing to rush off for." Her line of sight flicked in the direction in which her friend had gone.

He nodded, clearing his throat. He was well aware Megan and Jolie were sharing a suite. Separate en suite bedrooms, but with a communal living space in which he had treated Megan the previous evening.

"I don't want to crash Jolie's party," she said, the pale skin of her cheeks gaining a notch or two of color. "But I don't want any more alcohol." She looked conflicted.

"How about coffee?"

"Yes. That would be good."

Having ordered it, he found them somewhere to sit, pushing the red braided wrist tie beneath the cuff of his shirt as he took a seat. Although Mr. Valentine insisted it should be visible, Jim didn't enjoy feeling as if he were branded like a bull, so he hid it whenever possible. Megan hadn't made any mention of it. She didn't seem to be aware of its significance, which suited him perfectly. He did his best to steer clear of the guests who knew what it meant.

The coffee was good—hot and strong—and while they drank it, Jim discovered another commonality between them when he mentioned the diner he had found a couple of blocks away.

Megan loved diners too, albeit for different reasons. She said she loved their individuality, and the cultural heritage attached to them, the style of the interiors, the microcosm of life within their doors.

She laughed when he told her he mostly liked them for the food, but he didn't mind. He managed to make her laugh three more times before her cup was empty, before she looked at her watch. "I'd better go," she said.

"Let me walk you to your room," he said. He hoped it didn't sound too desperate. Too small-town boy trying hard to impress. But he wanted her to be impressed.

"There's really no need," she said, climbing to her feet, the tone of her voice starchy. "I'm sure I can find it all by myself."

He stood too. He'd blown it and offended her. About to try to clamber out of the hole he'd dug for himself, he was surprised when she touched his sleeve.

"I apologize," she said. "That sounded a bit harsh. I need to go." She headed toward the foyer. "Thanks for a great evening, Jim."

She was almost at the elevators when he caught up to her. "My pleasure. Don't forget to book another massage, if you'd like?"

"Maybe. I'll see how I feel." The gentle shake of her head was magnified by the swing of her hair. He was losing her attention. "Thanks, though," she said, smiling at him and pressing the elevator button.

He was running out of time, unexpectedly flustered at the prospect of not seeing her again. "Listen, it's probably a crazy idea, but how about I give you a head start on places to visit in the area?"

The elevator lights blinked, a countdown he had no control over.

"What do you mean?"

"Well, we could meet at the diner I told you about. Get something to eat. I could give you the lowdown on the area's hidden gems." He shoved his hands into pockets, trying to appear unconcerned by her reply. Trying not to think of the repercussions this could have on the complications he already had in his life.

The gold flecks in her emerald eyes dulled to match her expression as she frowned. The elevator door pinged. Then she said, "Okay. Yes. Why not?" She backed into the gaudy yellow light of the lift space. "What time?"

"Half past nine tomorrow?"

"Half past nine." She nodded, reaching out to the button for her floor. "See you in the morning, Jim."

The doors slid closed, leaving him staring at his mottled reflection in the brushed steel.

Running a hand through his hair, he puffed out his cheeks. Nothing like adding an unexpected layer of complexity to things. With a half hour before he was off the clock, he shuffled the red braid back down his sleeve in case he saw Mr. Valentine again and headed back into the bar.

Chapter Six

Andy Mossbury wiggled the inflated travel pillow around his neck. It was as hard as a rock. He'd over-inflated it. He pulled it off and adjusted the amount of air inside, squashing it between his fingers until he was satisfied.

Shoving it back around his neck, he shifted in his seat. Even though he didn't want to look like he was preparing to spend the night in his car, especially to the casual passerby or any cops who might be patrolling, this evening he'd made sure he was more organized.

Having taken over from the daytime guy tasked with watching Megan Wiseman a couple of hours ago, Andy had already munched his way through a cheeseburger with a side order of fries and slaw. The pickles which had been wedged between the bun and the cheese now lay amongst the wrappers in the abandoned paper bag in the footwell.

Not for the first time he questioned the logic of putting pickles on a burger in the first place. Who in their right mind ate them?

He should have asked the server to hold the green stuff, but he was in a rush to get back into position outside The Valentine Retreat. The teenage streak of fresh air in the Happy Burger franchise couldn't have looked less interested in customer satisfaction if he tried, so Andy went for the line of least resistance. He figured it would be both quicker and simpler to keep requests for the customization of his food to a minimum.

Shifting in his seat again, he arched his back to let a pocket of trapped air work its way back up from his stomach. He belched, then frowned and cracked a window. Maybe the apple turnover could keep until later. Let the burger settle for a while.

Instead, he poured himself some black coffee from the travel mug he remembered to make up *and* bring. Ten out of ten for planning ahead. He congratulated himself as he took a sip, then swore as heat bit at his lip. He recoiled, slopping liquid fire down his shirt.

"Goddamn it," he said, clutching the still half-full beaker in one hand as he batted at his chest with a Happy Burger paper napkin. His last clean shirt too. "Goddamn it," he repeated.

He should have been sensible and visited the laundromat earlier in the day. Even on Andy's sliding scale of cleanliness, the visit was well and truly overdue. The duffle bag containing dirty linen didn't bear unzipping. Added to which, if his final pair of "do-another-day" boxers and socks had fingernails they'd be struggling to hold onto that ambitious job description.

In other words, Andy needed to sort out his shit.

That was easier said than done. If what needed sorting was purely dirty laundry, he would have been in with a fighting chance. There was no doubt he would visit the laundromat at some point. His clothes would become clean and dry again. He wouldn't go so far as to press any of them, that was a sure-fire definite. Living on a friend's futon had a way of giving you an air of permanent wrinkle, whether you liked it or not.

Anyway, his personal hygiene, although definitely an issue at this point with coffee all over his last clean shirt, wasn't the real problem. It was a symptom of the problem, but it wasn't the root cause. He knew it was only a matter of time before he had to do something about the root cause. He had some decisions to make.

The sudden intrusion of a ringtone almost made him spill the coffee again. He dropped the dirty napkin, lodged the beaker against the windshield, and glanced around for the source of the noise. If this was it—the call he was waiting for from inside the hotel—he would have no time to do anything about his attire. He'd have to go in, coffee-stained shirt or not.

Ripping the travel pillow from behind his neck and throwing it into the back seat, he checked to see if his sports jacket was where he left it, on the rear parcel shelf. He could cover the worst of the stain if he zipped that up, he supposed.

Pushing a newspaper out of the way, he located the phone on the passenger seat, next to his high-end digital camera, and held it to an ear.

Adrenalin kicked in. His heart always rattled like a freight train when the game was afoot, and he fought to keep his breathing regular as he said, "Yes?"

"Andy? It's Rhonda."

He puffed out a breath as his heart rate returned to near normal. "Hi, Rhonda."

"Andy, I'm phoning on behalf of Mr. Onesta. He wants to know if you're in position?"

It was Onesta's PA, checking up on him. In Andy's opinion, Onesta's inability to trust any of William Wiseman's employees to get on with their jobs without the need for constant checkups said more about Onesta than it did any of those working under his direction.

Or perhaps he was under pressure to justify himself in the big man's eyes.

When Andy referenced the "big man," he meant Mr. Wiseman. Andy was ninety-nine percent convinced that Onesta held Wiseman higher up the pecking order than he did the good Lord Almighty.

"Is he still there? Or has he left you to it while he's out hobnobbing with local dignitaries?" Andy pushed the cuff of a sleeve, checking his watch. It was gone ten-thirty. "I can't believe he's still got you in the office, have you seen the time?" He didn't wait for Rhonda to reply. "Tell him I'm opposite the hotel with eyes on the door, as requested. Been here since nine this evening, so there's no need for him to try to short me on my hours, either."

She chuckled on the other end of the line. "I will make a note of that."

"Is he there right now?"

"That's correct."

"Did his date with the mayor fall through?" The corners of his lips twitched. Rhonda may work for one of the slipperiest men around, but she was well aware of the kind of animal he was. She had almost as little respect for Onesta as Andy did.

"I believe that may well be the case."

He could hear the smile in her voice. "It's a shame he doesn't realize there are so many products out there to combat bad breath."

This time she laughed out loud. "Shall I pass that information on to him?"

"Not until after I've been paid, Rhonda." Andy enjoyed chatting with her. He liked to think it was flirting, albeit of a very gentle nature because she always seemed to have a boyfriend in tow. "Actually," he said, "better make that after I've retired."

"No problem, Andy. I'll give Mr. Onesta the pertinent facts."

"Of which there aren't any. Nothing to report up to this point, apart from the fact I'm here, and I'm already bored and cranky. How many nights is this thing going to take?"

There was a muffled conversation on the other end of the line as she asked the question and received the reply. "Mr. Onesta says hang in there, Andy. Shouldn't be too long."

"Is that snake-speak for he's got no idea?"

"Something like that."

"Thought so." He hung up and tossed the phone back onto the seat, picking up his coffee instead.

It was cooler now, and he drank it without further incident.

Chapter Seven
Monday Morning

Megan faced the full-length window, taking in the view. Concrete, steel, and golden windows twinkled with reflected light. Another glorious city morning, with the sun already making progress on its well-worn arc into a clear sky. She checked the time. It would only take twenty minutes or so to walk to the diner. If she went.

It made far more sense for her to ignore the fact that she'd agreed to meet Jim. To stay put in the hotel and grab some breakfast with Jolie before they went out for the day. To keep things on an even keel, ensure the status quo and remain squashed into the box William had given Megan to live in when he agreed to the divorce.

She pulled in a deep breath. It had been easier to let the people she cared about think the divorce was an end to it. The final full stop in a badly punctuated sentence. But she knew, from the moment she instructed her lawyers and William heard about it, that it was going to be anything but simple. He wasn't the kind of person to agree to anything unless it was stacked in his favor.

However, there was no way she could survive under his stifling control for much longer, couldn't tolerate the string of lovers he did little, if anything, to hide. She realized that if she didn't leave him, she was going to lose the final strands of self-respect she had managed to cling on to. She would end up materially rich, but emotionally bankrupt.

Initially he'd laughed at her, reminding her that the pre-nuptial agreement she signed ensured she had no claim on any but the smallest fraction of his fortune. She remembered the look of triumph on his face. It was clear he was sure the threat of losing her lifestyle would be enough to persuade her to stay.

She made it clear she wasn't interested in trying to take a share of his money for herself. More than that, she didn't want her moment of fame in the press. She didn't even want any of the jewelry or artwork he'd bought her during their marriage.

The only thing she did want from him was a promise to continue to pay for Craig's care. The residential home William found for her brother was perfect. Close to her parents in Handleigh Parvill and more than equipped to give Craig the best life he could have, it was also privately run and fiendishly expensive.

The thought of telling her parents not only that she was divorcing the man out of whom they believed the sun shone, but that they would have to pay for Craig's care themselves—or move him—was too much to cope with. It would mean they would end up selling the family home to finance the costs, rather than take him away from the place he loved.

When his lawyers instructed hers that, subject to a few details, William had agreed to continue to support Craig's care costs, Megan had experienced a spike of hope. Perhaps she had misjudged William. Maybe she had been so far down her own rabbit hole by that point she had lost sight of a normal perspective on the situation. Then the lawyers went on to explain the details. The terms and conditions which would go hand-in-hand with the financial agreement.

It had William and his inability to let anything slip through his fingers written all over it.

If she wanted to secure Craig's future care, there was no option but to sign the super injunction and continue to live under William's control, albeit no longer under his roof. At the time, that had seemed the best option, she still believed that, but it made her acceptance of the invitation to meet Jim this morning a crazy one.

She enjoyed his company, that much wasn't in dispute. In fact, it was more than that. For the first time in a very long time, she'd felt a connection with someone new. By the end of the evening, she'd needed to force herself to drain her coffee cup and leave the bar.

That was exactly why she shouldn't meet him today. She should pretend she wasn't interested and forget the time or be otherwise occupied. She should knock this feeling on the head before it managed to get a toe hold, for his sake as well as her own. Things would be simpler that way.

She pressed her fingers to the glass.

"Morning."

Megan swung around at the sound of Jolie's voice. She'd been so deeply ingrained in her own thoughts she hadn't noticed Jolie's entrance into the room.

"Oh, hi. Morning." Megan did her best to smile.

"You okay?" Jolie tightened the cord on her robe. "You look a million miles away."

"I'm fine. Did you sleep well?"

"Not particularly." Jolie laughed. "But then, that was the general idea."

She'd almost forgotten about Chris. "Is he still here?"

Jolie shook her head. "He had to go get ready for an audition. He's an actor."

"I thought he worked for the hotel."

"He does that too. In between acting jobs." She ran a hand through her hair. "He's had speaking parts in a couple of films. And he's done a few horror things. Playing zombies mostly."

"That sounds cool. Are you going to see him again?"

"Yeah. Maybe." Jolie bit her lip. "I hope so."

Megan nodded, turning to study the view again. "I hope so too, then."

"How about you? How did it go with Jim?"

She crossed her arms, considering what to say. "He seems like a really nice bloke."

"Oh, please. Could you be any more vanilla about him? Don't give me that, Megan. I know you too well. I could see how well you two were getting on." Jolie stood next to her, staring out at the city. "Cut through that crappy British reserve for once, will you?" She rested a warm hand on Megan's elbow. "Tell me what you really think of Jim."

"He makes me feel like myself again." With her gaze fixed on the view, she searched for the right words. "For a while last night, I actually remembered myself, my life, the way it used to be. Before I got mixed up with William. He asked if I wanted to meet up with him this morning."

Jolie's fingers tightened around her arm. "That's fantastic. Isn't it?"

Megan shook her head and pulled away. "No, not really."

"What do you mean?" Jolie moved with her, not letting her run away, figuratively or physically. "You deserve to meet someone great."

"Why?" She wasn't sure she deserved anything of the kind.

Jolie looked confused. "We all do. Especially you, after what he put you through."

Megan shook her head. "Sometimes there are things that are more important than personal happiness, Jolie."

"Maybe. But that can't stop us from trying to grab a bit of pleasure, can it? Even if it is only for a while. Otherwise, what's the point?"

Megan shrugged. Jolie wasn't wrong, it just wasn't that simple for everyone. "Anyway, I'm not going."

"Why not?"

"He's just a guy I met. It doesn't matter." Compared to keeping her family stable and safe, meeting Jim at the diner didn't even factor on the scale of importance. It couldn't.

Jolie frowned. "That's stupid."

"Thanks."

"No, I mean it. Go. Enjoy a coffee or whatever with the man then we'll meet at the gallery later. Stop overthinking it. It doesn't need to be a big deal."

~ * ~

Jim struck out along the sidewalk. The sun slanted through the buildings, causing him to squint. Another beautiful day for the residents of and visitors to Los Angeles. Maybe a beautiful day for him too. Or maybe he was setting himself up for another fall. It was highly likely that a woman who stayed in a place like The Valentine Retreat wasn't going to be interested in a guy like him.

He stuck his hands into his pockets. The last thing he expected to happen when he took this job was to meet someone like her. The timing couldn't be worse. There was absolutely no way he could be looking for a relationship right now. Yet there he was, heading to the diner, hoping beyond reason that she would show up and bathe him in that smile of hers again. Trying to suppress the heady mix of excitement and nausea bubbling in the pit of his stomach.

The Tick Tock Diner stood on the corner of the block. Its red, striped awnings reached down over the full-height windows framing the building on both sides, giving the impression its eyes were partially closed, as though it was only just waking up. As he approached, the bustle of life inside became obvious. He pushed the door, the red neon "24/7" sign bright in his eye line. He scanned the length of the restaurant. There was no sign of her. The clock behind the counter read twenty-five past nine. There was still time.

He crossed the black and white checkered floor then took a seat on one of the chrome-legged, red vinyl-covered stools lining the counter.

"Hi there." One of the waitresses appeared beside him within seconds, placing a utilitarian white mug in front of him. "Coffee?"

"Thanks. Black is fine."

She filled the mug. "You want something to eat, sweetness?"

"I'm waiting for someone. Can I order when she gets here?"

"Sure you can." The waitress headed for her next customer.

Jim sipped from his mug and looked around. The diner was classic in its décor, with lots of chrome and red leatherette seating, and the tiled floor was scrupulously clean. It was crazy how much he wanted her to like it. Would it fit into Megan's expectations of an all-American diner? It fitted very neatly into his own. One glance at the dishes coming out of the kitchen was enough for that. Piles of waffles with blueberries perched on top, bacon, eggs, biscuits, pancakes laced with syrup.

Even the coffee was good. Well, to be honest it was good by diner standards, which wasn't necessarily saying a lot, but he'd tasted much worse. It was hot, strong, and very fresh. Noticing it was gone half past nine, Jim tried to keep his gaze away from the door. No way was he ready to accept she wasn't coming. Not yet.

A couple pushed their way into the diner, their faces unable to hide the argument simmering under a veil of unspoken civility. They headed for a booth to continue the confrontation. A middle-aged man with thinning hair and the beginnings of a pouch called his farewells to the cook as he pocketed his change then headed for the door.

Jim was on the verge of giving up and ordering some food when the door opened again. He felt for the counter with the base of his mug, setting it down as he realized it was her. She hadn't stood him up after all.

He slid from the stool. "You came."

"You didn't think I would?"

He shrugged. "I wasn't sure."

"This place is great. I can see why you like it."

He was glad she shifted the focus. "Wait until you taste the food."

She smiled. "Shall we find somewhere to sit?" She led the way to a booth against the inner wall of the building.

That was good, because it gave him the chance to get his stupid grin under control.

Chapter Eight

Anthony Valentine could hear someone whistling in the outer office. The theme tune to *James Bond*, unless he was very much mistaken. He'd be prepared to put a big stack of Franklins on it being one of his newest employees. He favored the wannabe actor, Chris Kimble, for the win.

Anthony wondered how long it would take the guy to work out how little anyone cared about his ambitions. Especially his current employer. Anthony would give him a while longer to focus on his actual job, rather than his pipe dreams. Time to work out which side his bread was truly buttered, before he seriously considered cutting the guy loose.

Management was full of tough calls, but he found that success came from taking them and twisting them to your advantage. So far the boy had performed well, but Anthony believed everyone would do well to remember how perilous life was, how quickly things could change. His phone beeped.

He sighed, swiveling around in his chair to take the call. "Thank you, Theresa. Send him in."

One glance at Benny had the big man primed. Anthony swung his chair away again, taking in the vista on the other side of the plate glass. He would let Benny deal with the formalities while he enjoyed the view a while longer. Management might have its trials and tribulations, but the view from his office wasn't one of them.

The door opened. The jangling of Theresa's bangles and her introduction of the visitor, Chris Kimble as Anthony had suspected, was unremarkable. There was no stopping his shoulders from tightening as he heard Chris say, "Thanks, babe."

Babe? Did men still refer to women in that way? Anthony shook his head. That needed sorting, without question. It was one thing to utilize women—and men, for that matter—to further your own ends, but there was absolutely no need to speak to them as if they were dirt.

Especially in his hotel. He drummed his fingers against the padded armrest as he took in the sun's light reflecting on the glass panels of the high-rise opposite.

Eventually he focused his attention on his employee. "It looks like a beautiful day out there, Chris. Beautiful and sunny."

"It is, Mr. Valentine." A nervous smile accompanied the reply.

Anthony nodded. To be fair to the young man, he did have a certain charm to him. All blond hair, blue eyes, and smooth, tanned skin. Perhaps he surfed in his spare time. He had that kind of outdoorsy glow to him. Chris rubbed his sweaty palms on his jeans.

Anthony encouraged a certain level of nerves in these red-braid meetings. Rather than offering Chris a seat, he left him standing awkwardly on the opposing side of the desk. It was imperative that boundaries were established early with the men who worked this section of The Valentine Retreat. Keeping them on the balls of their feet, certain in the knowledge that nothing but the best would cut it, could only be a healthy thing.

Having said that, his two latest employees—this young man, along with the newest acquisition, Jim Carenso—were shaping up to be what Anthony hoped would be a perfect fit in his organization. Both were dangerously good-looking and hot-blooded, but desperate for easy money. They were the kind of men whom women seemed to fall over themselves to get close to but were also men who struggled to back up their looks with any real substance. A winning combination where Anthony's hotel was concerned. Easy to manipulate. Easy to intimidate. Easy to cut loose, if necessary.

"It was good to see you in the bar last night. Did you enjoy yourself?"

"It's such an awesome atmosphere in there," Chris said, flashing a wider smile. "The refit is impressive, Mr. Valentine."

The irritation from the guy's ingratiating manner was tempered by his comment about the recent upgrade. The benefits of renovating a space designed to impress was never something to underestimate. As a hotelier, Anthony knew this fact better than most. High-end clients didn't tolerate tired décor. And he liked those customers.

He especially liked it when they took advantage of his red-braid service.

"So, enough of the pleasantries. You have information for me?" Anthony steepled his fingers beneath his chin.

"I hope so."

"It is what I pay you for, after all." He hardened his expression.

Chris cleared his throat. "The thing is, I recognize the girl Jolie's sharing her suite with."

"I presume this is relevant to me somehow?"

"She's booked in under a different name, but she used to be married to—" Chris took a couple of steps toward Anthony's desk, gesturing to the pile of magazines stacked on one edge. This month's selection of courtesy titles for the hotel's suites. "May I?"

"Of course."

He pulled the copy of *Living the Dream* from the pile, leafing through it until he found the relevant page. Turning the magazine to face Anthony, he pushed it across the desk. "She was married to this guy." He tapped a photo of a man Anthony instantly recognized. William Wiseman.

"Are you sure?" Anthony took hold of the magazine, his gaze racing across the write-up.

Not that he needed to read the accompanying rubbish. He knew exactly who William Wiseman was. But the news that his ex-wife was staying in Anthony's hotel, under a red-braid package? He couldn't believe what he was hearing.

"Yes. They divorced about six months ago. I like to keep up-to-date with celebrity gossip. It's important in my line of work. You never know when staying in the loop is going to come in handy at an audition."

Anthony sighed. Not the acting nonsense again. "Stop talking and start listening, Chris." A touch harsh, maybe, but this was important. "Let me get this straight. You are telling me that the woman you are entertaining is of no importance, but her friend's ex is worth tens of millions of dollars?"

Chris nodded. "Yes."

"Did I meet her last night? She was talking to Jim, if I remember correctly?"

"Yes. Exactly right, Mr. Valentine."

"Good. That's useful information, Chris." Anthony frowned as the guy continued to stand in front of him. Was he waiting for a postcard? "Was there anything else?"

"No, not really." Chris looked crestfallen. Like a dog who didn't get the pat he was expecting.

Anthony gritted his teeth. "Thank you. You can leave now."

"Oh. Okay." Indecision framed his face as he walked away.

"One last thing before you go." Anthony flapped the magazine down onto the desk. "My PA? She has a name, and 'babe' isn't it."

"Absolutely, Mr. Valentine. I didn't mean anything by it, honestly. It's just a turn of phrase."

Anthony pressed his hands flat against the surface of the desk and rose to his feet. "They all have names, Chris. I suggest you iron out a few of those kinds of *turns of phrases*. I expect my guests—indeed everyone in my hotel—to be treated with the utmost respect. I think using their actual names is a good place to start, don't you?"

He remained standing, his gaze tracking Chris as he left the room. Then Anthony sank back against the soft leather of his chair. He glanced at Benny, who was in his habitual place with his back against the office wall, expression neutral. Anthony wondered what his security and acquisitions manager thought about while he stood there. His presence was reassuringly formidable, even if it wasn't entertaining.

Anthony swiveled back in his chair to face the view. This news gave him a potential problem. He had a decision to make about his newest employee, Jim Carenso. Employed to be a red-braid entertainer, he had seemed rather slow to get up to speed with the basic requirements of the job. Anthony appreciated that it wasn't for everyone, that sometimes his choice of employee didn't work out so well. There had been a guy the previous summer—Paulo, if memory served—who tried to make trouble rather than accepting dismissal.

As a general rule, though, Anthony was more than happy to give the red-braid employees longer than most to bed in. He pressed one side of his lips together. *Bed in.* Apt choice of words.

But this news about William Wiseman's ex-wife caused Anthony a spike of excitement. It could be that the woman would take any of the red braiders, when she was ready. Or it could be that her interest was piqued by Jim in particular. If that was the case, Anthony needed to get the guy up to speed with the fullest extent of the requirements of his job.

Because a target like William Wiseman was far too good to have slip through his fingers.

Anthony studied the view for a while longer, then he took a deep breath. Decision made. "Benny, I need you to get me Jim Carenso. Tell him it's important."

Chapter Nine

Jim tried his best not to stare at Megan as she studied the menu card. He forced himself to look at the one in his own hand, although he already knew what he would have.

"I hope there's something that you like." The words gave him an excuse to look at her again.

She nodded, her focus still on the card.

"The pancakes here are seriously good. Really smooth and light," he said. He willed her to look at him, but she didn't.

He dropped his menu, taking hold of his mug instead. What was he doing? This was madness. There was no way the desire to get involved with anyone should even have a place in his head right now. Especially a woman staying at The Valentine Retreat, in one of the party suites. That information alone should let him know she wasn't interested in anything long term. Except she showed absolutely no reaction to his red braid the evening before. Was it possible she wasn't staying at the hotel for the same reason as her friend?

That was too much of a leap, even for him. Even if he wanted her to be staying at The Valentine Retreat purely for the spa treatments, while her friend enjoyed all the optional extras, wanting it didn't make it so. Nor did it change the fact he was employed as one of those optional extras, available to be selected at will, like a plate of sushi from a revolving display.

As if that wasn't bad enough, there was no way he could tell her the rest of it.

He sipped his coffee. He'd always managed to complicate his life, but this was going some, even for him.

Megan slid her menu between the sauce dispensers in the middle of the table and sat back against the banquette.

"You ready to order?" he asked. The choice was extensive, and she had taken her time to look through all of it.

"Oh, I'm probably going to have toast and jam."

He couldn't stop himself. "That's *so* British," he said. "Are you for real?"

She smiled, and he realized she was teasing him. "Nope, I'm joking. I might have the pancakes too. Especially if they're as good as you say they are."

"Okay. No pressure, then. But they are really good."

Once their food was ordered and their mugs topped up, she sat quietly, scanning the diner.

"I'm glad you agreed to meet me," he said.

"You said you were going to give me the inside track on what this part of the city has to offer. Hidden gems, remember?"

"I did, didn't I."

"I thought it would be worth the walk over here, as you proved yourself to be a bottomless pit of knowledge last night." She glanced at him and grinned. The gold flecks in her eyes seemed to shine all the brighter in the diner lighting. "This place is great, by the way."

He was in trouble, and he knew it. He couldn't take his eyes off her. He ran a hand through his hair. "Wait until you taste the food."

Halfway through his pancakes and deep into a conversation with Megan about the British obsession with tea, Jim was distracted by the buzz of his cellphone. Annoyed by the interruption, he lodged his cutlery on the edge of the plate, feeling around in his jacket pocket for his cell. The call was from Mr. Valentine's office.

"Sorry, I need to take this. It's the hotel."

"No problem," she said. She picked up her mug and fixed her attention on something across the diner.

"Mr. Carenso?" The caller was Mr. Valentine's PA. The gist of the call was that Mr. Valentine wished to meet Jim as soon as possible, about a red-braid matter.

Supposedly off the clock until later in the day, Jim frowned. "What time would Mr. Valentine like to meet?" With luck, he would be able to finish his food and his conversation with Megan.

"Straight away would be great."

That was annoying. However much he needed this job and to keep his employer happy, there was no way he wanted to cut short his time with Megan. She seemed to sense his indecision and pushed her mug to one side, beginning to gather her belongings.

He sighed. "I can be with you in fifteen minutes."

"Very good, Mr. Carenso. Mr. Valentine will be waiting for you." She ended the call.

Jim stared at his cell, trawling his thoughts for what his employer could need to talk about, especially at this time of the day. The requirements of his role had been explained when he accepted the job a couple of weeks ago. Had it only been a couple of weeks? Time spent in The Valentine Retreat had a strangely elastic quality. Maybe it would be a lecture about the braid wristband, about his lack of enthusiasm for wearing it in an obvious way.

He thought he'd been subtle about hiding it, but Mr. Valentine had made a point of referencing it the previous evening. Perhaps it would be nothing more than a rapping of the knuckles over that.

Jim abandoned the rest of his breakfast. Megan's plate was still half full too. "Not as good as you'd hoped?" he asked as he pushed his plate aside.

She smiled as she slipped into a soft suede waterfall jacket. "Not at all. Those pancakes were fantastic. You were right." The smile faded. "I don't have much of an appetite right now." She looked at his plate. "Anyway. Pot. Kettle. Black."

"I suppose.." He eyed his plate with regret. "Except leaving mine has absolutely nothing to do with a lack of appetite and everything to do with having to keep my boss happy."

"I should get going anyway. I'm meeting Jolie at the gallery soon. Plus, I've got your top ten list of off-the-grid must-visits to work through. Busy day ahead." Megan shuffled along to the end of the banquette, preparing to leave. "I'll get the tab," she said, glancing around for the cashier.

"No. Please. It was my invite. It's my tab."

She nodded. "If you're sure. Thanks."

He shuffled across too and stood. "Have you got plans for this evening?" He was sliding toward sounding desperate again. "I might see you in the bar?"

Megan shrugged. "I expect so. Jolie's keen to take advantage of everything the hotel has to offer."

He wondered if she was talking about the facilities or Chris. "And you're not?" Jim wasn't sure what he wanted her answer to be.

"Not really. This is Jolie's trip. I'm just here for the pancakes." The smile reasserted itself.

A man could get lost in that smile. "Glad I could be of service."

She headed for the door and he went to settle up, aware his attention stayed fixed in her direction long after she stepped out onto the sidewalk and disappeared along the street.

~ * ~

Ten minutes and a brisk walk later, Jim passed the front doors to the hotel and took the alleyway leading to the staff entrance. The difference between the two environments was tangible. The main street was clean and wide, already bustling with shoppers and tourists. Everywhere he looked there were signs of affluence, from the people walking past him, designer brand shopping bags swinging, to the cars and cabs moving slowly along the street, their suited occupants eager to get somewhere important.

By contrast, the alleyway was a lot less wholesome. The bare bricks lining the outside of the building were covered in graffiti, stretches of the walls heaped with piles of flattened cardboard. A trio of massive, wheeled dumpsters for the hotel's waste were set against the walls nearest the street. Here and there, he noticed gaps in the brickwork, where one had rotted out or some of the grouting in between bricks had fallen away.

It about summed up the whole hotel. Like two sides of a coin. One all shiny and expensive, the other dirty and rotten.

The condensed air from the heating system vented from a massive square stainless-steel box above his head. A side door flung itself open, allowing a junior worker from the kitchens to hustle out with a bucket of scraps. He was struggling with the awkward weight, trying not to spill any of it over his clothes. He glanced at Jim, his eyes full of concentration, his nod of acknowledgement barely perceptible. Jim nodded back. A loud, aggressive voice from inside the belly of the kitchen resounded through the doorway. "Hurry the fuck up, you wipe of snot."

The owner of the voice appeared in the doorway. A huge, florid-faced man sporting a tangle of facial hair, with a checkered cotton hat perched on top of a forehead slick with sweat and chef's whites stretched over his ample frame.

Jim slowed as he passed, the sound of the chef's labored breathing audible above the clattering of the young man struggling to open the food-waste dumpster. Without an offer of help, the chef berated the boy as he tried to lift the bucket to empty it without spilling the contents onto the alleyway.

"What the fuck are you looking at, pretty boy?" the chef spat, his anger spilling out toward Jim.

The young worker, glad of the distraction, scurried back into the comparative safety of the bowels of the building.

"Just wondering if I'm about to witness you having a cardiac arrest, that's all," Jim said, sticking his hands further into the pockets of his jeans.

The chef flung Jim a venomous look, stepping out from the doorway. He came close enough for Jim to be able to see the veins throbbing in the guy's temples, his fists clenched in anger. Jim held the chef's gaze for a few seconds longer, then carried on toward the staff entrance.

"You need to learn to keep your smart mouth the fuck away from me, pretty boy, or I'll rearrange your features for you. Then Mr. Valentine won't be so pleased to see you, will he?"

Jim laughed out loud but kept walking. The guy had a point. That would really mess with his plans for this job. He couldn't have that. He punched the code to gain access to the building and closed the door behind him.

In the lobby beside the staff canteen, he paused to feed some money into the vending machine. To his frustration, the machine clunked and made encouraging whirring noises, but the can of fizzy soda he wanted remained resolutely in position inside.

"Goddamn it," he said. The combination of his confrontation outside and the prospect of a meeting with Mr. Valentine had made his mouth uncomfortably dry.

"That crappy thing tried to steal my money too."

"What's wrong with it?"

"No idea, man." Richie sauntered across to the machine, delivering a deft kick to the bottom section of the machine's right-hand side. The can of soda dropped into the slot. He handed it to Jim. "There you go."

"Thanks."

"No problem." Richie leaned against the wall.

Jim wouldn't have been surprised if the whole thing had shifted slightly as he applied his full weight. He wasn't a small man, but Richie dwarfed him, the guy making the most of every inch of his impressively muscled frame. His reputation as one of the most popular red-braid workers preceded him. Jim already knew he was one of the boss's high rollers.

"Listen, I'd better get going. I have a meeting with Mr. Valentine," Jim said. He lifted the can of soda. "Thanks again."

"Sure." Richie stepped toward him, reaching a hand inside his jacket. "Before you go, Jim, a word to the wise?" He pulled at a plastic bag until its contents were visible—a brightly colored range of pills in a variety of shapes and sizes. "Sometimes this job is all gravy, man. You know what I'm saying?" Richie let out a slow, inhaled sort of a laugh. "But not all the time. Sometimes even the best of us need help." He patted the bag. "I've got just the thing for that, whatever the need." The bag disappeared again. "I wanted you to know I can always help you out." He zipped up his jacket and walked away.

Jim headed for the staff elevator, draining the soda as he waited for the correct floor. His gaze traveled to the top left-hand corner of the stainless-steel box as he tipped his head back. He'd noticed it before, a tiny corner of black against the shining silver of the rest of the space. Almost as if whoever had constructed the lift had made an error when they cut the final sheet of metal.

The doors slid open, and he made his way into Mr. Valentine's outer office. The secretary was waiting for him, visibly relieved by his arrival. "I'll let him know you're here," she said, gesturing for Jim to take a seat.

A few moments later he was being ushered into the office. He didn't get any further than the doorway before coming face-to-face with Mr. Valentine's security.

"Stop there and take your jacket off," Benny said.

Jim slipped out of his jacket and watched as Benny checked the pockets. Then he gestured for Jim to hold his arms out.

"Don't move," he said as he frisked him.

Chapter Ten

Anthony slipped his black notebook back into the office drawer as Benny patted down Jim in the doorway and took away his phone. Lining the book up in its correct place between the box of pencils on the left and the discrete Smith and Wesson on its right, Anthony slid the drawer closed and locked it.

He supposed the notebook could be described as a guilty pleasure. The act of taking it out and looking through it—or, even better, being able to add information to it—certainly gave him a rush. Should that make him feel guilty? He had worked hard to eliminate the guilt which had attached itself to so many of his positive emotions for countless years.

Perhaps he should view the notebook in simpler terms. It gave him pleasure. There. Nothing wrong with that statement. He enjoyed reading the names listed within, studying the simple handwritten accounts of who and when and how much, daydreaming about what they might have and what he might take.

William Wiseman was on his list. Had been for a long time. And now, as Anthony waited for Benny to finish checking Jim for recording devices or wires, he couldn't deny the prickle of adrenalin which accompanied the thought that another one of the people on his list might have come within reach.

"Good morning, Jim. Thanks for coming in so quickly." Anthony gestured toward a chair. Usually, he would have kept Jim standing, but he wanted to get the man to relax. Now was not the time for intimidation. The business at the door with Benny was bad enough. Necessary to negate the possibility of leaks, but intrusive and intimidating, nonetheless.

Jim eased himself into a chair.

"Your cell is on Theresa's desk," Benny said as he shoved Jim's battered brown leather jacket onto the back of the chair next to the one he'd taken a seat in.

"Thank you, Benny." Anthony waited until Benny settled into his usual spot against the wall. Not for the first time, Anthony considered whether Benny sucked on razorblades to achieve his gravelly tone of voice. "So, Jim. You are probably wondering why I wanted to see you."

Jim nodded. He fidgeted in the chair, his gaze darting around the room. Nerves, Anthony presumed. Nonetheless, the guy held himself well. Anthony had always believed you could tell a lot by the way someone held themselves. Although Jim had taken a while to get into his stride with the job, Anthony liked him. He was clearly doing his best to appear confident, despite the unconscious display of nervousness.

In many ways, Jim reminded Anthony of a younger version of himself. A memory surfaced of a time in his life when he struggled to appear confident and in control enough to cover his own boiling pot of insecurities.

"Well, there's nothing to worry about. I want to say that up front," he said, relaxing back into his chair.

Jim's shoulders dropped an inch or two. "That's great. Because I really need this job, Mr. Valentine."

He'd told Anthony his story of large debts accrued in a short space of time due to a spate of bad decisions. Money owed to the wrong type of people, the type of people who added interest at an ever-accelerating rate. The kind of people whose ranks Anthony could have joined, almost did join, as a young man.

Except he had always known he wanted something more than to end up grubbing around, collecting payments from terrified business owners anxious to avoid having their shop windows smashed and their stock trashed. Laundering drug money for the families and trying to hold territory against the less principled but equally organized groups springing up all over.

With origins in Eastern Europe and Asia, these groups had their feet firmly on American soil, and their hands resolutely squeezing the families' traditional pursuits dry. There was no way he was prepared to end up like his father.

"I appreciate you telling me this job is important to you, Jim. That is exactly what I like to hear. The feedback we have received so far, particularly about your spa work, has been extremely positive." Anthony gave a fleeting smile. "But it's the red-braid service I want to focus on today."

Jim shifted again in his seat.

"I've noticed on occasion that your braid isn't visible while you are at the hotel, especially in the bar. I am sure it's an oversight on your behalf. If it is a sign of nerves, then let me assure you, I understand. Don't get me wrong, I never expect any of you to leap in with both feet right at the start. I know it takes time to learn the ropes, gain a bit of confidence." Anthony leaned forward to emphasize the authenticity of his words. "In fact, I keep a special eye on any employees who do dive straight in. Because as a rule of thumb at The Valentine Retreat, the onus is always on the members of the fairer sex to make their wishes known to you, not the other way around. Over-enthusiasm can be an unattractive quality. I've always thought the line between it and desperation rather too thin to be accurately drawn."

"I understand. It's just taken a while longer to settle in than I was expecting."

"I accept that, Jim. Totally get it. But you must remember, you're only giving them what they want. What they desire. What they crave. What can possibly be wrong with that?"

"I see that. I promise I'll step up."

"That's exactly why I wanted to see you. Thing is, you seemed right at home in the bar last night. You are exactly the type of man I want to see wearing my braid, entertaining the lady guests. In fact, the woman you were speaking to appeared extremely relaxed in your company. You have an easy charm to you, Jim, has anybody ever told you that?"

"On occasion." He smiled, only for a second or two, then shut it down.

Anthony was right. The confidence was there, the guy just needed drawing out. "Nonsense, Jim. 'On occasion?'" He relaxed back into the chair, shaking his head. "Too modest for words. No. You, young man, have what I want. I saw it right from the start. You have what it takes to make it big here at The Valentine Retreat. Think Richie and multiply. More women than you know what to do with." Jim's expression shifted, as he hoped it would. "How does that sound?"

Jim nodded.

"Good. And, Jim, because I can see such promise in you, I am going to do something I never normally do."

"Oh?" Jim looked nervous again. "What's that?"

"The woman you were with at the bar, do you know who she is?"

"Who, Megan?"

"You aren't one for celebrity gossip, then?"

"No. Why? Who is she?"

"It's not so much who *she* is, rather who her ex-husband is."

"Oh, okay. She said she recently divorced."

"Her ex-husband is William Wiseman. Have you heard of him?"

Jim shook his head. It was clear from his expression that he was nowhere near cottoning on. Why would he? The part of the business Anthony intended to bring Jim into the loop on was one he kept from the newbies until he was sure he could trust them implicitly. That usually took a lot longer than two weeks.

There was no doubt that the money earned from the red-braiders was a sweet addition to the hotel, the service a discreet ripple of excitement reserved for the rich and frustrated women of Los Angeles and beyond. After all, if it were deemed acceptable for their husbands to have mistresses or hookers—or both—on tap, why couldn't the wives enjoy some fun of their own? Satisfaction, discretion, and safety all guaranteed, and a luxurious setting to boot. In certain circles, The Valentine Retreat had become the worst best-kept secret, and Anthony liked it that way.

For the most part, the hotel had remained out of reach of the authorities. After all, the guests weren't paying for the sex; they were paying for the room. And the red-braiders weren't paid to have sex; they were paid to entertain. The hotel could hardly be held accountable for what two consenting adults got up to behind closed doors, now could it?

Jim knew he'd signed up for all of this. The importance of remaining discreet had also been made very clear. Anthony never directly threatened his employees—that wasn't his style. Instead, he allowed word to get around about what happened to people who contacted the press, or any other challenging sector of the authorities, like the police. It was usually enough to deter any troublemakers. Usually.

But what Jim didn't know about was the part of the business Anthony was going to reveal. The jewel in the crown, as it were.

"I know you have some debts you are keen to clear," Anthony said, setting the honey in the trap.

"I have, Mr. Valentine." Jim stared at the floor for a few moments, then ran a hand across his forehead.

"There's absolutely no need to feel embarrassed. We all make mistakes." He waited until he had Jim's attention again. "The thing is to put those mistakes right. I can help you to do that, if you help me."

~ * ~

Jim stared at the man, trying to figure out what Mr. Valentine meant. The amount he had given for his debts was huge, and the need to work at The Valentine Retreat to pay off those debts was inescapable for the foreseeable future. Mr. Valentine was already helping Jim with the substantial paycheck the red-braiders received. Was the man telling him there was a way to earn even more?

And how could it be connected to Megan? "I'm sorry, Mr. Valentine. I don't understand."

"Let me fill you in."

Mr. Valentine explained how fantastically wealthy Megan's ex-husband was. He flipped the open magazine on his desk so Jim could see the article. As he read it, Mr. Valentine explained what he was alluding to.

"All I need you to do is to keep your ears open and your brain focused. Get as up close and personal as you can with her and let her talk. Encourage her to tell you all about how terrible her husband was. Once her guard is down, you will be amazed by the sort of information you can harvest."

"Information?" Jim slid the magazine back onto the desk.

"Types of security systems installed, positions of safes, even gate codes—especially if they relate to birthdays or memorable events. The type of art on the walls, the amount of cash in the vault, the number of diamond necklaces she didn't get awarded in the divorce settlement which still languish within his property. All available on an endless sea of regret and ready to be netted if you get the tide right. Give her your undivided attention, a shoulder to cry on...quite frankly give her whatever she wants, and you will be amazed at what she will give you."

"But why would you want to know those things?"

"What's the saying, Jim? Knowledge is power. The Valentine Retreat is not my only business interest, and this kind of information can be a useful tool in my other endeavors. There's no need to be intrusive, and it's imperative you aren't obvious. It's just that nuggets of information are as useful to me as nuggets of pure gold would be to you at present, with your debts."

Jim frowned. He hadn't been expecting this. Sweat prickled at the back of his neck and under his arms.

"Put it this way, Jim." Mr. Valentine steepled his fingers beneath his chin. "Bring me useful information about William Wiseman's assets, and I will see what I can do about the people who are chasing you for money. How does that sound?"

It was exactly the kind of thing Jim should want to hear. After all, he wanted nothing more than to get "up close and personal" with Megan. But not like this.

The problem was, whichever way he looked at it, he couldn't escape the fact he had so much more at stake here. Meeting a woman who piqued his interest like no woman had done for years and the knock-on effect of that—which was causing him to doubt his ability to do this job—was only a tiny part of it. This was a new complication added to the list.

It didn't matter that his mouth was dry, and the palms of his hands were slick with nervous sweat as he nodded to Mr. Valentine. It didn't matter how he felt about having met Megan or what she might mean to him one day. He told Mr. Valentine he would be totally up for the challenge, that he was thankful for the opportunity.

Because however Jim was feeling made no difference. It was out of his control. He had to do this job, whether he wanted to or not.

Chapter Eleven

Megan was out of breath by the time she reached the art gallery. She could have grabbed a cab, but after leaving the diner she wanted time to process her thoughts. A brisk walk had seemed as good a way as any to achieve that.

Jolie wasn't outside the gallery, which was tucked discreetly between a bustling clothing store and an artisan craft shop. Instead, she lingered in front of the craft shop, whose window drew the eye with a vibrant display of printed silk scarves and a fabric rainbow of tiny stuffed elephants making their way up a gray papier-mâché mountain.

"Look at that little guy," she said as Megan approached, pointing to a turquoise elephant, its ears fanned out and trunk snaking up into the air. "It's so cute."

"Do you want to go in?" Megan said.

She wanted to get into the gallery and see the art, but Jolie was right, the elephant was cute. The turquoise fabric shone with silver flashes from the thread creating an intricate pattern on its surface.

"No. Have you seen how much they are? It's not like I need one."

"I suppose not. It would be good to have something to remember our trip, though." She twisted her head in an attempt to read the price ticket, then gave up as Jolie turned her back on the display. Her friend seemed distracted. "Are you okay?"

Jolie brightened. "I'm fine. I left my phone at the hotel, that's all."

"We could go back and get it before lunch if you'd like?"

With a plan in place for the phone's retrieval, they headed into the gallery. As they stood in the atrium, it became clear that the gallery's footprint was much larger than it appeared from the front. The thought sent a shiver through Megan. A treasure trove waiting to be discovered. "Where shall we start?" she said.

"How about we start with you telling me how it went at the diner."

Megan was surprised it had taken her this long to ask. She had almost convinced herself she wouldn't meet Jim until Jolie had persuaded her otherwise. Her argument was logical; it didn't have to be a big deal. People met others for a cup of coffee or brunch everywhere, every day of the week. It didn't always have to mean something.

Except that as Megan sat opposite Jim in the diner, she wasn't sure she wanted their meeting to be no big deal. She was beginning to feel like she wanted it to mean more than that.

In the months since the divorce, she had done her best to get back on an even keel. To persuade herself that she could cope. She convinced herself she was fine on her own. That she just needed time and space and distance from the rest of the world in order to try to make sense of her place in it. To figure out how to make it work, within the restrictions of William's agreement.

Most of its details hadn't worried her. Much of the overly wordy document was to do with her agreeing not to interact with the press, not to put anything defamatory about William or any of his business interests on social media, not to bring any kind of negative attention to him or his businesses. No DUIs or other trouble with the authorities, no fraternizing with anyone with a criminal record, no engaging in illegal activities. No paying for sex.

The lawyers remained impassive as she laughed out loud at that clause, then began to cry. It was put in for effect, Megan was sure about that. To upset her. It worked.

Once she'd recovered her composure, she hadn't cared too much about any of that section of the agreement. None of it seemed relevant to the way she planned to live her life. The rest of it was harder to swallow. For the monetary agreement to remain in place, she was required to continue to reside in the States. And should she wish to enter a new romantic relationship, it would have to be sanctioned by William's lawyers before the news became public.

It didn't take a genius to work out that the chances of William's lawyers making that an easy process were slim. She could imagine them investigating the hell out of anyone unfortunate enough to fall for her, intimidating them until they ran for the hills.

At the time, she hadn't been too concerned about what she signed. To be honest, with the way William had come to make her feel during their relationship—the way the mention of his name or the thought of him still paralyzed her—the last thing she was interested in was looking for someone else. So, if her family remained unaffected, she had been content that finding someone new would stay on her "Wednesday after never" to-do list.

And yet, Jolie's constant encouragement to start dating—sometimes gentle cajoling, sometimes rather more pointed and graphic—had been striking more of a chord with her lately. However hard Megan insisted she was going to end up an old maid, living in Connecticut with a hundred cats, she wasn't sure she meant it any longer.

Meeting Jim had accentuated her unsettled emotions. She wasn't sure she'd ever found anyone quite as easy to talk to. Or as easy to look at. It wasn't even that; it ran deeper. Impossible to vocalize properly, but when she walked into the diner earlier and Jim looked at her, it was as if the rest of the world faded into insignificance.

Maybe that was what Jolie meant when she said that you knew.

"Oh, you know," Megan said glancing around at the walls packed with paintings. "It was fine." Her cheeks burned at her blatant understatement, but she hoped Jolie would work out what she was struggling to find the words to say.

Jolie stared at her for a few moments, then drew in a soft breath. She squeezed Megan's arm. "Well, that's a lot more than fine, then," she said.

Half an hour later, having soaked up some of the best pieces hanging on the walls, they stood shoulder-to-shoulder, staring at a bold mixed media on canvas. The work reminded Megan of a contemporary Spanish artist she liked.

She glanced at Jolie. "This one is definitely my favorite."

"Does it upset you that you can't buy this kind of stuff any longer?"

Megan sighed. The free rein William had given her at the beginning of their marriage to buy pieces of art seemed like a distant glimmer. It had been fun. She'd learned eventually that he let her do it because he recognized she had a better eye for an art investment than he did.

"Not really," she said. "I miss the art, probably the Degas the most. I chose it because I loved it, you know. Not because of what it was worth."

"Does he still have it all?"

"I imagine so. You know what he's like."

"Yes," Jolie said. "I do." She edged away from the painting. "Shall we make a move?"

Megan frowned. Jolie loved spending time in galleries almost as much as she did. "Of course. Are you sure you're okay?"

"I'm absolutely peachy. I just want to go get my phone."

They headed for the door. Something hovering around the edges of Jolie's expression didn't match up with her words. Megan knew better than to push her, though. Her friend would tell her, eventually, if something was wrong. Megan had always been the one who kept things buttoned up tight in this friendship, not the other way around.

~ * ~

Andy couldn't believe the daytime PI had gone home, claiming to be sick. The guy had only been outside the hotel for a couple of hours. What a lightweight. The call came in from Onesta, telling Andy to get back to The Valentine Retreat and pull a double shift. Unbelievable. He would like to see that suited bastard try to sit in a car for nigh on twenty-four hours. Idiot.

He had managed to make it to the laundromat before the call came in, so at least he had a fresh shirt to wear. No such luck with refilling his insulated mug, he hadn't thought of doing that. His thirst grew with every passing minute, and there was absolutely nothing to report. There hadn't been any sign of Megan Wiseman since he pulled up opposite the hotel. No one had phoned. Nothing was happening. Except his mouth was dry, and his stomach was growling, and if Onesta was expecting Andy to sit here for another million years, he would need food and drink. Plenty of it.

He threw his car door open, wincing as he swung his legs out. His camera was covered and out of sight, a newspaper hiding it from view. Pulling himself from the car, he smoothed his creased shirt and checked his wallet was in his pocket. He was only going to be five minutes—there was a deli just around the corner.

He grabbed his phone from the dash, slammed the door, then waved the key behind himself to lock up as he headed along the sidewalk. If something happened in the five minutes he was away it was tough luck. He was doing Onesta a big enough favor as it was.

Not that Onesta would see it like that. Especially if something important occurred while Andy was stocking up on snacks. He picked up the pace, shooting into the deli and heading for the cold counter. He selected a pre-packed pastrami and cheese sandwich on rye. Adding a bag of salted pretzels and a slice of chocolate cake to the pile, he asked for a black coffee to go.

As the girl placed his food into a brown paper bag he drummed his fingers on the counter with irritation. Why was it that when you were in a hurry your purchases were packed with the utmost care, no matter how long it took? Saunter in with time on your hands and you found everything was slung into a bag without so much as a backward glance.

Eventually she was finished arranging his purchases. He took the bag and disposable cup and shot back down the street. He slid the bag of food onto the passenger seat, lodging the cup on the dash as he glanced across at the hotel. Nothing happening. What a surprise.

He lowered himself into the driver's seat, propping his phone onto the dash beside the coffee as he yanked the car door shut. Not for the first time, a wave of futility washed over him. Was this what it had come down to? Was this what he had lost his family for? So he could spend all the hours God sent watching other people living their lives, while his own slipped further and further away from him.

He scanned the street again, his gaze passing over pedestrians as he reached into the bag for his sandwich. The sandwich never made it out of the bag, however, since a couple of women walking toward the hotel caught his eye. Megan Wiseman and her friend.

There had been no report that the woman had even left the building. Although it was entirely possible, he supposed, that the daytime guy might not have even bothered to turn up. To be fair, Andy hadn't hung around to wait for him. He'd had an important date with a washer and dryer, after all.

"Damn," he said under his breath as he retracted his hand from the paper bag and felt for his camera instead.

The sheaf of newspaper cascaded into the footwell. He brought the camera up, as slowly and unobtrusively as he could, fixing his eye to the viewfinder, fiddling with the focus. There was no doubt it was Megan.

He snapped a couple of shots, more to check the focus than for any practical use. As he checked the photos for clarity, the women climbed the front steps. Halfway up, Megan paused. He raised the camera again to see her attention shift, taken by something or someone to her right. Keeping the camera on her, the zoom made it possible for him to see her speak to her friend. The friend duly replied and disappeared into the hotel.

Megan skipped back down the steps. He could see her saying something—it was a greeting. "Hi there," or something similar. He moved his camera to the right, panning across the street to see who she was talking to. A man, dressed casually in jeans, with a brown bomber jacket and a crisp-looking blue shirt. Andy shifted against the crinkles of his own shirt as he wondered if that guy pressed his own clothes or if he used a laundry service.

Either way, he was tall, with dark brown hair. Early thirties, if his confident, loose gait was anything to go by. He fiddled with the camera lens again as the man smiled and he and Megan started to chat. The guy took his hands out of his pockets and looked as if he was about to hug her. Instead, he ran a hand through his hair.

Megan inched closer to him as they talked. Then the guy panned his vision up and across the street, almost directly at Andy's car. He took a couple more shots of the two talking, then dropped the camera from sight.

A moment or two later, he put it back up again, focusing on the guy. Frowning at the length of time it took the lens to shift in and out of focus, it began to dawn on Andy that he recognized the man. He was completely out of context there, outside The Valentine Retreat; that's why it had taken Andy a while to realize. He was sure now he knew who it was.

He hadn't seen the guy for a while. Their paths had crossed during a job Andy worked a couple of years ago. But it was undoubtedly him. What was his name? Jim. Yes, Jim something. With a few more shots of them both in the can, Andy lowered the camera. His brow furrowed as he finally remembered the guy's full name.

Officer Jim Carello. That was it. Andy was confused.

Why was Megan chatting with a cop?

Chapter Twelve

Jim had left his meeting with Anthony Valentine like a scalded cat, shrugging back into his jacket and grabbing his phone from the secretary's desk with sweaty palms. Shoving it into a pocket, he made his way to the elevator.

He took a deep breath, trying to stay calm. Going into the meeting, his overriding concern had been about losing this job, about the cover so carefully created for him by the department being wasted because he hadn't been enthusiastic enough with his red braid. Instead, what he'd learned in that room propelled him toward the elevator with a sense of urgency he hadn't been expecting.

Sucking in more air, he waited with growing impatience for the doors to slide open, not daring to look anywhere but directly at the brushed steel. He wiped his palms on the sides of his jeans as the elevator doors pinged. No one else was in the space.

Once sealed inside the metal box, his gaze flicked up and around the inner edges of the ceiling panels. He saw it again. A tiny triangle of black against a sea of steel and mirror. There was without doubt a camera hidden in the front top left corner. How many other cameras littered the building, unobserved but in turn observing everything that went on? He kept his game face firmly in place, but Jim's mind was racing.

This could be the break his department had been looking for. The Valentine Retreat had been a thorn in the city's side for as long as anyone cared to remember, but with the way Anthony had things set up, the hotel dangled frustratingly out of reach. Nobody in the vice squad was under any illusion about what went on inside that building. However, finding a way to prove that money was changing hands for sexual favors had remained elusive.

A rare cross-department information dump a couple of months prior—following a house invasion turned murder up in Sunset Heights—had brought up an interesting but tentative link with The Valentine

Retreat. Tentative, but after some digging, persuasive enough to prompt some serious action.

Chief Jackson, head of vice, decided the time was right to get someone inside Valentine's organization and have that person become a cog in the right part of The Valentine Retreat's wheel. To find out how the place ticked and gather proper intelligence, rather than the secondhand gossip floating around.

Once they knew the lay of the land, a plan of attack could be formulated. If there was another angle to Valentine's business ventures, they needed to know about it. They needed a way to bug his office, perhaps with Jim there to ask all the right questions. Or to find a weak link in Valentine's chain Jim could cultivate then lean on to provide evidence. A disgruntled sex worker, maybe, with an axe to grind in the privacy of an interview room in the precinct building.

Chief Jackson asked all the guys in vice for volunteers, but there were only a couple of members of the department who fitted the criteria. Single, interested in women, and under forty left Jackson with the choice of Jim or Phil Green. Phil was only recently back at work, recovering from an automobile accident, strapped into a back brace and relegated to desk duty for the foreseeable future.

The rest of the department had no trouble having some fun at Jim's expense. He'd been ribbed for days about brushing up on his chat lines, asked questions about which parts of his anatomy he was planning on getting waxed. One morning he arrived at the precinct to find somebody had left a box of cherry-flavored condoms on his desk. Went with the territory.

But Jim wasn't joking around now. With this latest information, the whole deal had become a lot more serious.

As he strode from the elevator, it seemed more likely than ever that they had been on the right track with the recent Branscombe killing. The mansion on Sunset Heights remained a crime scene, a place where the divorced house owner lost not only a vault full of cash, but also his life. It looked highly probable that the place could have threads which would ultimately lead back to The Valentine Retreat, especially after what he had just heard.

He needed to get to the precinct to explain to Jackson what had taken place in the meeting with Valentine so they could formulate a new plan. Jim had hoped he could slide under Valentine's radar with the whole red-braid thing for a while longer. That option just evaporated.

But there was no way he was going to attempt to seduce Megan in order to find out information for Valentine. Not that he didn't want to get close to her—there was nothing he wanted more—but not as a part of his job. And not while she was unaware of what was going on. His eyebrows arched as he considered what Jackson would make of that.

Jim hurried through the staff corridor, pushing out into the alleyway with one hand whilst wrapping the other around his mobile. His intention was to phone the precinct, to tell them he was on his way in. True to form, the angry chef from the previous afternoon stood near the dumpsters, smoking a cigarette. Jim slipped the phone away, shoving his hands deep into his pockets. The last thing he needed now was a confrontation with that Neanderthal, so he averted his gaze and kept moving.

The chef pulled a deep drag from the cigarette, then shredded the rest of the butt on the dirty tarmac with a scuff of his boot. "Yeah, you keep on moving, pretty boy, if you know what's good for you. Your sort are all the same, all talk and no trousers. Well, not the right kind of trousers, anyway." The chef laughed at his own joke, the sound resembling a drowning dog. More of a gurgling bark than a laugh.

Jim would have enjoyed wiping the smirk from the guy's face. As he kept moving, he consoled himself with the thought that if they managed to get The Valentine Retreat closed for good, that unnecessary grouping of DNA would get what was coming to him soon enough anyway.

He popped out of the alleyway into the sunshine of the street beyond. He reached again for his phone, thinking he would walk for a block or two before he grabbed a taxi. He was almost certain Valentine would have no reason to have him watched, but it never hurt to be careful.

Then he saw her on the steps at the front of the hotel. She'd already spotted him, her lips curved into a smile.

The mobile disappeared back into his pocket for the third time. "Hi," he said.

"Hi there." She skipped down the steps to meet him.

"Did you change your plans? I thought you were going to a gallery."

"We did, but Jolie couldn't settle. She left her phone here, and it seems she can't survive without it. I mean, how else is she going to check Twitter for vital bits of gossip?"

Jim wondered what her lips would feel like against his. Whether they would be as soft to the touch as they were to the eye. Her expression prompted him to think she might have asked him a question. He took his hands out of his pockets. At this rate she was going to be convinced he was hard of hearing. "Sorry?"

She shrugged. "It's fair enough. I feel lost without my phone too, to be honest. Anyway, what are you up to? How did your meeting go?"

"It was fine, thanks." He studied her, waiting for her to notice his deliberate use of the word.

She laughed. "Very funny." She inched closer. "Was it really okay?" A look of concern flitted across her eyes.

"The meeting went well. Honestly. I'm heading off to run a couple of errands."

She nodded, her gaze chasing an invisible firefly out of both their lines of sight. "I might see you this evening, then?"

"I hope so," he said. He needed to get to the precinct, but this conversation was important to him, and it seemed to be to her too.

The gold flecks shone in her eyes. Everything swirled around in his brain, a molten lava flow of the problems he faced. One look at her had him likening her to a rescue helicopter, appearing in the nick of time to lift him free of the mess he was making of his life. Except she wasn't. What she was, in fact, was a piece of jigsaw from a totally different puzzle to the one he was knee deep into solving. Although he had no way to make the piece fit, he was determined to hang on to it.

"Found it."

Jolie headed back out of the hotel toward them, waving her phone.

"Am I interrupting something?" she said. "I do hope I'm interrupting something." She studied them in turn. "I am, aren't I?"

Jim took a step back. "I'll let you ladies get going. See you later, Megan?"

Megan nodded, grinning as Jolie linked an arm through hers and led her to the curb. On reaching the far side, Megan held up a hand in farewell as vehicles crisscrossed between them.

He took a deep breath and ran his fingers through his hair as his own smile matched hers. Then he glanced back at The Valentine Retreat, his grin fading as he set off along the street. He still had his job to do.

~ * ~

A cab took Jim most of the way to the precinct building, then he jumped out and walked the last couple of blocks. Out of habit, he scanned the sidewalk behind him every now and again, just to be sure. There was no sign of a tail, so he pushed through one of the double doors leading into the building. Nodding to the uniform at the desk, he punched the door code and moved from the public lobby into the heart of the station. A call to Chief Jackson made from the cab had ensured his boss would be waiting for him.

On the third floor, he passed a couple more uniforms and headed across the open-plan workspace. His desk was as he'd left it: a mess.

Paperwork wasn't his strong point, never had been. He preferred to be out there, chasing a lead. One day he'd get good at admin, he told himself. One day, when he was all settled down and no longer wanted excitement and adventure, maybe then he'd be the division's most organized cop. His report writing headaches would be a thing of the past.

For now, the mess on his desk was one of his defining characteristics. It would remain something for his boss to chew him out about once life returned to normal.

The room was empty, apart from Phil Green. He was slotting files into one of the massive cabinets against a wall. "Hey, Jim."

"Any chance you could make a start on my desk when you've cleared your own?" Jim waved a hand at the lopsided stack of files on the surface of his desk.

Phil swore at him, and Jim supposed he had a point. "How's your back?"

"Hurts like a hot poker up the butt." Phil slid the cabinet drawer closed. "How come you're here? I thought you were up to your elbows in sex toys."

"Hilarious. You should do stand-up. I'm here to see the chief."

"He's in his aquarium." Phil pointed toward the glass-fronted office at the far end of the space.

Luther Jackson's office afforded him a complete view of his department. An ongoing complaint among Jim's colleagues—the glass rendered it impossible to kick back and eat doughnuts when they were at their desks.

He was halfway across the space when Luther noticed him. He ended a phone call and stood, gesturing for Jim to come in. "Good to see you, Jim. Take a seat." The familiar New Orleans twang embellishing his gruff tone grounded Jim in a way he'd been missing since he'd been at the hotel. "Coffee?"

"Sounds good."

Chief Jackson turned to the coffee machine in his office. A perk of his rank. At least, that's what he told the troops. Jim thought the investment in a machine had more to do with the chief's disdain for the department coffee than anything else.

"Got new beans," Jackson said, looking at the machine. "Did you know you can get them mail order? These ones are Guatemalan. Should taste of..." Grabbing the foil packet, he stared at the label, then shoved the bag in Jim's direction. "Read it, will you? Forgot my damn glasses."

He eyed the details on the packet. "Cookies, dark chocolate, and plum," he said. He would settle for it tasting of coffee, to be honest. He handed it back.

"Always good to expand the palate, don't you think?" Jackson said, propping the bag beside the machine.

He ran a hand over his salt-and-pepper buzz cut. A number four, Jim reckoned; not short enough to see the scalp, but low maintenance. It about summed the chief up. He was fit and trim for his age, but he was the kind of man who didn't hold with standing in front of the mirror for longer than was necessary.

"Right. Watch this baby work." Jackson shoved a department mug underneath the spout and pressed a button.

Jim was well aware of how the chief's coffee machine worked. However, he appreciated the time it was giving him to decompress slightly, to get his thoughts in order. Jackson passed him the mug, then took another to fill for himself.

The chief sank into his chair, taking a measured sip from the mug before he fixed his eyes on Jim. His expression was expectant. He didn't speak, but Jim could tell what he was thinking. Why had he come in?

"Things have changed," Jim said.

Chapter Thirteen

Andy was glad of the excuse to get out of his car and follow Megan and her friend. He tailed them at a discreet distance, losing track of time as he pondered the possibilities associated with Megan Wiseman and Jim Carello.

It was clear she knew the cop, but Andy couldn't work out why the two of them would be meeting outside The Valentine Retreat. Initially he'd assumed it was a chance meeting. One of those "haven't seen you in a while" conversations.

However, he couldn't escape the sense that the two of them were more than mere acquaintances. Many years spent watching people helped Andy to pick up on the subtle body language displayed. Sometimes he had a sense of what was going on between two people before they even knew it themselves.

The number of times he held his camera up, ready before the first punch was thrown or the first kiss was accepted. It was something he prided himself on, if he was being honest. One of the reasons he had been employed regularly by Mr. Wiseman's organization. After all, William J. Wiseman only tolerated employees from whom he got results.

However, this didn't really add up. Okay, a couple of days tailing Megan wasn't long enough to find out much about the woman or about her current life. Maybe she and the cop were an item. Maybe she'd been keeping it under the radar. There had certainly been no mention of it in Andy's briefing notes.

He shook his head as he walked. No, that wasn't it. There hadn't been the level of familiarity you would expect from that kind of a greeting. This had been an awkward and yet highly charged exchange.

Something didn't make sense.

He did trust his instincts, though, and the bottom line was that those two were seriously attracted to one another. The air all but crackled around them.

He paused at an intersection, waiting for the "walk" sign to light up. There was no hurry; the two women had stopped partway up the next block and were discussing one of the many store window displays. He sauntered across the street and took out his phone, pretending to look at messages until they walked on again.

A thought crossed his mind as he stared blankly at the screen. "Hang on," he muttered under his breath. "What if…?"

It occurred to Andy it was possible Megan and the cop might have met *at* The Valentine Retreat. He pocketed his phone. The backs of the women's heads bobbed as he trailed them along the street, whilst his brain whirred. He waited patiently for the swirling shimmers of his thoughts to coalesce.

He wasn't privy to the reasons behind the job he had been employed to do. Perhaps he should have wanted more information, perhaps his scruples should have made more of an effort to make themselves heard. He'd allowed the temptation of the money he would earn to override everything else, again. But when a person had felt his back against the financial railings like Andy had in the past, it was hard to turn down the opportunity to make some easy money. And this was easy money when all was said and done. A sitting target requiring nothing more than dogged patience and a bit of good luck.

He wasn't sure why William Wiseman would want photographs of his ex-wife in bed with another man. Perhaps he should have asked. He knew he wouldn't have been given the job, though, if he'd probed for information not already included in his briefing. He would have been given nothing more than a stonewalling. Maybe it was better not to know.

If the shimmers of thoughts had coalesced into something logical inside his brain, though, this whole scenario had taken on an entirely different slant. If Megan and Jim had met inside The Valentine Retreat, then surely that could only mean Jim was working in the hotel, and Andy was in danger of stumbling into the center of a police sting.

If Jim Carello was there undercover and that was how he and Megan had met, it seemed highly likely the man he would photograph her with would be Jim. They had taken painstaking care to stand close enough to make it difficult not to touch one another, even accidentally, during their conversation outside the hotel.

Andy wasn't a betting man. Had he been, he would have happily wagered that those two had not yet entered a relationship of an intimate nature, but it was definitely on the cards.

His thoughts finished coalescing and began kicking. Although he didn't have a full understanding of the reasons behind the request for the photos, it seemed likely the fact that the guy was a cop might have some bearing on their usefulness. If he *was* working there undercover, he wasn't a proper bona fide employee of The Valentine Retreat, and Andy couldn't be sure how this would impact their significance.

He sighed, banging a fist against his thigh. Now he didn't know what the hell he was supposed to do.

The women took a table outside a restaurant. The kind of place Andy would usually walk straight past, with a menu heavily influenced by salads and fish and with wheatgrass smoothies on tap. Once inside, he managed to bag a table with a great view of the two women through the glass. Salad or fish might not appeal, but it wouldn't hurt to check out the menu whilst he was here. There was bound to be something more substantial available.

He ordered a Spanish omelet, then pulled out his phone. Now would be a good time to clarify his position with Onesta. He needed to know where he stood if the guy he ended up taking photos of Megan with ultimately turned out to be an undercover police officer. Onesta was the legal eagle, and Andy wanted to be sure he wasn't going to end up on the wrong end of a lawsuit.

There was something else playing on his mind. If the cop was at The Valentine Retreat undercover, there was no way Andy wanted to mess up a police operation. He did not want to be responsible for putting that cop, or Megan, in danger by blundering in at the wrong moment with a camera.

He frowned, lodging the handset on the table. Was he overreaching? Perhaps he should wait. See how this thing played out for a while longer.

But how would he know? There was no way for him to find out anything more before it was too late and he was propelling himself into the room, taking compromising photos of a police officer.

Picking up his phone once more, he scrolled down the contacts list until he reached Don Onesta. The shake of Andy's head was involuntary. That name had to be God's joke. Honesty? Not something which featured highly in Onesta's world. Getting results and keeping William Wiseman happy were all he cared about.

The phone rang a few times before Onesta's PA picked up.

"Hi Rhonda," he said. "It's Andy. Can I speak to him?"

"Sure, Andy," Rhonda said. He could hear the smile in her voice. "I'm sorry, though, I'll have to ask you to hold. He seems to be particularly busy today."

"Of course he is." He knew the drill; Onesta always made callers wait a while. It was one of his psychological parlor games. Annoying, but unavoidable. On the plus side, it did give Andy time to chat with

Rhonda. "How are you?" he asked.

After a minute or so, she put his call through. He flicked some dirt from under a fingernail as he waited to hear Onesta's slippery tones, glancing habitually at the women eating lunch.

"Andy? Do you have good news for me?"

Andy could imagine the man flattening his tie with one hand, ensuring it lay flush to his expensive, tailored shirt as he pressed his phone to his ear with the other.

The uptick in his voice failed to disguise his eagerness for news that Andy had the photos they wanted. "No, Don. I don't."

The ice-cold silence at the other end of the phone sliced through the warm atmosphere of the restaurant. "So why are you calling?"

Andy picked up a fork, cutting a section from the edge of his newly arrived omelet. "The situation here is more complicated than we initially thought." He raised the forkful to his mouth, then lodged it back onto his plate. "Listen, Don, I need you to clarify something for me."

"What's that?" The exhalation of breath accompanying the words magnified the annoyance already clear in Onesta's voice.

"These photos you want me to take. Does it matter who's with the woman when I take them?"

"How do you mean?"

"Thing is, I've recognized someone here. He appears to know Megan, and I think there might be something going on between the two of them. I think it's possible he might be working in the hotel."

"I don't get your point, Andy. Where's the issue?"

Sweat pricked under Andy's arms. Should he say anything about the cop or should he play dumb? Pretend he hadn't recognized him after all? Hope that taking illicit photos of a police officer wasn't a criminal offense?

But what if there was an undercover operation going on in the hotel? What if Megan got herself caught up in the center of it? Andy blundering with a camera was hardly going to be a good thing, was it? Maybe Onesta should wait for another opportunity.

Andy took a deep breath and said, "The guy I recognize? I think he's a cop. That's my issue."

He listened to the silence, quiet enough to hear Onesta's cogs turning. Eventually, he said, "So what?"

It was clear from his reply he didn't grasp the extent of the possible situation.

Andy huffed. "Listen, I know you don't tend to get your own hands dirty in your line of work, but you need to understand something. There's no way I'm treading on the coattails of a police operation. If they're about to sting The Valentine Retreat, I'm not prepared to go steaming in and get in the way. And what about Megan? I'm wondering if we should reassess and weigh the risks involved."

He was coming on a bit strong, but he needed Don to grasp the gravity of the situation. It was all very well for Onesta to issue directives from the safety of his office, and Andy had been under no illusions when he took this job. However, adding the police into the mix could turn this whole deal nuclear.

There hadn't been much to find about Valentine on the internet, apart from on the glossy hotel website. If you looked hard enough—and Andy had—Valentine's roots showed, as clearly as a graying head of hair whose owner had been denied access to a bottle of hair dye. Valentine's roots were Mafia-tinted, even if he pretended they weren't.

"I wonder how important this photo is right now," Andy said. "I wonder if I shouldn't just cut and run and do this whole thing another time."

He didn't say it, but after what the ex-Mrs. Wiseman had been through, he was of the opinion she should be allowed an uncomplicated weekend with a new guy. Let the woman enjoy herself for a few days. Better still, let the woman get on with the rest of her life. However, it was clear that Wiseman hadn't finished with her; otherwise Andy wouldn't be on this damned assignment. He wouldn't be sitting at some fancy restaurant watching his omelet congeal while Onesta practiced his heavy breathing on the other end of the phone.

"Andy, you listen very carefully to me. You need to stay exactly where you are. You stay on this job, do you hear? If you want to get paid, you'll see this thing through. I'll speak to Mr. Wiseman, get the cop sorted and out of the picture. It won't be a problem for long. Mr. Wiseman plays golf with the chief commissioner."

There was another angle to this, which had also passed Onesta by.

"I don't think you're fully understanding what I'm saying, Don. After what I saw earlier, I think it's possible it's the cop who Megan's spending her time with. If she were sleeping her way through every man in the hotel I'd have already got the call, but I haven't." Onesta clearly hadn't bothered to remember what type of a woman Megan was. She wasn't the one who had slept around. "What I don't think you understand is, without the cop, I think it's unlikely I'm going to get my picture. If it is the cop she's interested in, will the photo give Mr. Wiseman what he needs?"

The cogs finally seemed to be whirring. "Shit," Don said.

Andy had never heard the man swear before, not even so much

as a "damn." He thought the line had gone dead, but then Rhonda said, "Andy, I don't know what you just said to him, but he's told me to tell you to stay on it for now, and he'll get back to you very soon. He looks as white as a sheet, and he's locked himself in his office. I've never seen him so ruffled."

He grinned. Nothing more enjoyable than bringing that cocky moron down a peg or two. Sticking his fork back into the slice of omelet, he said, "Okay, Rhonda. I'll do that. But tell him not to take too long, will you?"

Chapter Fourteen
Monday Afternoon

Megan and Jolie stayed at a table outside a restaurant called The Quiet Woman long after they'd finished lunch. Megan's grilled salmon with coconut rice was so delicious she ate almost all of it. There was something about eating in the fresh air—food always tasted better.

As she sipped Amstel light from a chilled glass, it occurred to her that she hadn't thought about William at all during the meal. For the first time in what felt like forever, she watched the world walk past from the seclusion of her sunglasses without his shadow at her shoulder. The only shadows in existence were the ones cast by the large canopy set up to shade the tables nearest the restaurant building. The sun was high in the sky, so high it was making its mark on every part of the street.

For the first time in as long as she could remember, her thoughts were filled with something different. And these thoughts weren't hovering around the edges of her mind, like timid butterflies. They were front and center. They were bold, strong, and as exciting as they were unfamiliar. They were about Jim. About the prospect of seeing him again later that day.

Jolie's phone rang. She rummaged around in her bag to locate it, pulled it out, and glanced at the screen. "Do you mind if I take this?"

Megan shook her head. She was enjoying herself and would be happy to sit here all afternoon, whilst her thoughts about Jim ran riot behind the safety of her dark glasses.

Jolie pushed her chair back, walking away from the table as she answered her call. Megan took another sip of beer, her attention taken by something glinting in Jolie's open bag. Intending to zip it closed, she put her glass down and leaned across.

As she tugged the sides of the bag together, she couldn't help but peek inside. Jolie's bag was always full of junk. There was no way the weight of it didn't give her friend backache. But it wasn't any of the usual items which had caught the sun's reflection. It was a blue, fabric elephant with silver threads and sequin decoration. A remarkably similar elephant to the one Jolie had been looking at in the craft store window earlier.

Jolie stood a short distance down the street, her bouncy blond hair moving as she had what looked to be a very animated conversation, but she wasn't smiling. Megan picked up the toy elephant. Jolie had made a point of saying she didn't want to go into the craft shop, that she didn't need the trinket. She hadn't said she'd already gone in and bought one. Why had Jolie hidden it from her?

Megan supposed it was possible her friend had bought it for her as a surprise gift, but she doubted it. Jolie knew how little Megan valued belongings since her time with William. He valued ownership above all else, whether it had been ownership of wealth, belongings, or people. She had been carried along on his wave for a long time. Hard to imagine who wouldn't have enjoyed collecting the art, buying clothes, being given jewelry, and reveling in the ability to have whatever they wanted. The joy of ownership paled when she realized she herself had become another piece of inventory, expected to perform her role in an exemplary fashion and to accept William's demands without question.

She shook her head to clear away the thought of him, replacing the elephant. After the sugar shaker incident in the café the previous morning, Megan had a feeling she knew exactly how the elephant had found its way into her friend's bag.

Her light fingers had always been there, right from when they had first met in high school. It had been insignificant things back then. Items Jolie could pawn for a couple of dollars here or there so she had enough money for lunch. However, when she spotted Jolie pocketing a gold-plated lighter left lying on a table at the event where she met William, Megan realized how deeply Jolie's tendencies ran and how much trouble they could get her friend into.

Once Megan was with him and money was no longer an issue, it would have been easy to have subbed Jolie every now and again. Except that a hand-out wasn't what her friend wanted. In fact, the offer made Jolie angrier than Megan had ever seen her. Eventually she realized it wasn't about the money Jolie got from pawning the things she stole. While it might have started because of her need for quick cash, it had developed into something else.

What could have caused Jolie to fall back into a pattern of behavior she adopted when she needed a sense of control?

She picked up her beer, but the enjoyment from its bubbly tang was gone. Eventually, Jolie re-joined her.

"Sorry about that," she said, slipping her phone into her bag. A furtive shuffle to hide the elephant under something else and a glance up at her told Megan her suspicions were correct.

"I saw it," she said.

Jolie frowned. "Saw what?"

"The elephant in your bag." Megan pushed her glass of beer to one side. "What's going on? First the sugar shaker and now this?"

"What do you mean? I bought it earlier." The pulses of crimson on Jolie's cheeks confirmed the lie.

"You told me you didn't need one."

"No. I told you I didn't need another one."

Now Megan was convinced there was something wrong. That wasn't what Jolie said, and they both knew it.

"Don't look at me like that." Jolie crossed her arms. "It's not a big deal. Leave it alone, will you?"

"All right. But I know when you're not telling me everything."

Jolie ran a hand through her hair, her tense features loosening a little. "Yeah, maybe. Like I said, though, I'm perfectly okay." She didn't elaborate. It seemed the conversation was over.

Megan recognized the expression, the tightness which didn't match up to the reassuring words. She'd done it far too many times herself when she was hiding what was going on with William. When the relationship turned sour, she continued to pretend everything was perfect. When Jolie complained they could no longer swap clothes because Megan's were all too small, she could have told her what he was making her endure. Instead Megan smiled and told Jolie how successful her diet had been. How much fun it was to be able to shop for a whole new wardrobe.

Trying to explain, even to her best friend, what was going on became an impossible task. Especially when she wasn't sure herself.

It began with a negative comment here or there about what she ate, what she wore, how she styled her hair, whom she spent time with. After a while, it didn't seem to matter how thin she got, William would frown at her menu choices. However carefully she planned her week, he insisted on checking her diary. Regardless of how often she had her hair or her nails done, nothing was ever quite right. Whatever her point of view was on anything, he would laugh and contradict her, brush her thoughts and opinions aside as if she were being ridiculous.

When she thought about it like that, with the privilege of hindsight, she was amazed she stayed for so long. But the truth was that it was a gradual slide from the fairy-tale beginnings into the straight jacket she ended up wearing. She knew she had to leave, but William had always explained his behavior away. He had no difficulty making it seem as if he were doing it all to keep her safe. That he had her best interests at heart. That it was because he loved her so much and it was purely due to her own inability to deal adequately with situations. After a while, she was disorientated enough to question herself. Question the legitimacy of what she thought she knew, second-guess her every emotion.

But there was no way to misinterpret the existence of his other women. There was no way he could explain them away, was there?

She remembered the day she finally broke. They were standing in his wardrobe room. As his hand settled on a silk tie with a yellow and royal blue checkered pattern she finally plucked up the courage to confront him.

"I know you've been sleeping around," she said, determined not to allow her voice to crack. She held the fingers of one hand firmly within the other to stop them from shaking. "How can you keep saying you love me if you need them too?"

"Megan, please. I love you, but you can be so naïve," he said, pulling the tie from the rack. "There's a world of difference between love and sex."

They might as well have been discussing new tiling for a guest bathroom.

He flicked up his collar, the look on his face in the mirror one of total concentration as he scrutinized himself tying a perfect knot and smoothing his shirt back into place. It was as if he considered a single sentence enough to explain away months, maybe even years, of one-night stands. The expression on his face was still burnt clear in her mind, as if she'd totally missed the point and was making a fuss about nothing.

She stared at him until he sighed and said, "I chose to marry you, didn't I? Because I wanted you. That's all that matters. The rest of it is none of your concern."

"Yes, but…"

"The thing is, Megan, if I wanted out, I could get rid of you like that." His expression hardened, and he clicked his fingers together. "You must know that, right?" He slipped into an immaculate navy suit jacket and walked toward her. He poked her in the collarbone. "Pouf. You're gone." Then he enveloped her in his arms. His breath was warm against her neck, but his body was tight and distant as he whispered, "So, it's just as well you make me happy, isn't it?"

Megan shivered even though she was sitting in bright sunshine outside the bustling restaurant.

"What's up with you?" Jolie said. "You look like you've seen a ghost."

"Shall we go?" Megan didn't want to spend any more time thinking about William. "But I meant what I said. If you want to talk about anything, you know I'm here for you."

Jolie checked her watch. "Sure. I know. So, what do you want to do? Did Jim give you his top sightseeing tips at the diner, or were you too busy trying to keep your hands off one another?"

Megan shouldered her bag and stood abruptly. "It wasn't like that. I like Jim, he's fun to be around. There's nothing more to it. Like you said, it doesn't have to be a big deal."

Now who was lying?

Chapter Fifteen

Jim drained his mug and set it down on Chief Jackson's desk. Cookies, dark chocolate, and plum were a better combination of flavors for coffee than he'd initially given them credit for.

Jackson cradled his drink, his attention never wavering from Jim's face. "So what you're saying is that the basic set up is as we assumed it to be?"

"Right."

"And as we suspected, he has his office swept for bugs regularly?"

"On a daily basis, according to housekeeping."

"What about wearing a collar microphone? The tech guys are nearly through with the requisition order. We should have one in the next couple of days."

"That's certainly a better option than trying to plant a device or wearing a wire. But we get frisked before we're allowed into his office, so it would still be a risk."

Chief Jackson frowned. "Okay, maybe we need to rethink that. You haven't managed to pinpoint anyone working the red braid who might crack?"

"The thing is, even if they did, I don't think it would help us. The guests only pay for the room, not the extras. As Valentine likes to say, he's not responsible for what goes on behind closed doors between two consenting adults. Payment for sex is never directly spoken about."

"It's semantics, though, isn't it? Whether they're paying for the bed or the body in it, the result is the same."

Jim nodded. The frustration on Jackson's face was clear. "But lawyers love semantics, don't they?"

"Too true," Jackson said. They both knew there was absolutely no point bringing a case against Valentine unless it was loaded with rock-solid proof. "Upstairs are going to hate this." He sighed.

"That's not why I came in," Jim said. "There have been a couple of developments since we last spoke."

Jackson lodged his mug onto the desk, his dark gaze sharpening. "Thank God. What's happened?"

"One of the other red-braid guys referred to someone who worked at The Valentine Retreat until late last year. Apparently, he upset Valentine, and no one at the hotel saw him again. I got the impression there was more to it than him losing his job."

Jackson raised an eyebrow. "You think they got rid of him?"

"I suspect so. The worker I spoke to got nervous partway through the conversation and clammed up. But that Benny character is never more than three feet away from Valentine. Valentine calls him a security expert." Jim mimed quotation marks as he said the words. "He's clearly more of an enforcer. I'm ninety-nine percent sure he's carrying. Have you got an ID on him yet?"

"He doesn't come up on any of our databases. Quite remarkable when you think about it."

"Yeah. Round of applause to him for remaining under the radar."

"Probably why Valentine employed him in the first place."

"Let me know if you find anything on him," Jim said. "Anyway, the guy who disappeared was called Paulo. Nobody could remember his full name."

"Nice." Jackson made a note of the name. "I'll get missing persons to trawl through the records." He shook his head. "Not sure where it will get us, though, even if we identify him."

Jim was fully aware of that. People went missing all the time. If they were lucky, their absence was noticed. Mostly, they slipped through the cracks. LA might be called the City of Angels, but a more accurate description would be the city of people who made a point of looking the other way.

Chances were that Paulo had moved here to find work. Probably the only person who even noticed he was gone was his landlord, chasing for rent that would never be paid. By now the room would be rented out to someone else, a new somebody for nobody to remember, with Paulo's existence black bagged and consigned to a dumpster months ago.

"There's something else." Jim was glad he'd saved the best for last. He'd brought nothing of real use to the table until now, a fact which hadn't escaped his notice. "I met with Valentine earlier. He has a special job for me."

Jackson shuffled to the front of his chair. "Well that sounds more promising."

It was promising. For the first time, they might get ahead of

Valentine. With what they already knew about the Branscombe killing, what Valentine asked Jim to do looked like it might fill in some of the blanks.

But it involved Megan, and he wasn't sure he wanted to get her tangled up in something like this. Especially without her knowledge. Being undercover gave him grounds for more leeway than usual in the way he could operate, but it wasn't really the rules which were bothering him. His hesitance was more due to the fact he was already betraying her trust. It wasn't as if he could tell her who he really was. Rule number one of being undercover: never reveal you're undercover. That was the way to get people killed.

He was first and foremost a police officer. He had never wanted to do anything else; it was what got him out of bed in the morning. First, second, and last on his list of priorities, it had been the focus for his life ever since the day after his tenth birthday.

He had been with his mother, on their way home from the supermarket, the car idling at an intersection. Three men came at them, all wearing balaclavas and wielding bags and weapons. Jim had never seen his mother so scared, her hands shaking as she locked the doors and told him to get down on the floor of the vehicle.

From his position wedged between the front and back seats, he noticed the car-jackers' attention taken by something outside the vehicle. There was muffled shouting, partly from the men looming over the car, but also coming from somewhere else.

Utterly terrified those men were going to shoot his mom or drag her out of the car in front of him, that day was the closest he'd ever come to losing control of his bodily functions. If the other men, the ones approaching the car, were also intent on taking from them, then he couldn't see a way out. When his mother began thanking God, he peered out. Brave enough at last to look to see who else was approaching their car. It was the police.

In the aftermath, Jim realized he wanted to be like them. The good guys arriving to arrest the bad guys and keep everyone else safe. A simplistic view, no doubt, but he was young and had almost crapped himself with fear. That feeling was a hard one to shake. In his pre-pubescent mind finding a way to keep his mom safe became his priority. Back then, the only other option for achieving that seemed to be becoming Superman, and Jim couldn't fly.

As the years progressed, the desire to protect grew stronger. To do something that mattered to other people became hardwired. Plus, he wanted to care about what he did. He still craved all those things. The trouble was the reality of things in adulthood were never quite as clear-cut as they appeared to a ten-year-old.

"Have you got trapped wind?" Jackson said. "Am I going to have to waterboard the information out of you or are you going to tell me what Valentine wants you to do?"

"Yeah. Sorry. The thing is, I've been spending time over the last couple of evenings with a particular guest. Her name is Megan Wiseman—or at least that was her married name. She's divorced now. She's booked in as Megan Leadbetter."

Jackson shook his head. "Should the name mean something to me?"

"Not necessarily. Her ex is William Wiseman. He's a business tycoon, apparently."

Jackson noted down the names. "Okay. We'll check them out. Well, when I say 'we' I mean someone in the department with more time on his hands than most." He grinned, his line of sight passing out through the glass front of the office and alighting on Phil.

"Anthony Valentine certainly knows who he is. I think this could be our way in to nailing him."

"What do you mean?" Jackson's expression sharpened again.

"We were right about there being more to Valentine than purely the solicitation of male employees."

Jackson listened in silence as Jim outlined what he had learned about the screening of guests. The garnering of information under the guise of pillow talk, which could only be for one reason: the other branch of Valentine's tree, up until recently hidden from view. The high-class heists.

By the time he finished explaining, writing covered Jackson's notepad. "And this Wiseman woman fits into this somehow?"

Jim squirmed in his chair. This was going to be the difficult thing to explain.

"Spit it out, Jim. For the love of God." He cocked his head to one side. "Hang on. I get it. Valentine wants you to pump this woman tonight, for information about her ex, right?" He chuckled, then his expression straightened. "Sorry. Bad choice of words, but you know what I mean."

"Yes. I know what you mean, and you've got it about right." Jim paused. "In return he said he will sort my 'problem' with my creditors. It might be worth getting them off the streets for a few days in case his solution is a permanent one." Although none of the loan sharks he mentioned to Valentine were upstanding members of the community, he didn't want to be inadvertently responsible for their deaths or have his cover blown by one of them squealing that they'd never heard of him.

"This is a perfect opportunity to get myself into the right place in Valentine's organization. It's just that…"

"Just what?"

The concentrated gaze of his chief bored into him, and the heat rose in Jim's cheeks. "Megan has no idea what's going on."

Jackson frowned. "If she's there and she knows about the red-braid workers, she can't exactly cry foul."

"I don't think she knows, though. That's my point. I think her friend knows about it, but from what Megan's said I'm sure she thinks the hotel is like any other."

Chief Jackson drummed his fingers on the surface of his desk. "Does this have to be a problem? Can't you find a way to sweet-talk her into giving you something useful for Valentine?"

"I'm not sure I'm prepared to do it. That's the bottom line. She's innocent to what's going on, to all of it. And I—" He broke off, unable to complete the sentence without giving away his feelings for her.

"Jesus Christ, Jim. I'll wait while you climb into your suit of armor, shall I? Why don't you give it a polish while you're at it? Want me to hold your horse?" Jackson fed more beans into his machine. With his back to Jim, his shoulders drooped, and his tone softened. "The thing is, we've never had something as promising as this on Valentine before. You know that as well as I do. Michael Branscombe was best friends with the chief prosecutor, for God's sake. You can imagine the kind of pressure that's creating." He turned around. "This is your chance to get yourself right up in Valentine's estimations. Don't lose sight of the fact that we need to nail this bastard. That's the end goal here. I think we might have to accept some collateral damage if it means we get the results we're after. I'm not saying you have to seduce the woman, Jim. I'm saying get her a bit drunk and see what you can find out."

Jim's jaw tightened. He couldn't help it. "I won't do anything which might put her in the firing line with Valentine. I think that man is capable of anything if it gets him what he wants."

"It sounds like she's going to be in the firing line then, with or without any help from you. She'll be safer with you there to watch her back, don't you think?"

Although he knew when he was being played, Jim also recognized the chief was making sense. Up until two days ago, this was the kind of break they'd all been praying for. A way to gain proper intelligence about Valentine and a ticket into his inner circle. This was exactly what Jim wanted, right up until the moment he met Megan. It was what he still wanted. He needed to get the job done. He had to work out how to do it without ruining any chance he might have with her.

"I haven't taken my eye off the ball," he said, running a hand through his hair. "I know how important this is to the department. Megan's only booked in to stay a couple more nights. Let me see what I can do, and I'll be in contact tomorrow."

"That sounds good to me."

"There's one other thing. Is anyone else being watched in that place? There's been a car parked opposite for a couple of days now. I think it might be press or a private dick. I wanted to check it's not one of ours, is it?"

Chief Jackson shook his head. "No, we made sure the place was clear before you went in. Maybe it's a PI, as you say. There's bound to be people frequenting that place being tailed by disgruntled partners, I suppose. Keep out of it, though. Stick to the plan and maintain your focus."

"I will." Jim headed out of the office.

Maintain his focus. As he pushed through the glass-plated swing door, he couldn't help but wonder how the hell he was going to manage to do that.

Chapter Sixteen

After lunch, Megan and Jolie headed out through the park. They wandered along meandering tarmac paths and passed through grassy swathes of a wildflower meadow, a microcosm of nature with skyscrapers the ultimate backdrop behind the groups of mature trees. They'd agreed that neither of them were keen to pound more sidewalks; a gentle afternoon was much more appealing.

Megan had Jim's list of the places in this part of the city he liked best, including a shop which stocked nothing but vinyl, with a huge section dedicated to the eighties, and an ice cream parlor with fifty-six different types of toppings. Yes, he said, he had counted. As they sauntered along one of the paths she realized she was guarding his list. She wanted to see all the places he had mentioned, but she wanted to see them with him.

For now, she was content to stay in the sunshine. She wanted the anonymity of fresh air and space and time to collect her thoughts. After a while, she found she wasn't really looking at the scenery, although the rainbow of flowers speckling the long grass was beautiful. She was observing the people.

As they walked, they passed parents with their children—babies in strollers, toddlers strapped into harnesses with leashes attached to adult hands like leads on dogs, kids bombing around on primary-colored trikes, or learning how to roller skate. Couples of all ages winding their way through the park, some arm-in-arm, some laughing, some arguing. Joggers in brightly colored activewear, with headphones on their ears and expressions of determination on their faces as they shot past. Groups of friends congregated on benches, joking around, enjoying one another's company in the balmy weather. Others were dressed in sharp suits, walking with purpose, checking watches and clutching bags and briefcases as they hurried toward the places they needed to be.

They were just people going about their daily lives. All with their own worries and fears, Megan didn't doubt that. Each human a microcosm of swirling emotions. But unlike her, they were actually living. Seizing the day and squeezing as much out of it as possible. They were taking decisions, making plans, hoping, and dreaming. They were *being* rather than *existing*. That was how life had felt to her for so long. As simply existing.

She went through the motions—she ate, slept, exercised, and talked to people—but she didn't connect with any of it. Like a reel of film, she watched as if it were happening to someone else. Sometimes she considered what the girl would do next then she would remember she *was* the girl.

But something was shifting in this existence of hers. Like an emotional earthquake, barely registering on any external scale but sufficiently powerful for her to be unable to ignore it. Unable to ignore how she was feeling about a man she had only just met. A man she barely knew. A man who was causing her to question the existence she had decided was acceptable to inhabit.

~ * ~

At the lake in the center of the park, Megan paused and leant against the twisted iron railings. She fixed her gaze on the water. A few ducks floated here and there, eyeing her for her potential merits as a provider of food. Jolie leant over the railings beside her. She too had remained uncharacteristically quiet since lunch, presumably absorbed by her own thoughts.

She threw a small pebble into the water. The concentric ripples spread out from the site of impact.

"I want to ask your honest opinion about something," Megan said.

"Sure." Jolie turned to face her. "About what?"

"I think I might ask Jim for his number, see if he wants to meet up sometime. Away from The Valentine Retreat, I mean. What do you think?"

"I thought you were seeing him tonight?" Jolie looked confused.

"I am."

"But you already know you want to keep in contact with him after we leave? You like him that much?" Jolie's blonde hair bounced as she spoke.

"I think so."

Her friend shoved her dark glasses up amongst her curls, her expression hard to read. "There was me thinking I was booking you a bit of fun for the weekend."

"What do you mean?"

Jolie's cheeks colored. "Nothing." She threw another pebble. "I just asked whether they had any tall, dark, and devastatingly handsome massage therapists when I made the booking for you."

"He's not all that handsome," Megan said.

A duck, braver than the rest, paddled toward them.

"Are you joking?" Jolie fixed her with a look.

Megan smiled. "Well, okay, he is easy on the eyes. I'll give you that. But it's what he's like on the inside that counts."

Her friend's face lit up with a naughty grin. "How would you know? You haven't let him inside you yet."

"Oh my god. Really, Jolie? Such a way with words."

"You did kind of walk into that one," she said. "If I'd known, I would have booked you a happy endings massage, saved all the messing around." She grinned even harder.

Megan chose to ignore the comment.

"For what it's worth, I think getting his number is a great idea." Jolie paused, waggling a hand at the duck. The bird took offense and flapped away across the water. "But there's no need to rush into that, is there? We're here for another couple of days, after all. You've got loads of time to ask him for his details. You might as well find out if he's worth the effort first."

Megan frowned. Jolie might be a bit brash at times, but she didn't shy away from saying it as it was. Nor did she hide herself away. She strode right up to life, grabbed it by the scruff of the neck, and gave it a good shake.

That attitude might be currently out of Megan's league, but that didn't stop her from admiring her friend. Whatever was worrying Jolie, she wasn't letting it dominate her. It was high time Megan refused to allow negativity to crowd in and ruin things for her too.

She made a firm decision as they walked on through the park and bought ice creams from a vendor with a huge cold box strapped to the front of his vintage tricycle. Whatever the complications, nothing was going to get in the way of her enjoying some time with Jim.

Who would even know? It had been ages since anyone had followed her. The paparazzi had given her up as a boring target months ago. She'd become exceptionally good at keeping her head down.

Jolie had encouraged her time and again, but for the first time since the divorce, Megan could see herself enjoying the company of a man. Even if it would only be for a few days.

Plus, if William never found out he wouldn't be able to spoil it, would he?

Chapter Seventeen

Some days Andy had to admit he enjoyed his job. Those days tended to be fewer and further between than he would like, but this was shaping up to be one of them. A decent Spanish omelet in the restaurant, then a gentle amble in the sunshine and an ice cream? Couple that with having a go at upsetting Onesta's digestion and you had a day well spent, in Andy's book.

It looked like Megan and her friend were heading back in the direction of the hotel. He hung as far back as was practical. It was unlikely there would be something worthy of photographing in this setting, but after Megan's meeting with Jim Carello earlier, Andy wasn't taking anything for granted.

His cellphone chirruped from the depths of his jacket. He threw the end of his ice-cream cone into a trash can and reached into a pocket, checking caller ID before he answered. It was Don's office. He'd taken his time.

"Hi Andy, it's Rhonda here. Could you hold for a second? Mr. Onesta is very keen to speak with you, but he's on the other line right now. He won't be long."

Andy snorted a laugh. He could hear the tell-tale tone in Rhonda's voice. She was feeding him a crock of shit, same as she usually did. Onesta was probably in his office playing with one of those indoor golf practice mats, trying to get the little white ball into the little green hole. Chances were he was gunning for an invite to join William Wiseman and the chief commissioner on the golf course, so Andy supposed he needed all the practice he could get.

"No sweat, Rhonda, I know the drill. Never known anyone who works as hard as your boss." He laced his voice with as much sarcasm as he could manage and was rewarded as he heard her chuckle.

"Thanks, Andy," she said. "I'll put you through as soon as I can."

"Oh, please don't rush," he said. Away from the park now, he picked up his pace, heading back toward the hotel. The women crossed the street ahead of him and turned a corner.

She laughed again. "How are the kids?"

He jogged until Megan and her friend were back in view, then fought to get his breath under control as he said, "Kids are great, when I get to see them. Linda's still playing hardball over visiting. Can't blame her, I suppose. She put up with me and the job for long enough. Can you believe Rory's twelve next week? Seems only yesterday he was learning to ride a bike. And Emma is cute as a button. Coming up on eight and already sassy as hell." Like her mother, he almost said. "Anyway, how's your latest beau? What's this one's name, is it still Eric?"

Rhonda groaned. "Stop it, Andy, you make me sound like a serial hussy. His name was Eric, as well you know. Then I found out he still lives with his mother, and I couldn't stop it all going a bit *Psycho* in my head, so I dumped him. Shame, really, he had a nice car."

It was Andy's turn to laugh. "Well, how about I swing by the office next time I'm in the area. Let me take you out for something to eat. I can't promise you a nice car, but I can absolutely guarantee I don't live with my mother. Think about it?" He didn't elaborate on his current living arrangements. Some things were best left to the imagination.

"I will, Andy. I'll definitely think about it." Rhonda's tone changed, taking on a business-like edge. "Okay, Mr. Onesta is ready for you now. I'll put you through."

Andy waited for the click of the call being transferred, and her warm voice was replaced by Onesta's. "Thanks for holding, Andy," he said.

"Did you get your hole in one?" Andy couldn't help himself.

"What?" The frown was clear in Onesta's voice, but he chose to ignore what Andy insinuated. Instead, he said, "Listen, Andy, I've spoken to Mr. Wiseman, and we feel the best course of action is to end your shift as soon as possible. Mr. Wiseman is mindful of the fact you've been stationed outside the hotel for rather a long time, and he agreed with me it's only fair to give you a break."

Andy watched Megan and her friend climb the steps to The Valentine Retreat before he headed back to his car.

"So you're pulling the job?" Even as he said it, Andy could hear the surprise in his own voice. Had his opinion actually mattered?

"Not exactly. Kenny Johns is on his way to take over from you. If you can stay put until he arrives, then you are free to leave. Email my office with your hours and details of any expenses, and they will be paid in the normal way. Mr. Wiseman has authorized me to give you a special bonus, a one-off payment, in acknowledgement of your fine work to date."

Andy wondered why Onesta kept referencing Mr. Wiseman. On day-to-day jobs the man couldn't wait to grab the decision-making glory for himself. Perhaps he thought it gave his words added weight, because normally Mr. Wiseman had no interest in something as menial as a PI's workload. Andy popped the lock on his car and climbed in.

"So what's happening with the cop?"

"Oh, that's all been taken care of. He's not of importance, and it's no longer something you need to concern yourself with, Andy."

Onesta was doing his best to sound light, almost disparaging, about the information Andy had brought him. But the underlying slippery tone was inescapable. He was being fed a line. Being paid off with the promise of some extra cash.

The whole thing made him uneasy. "Listen, I'm quite happy to come back later, take up position again once I've had a break, if you like?"

"Absolutely no need. As I say, Mr. Wiseman has it all under control. He wanted me to thank you for bringing the situation to his attention and he is immensely grateful to you for everything you have done thus far. Okay? We'll be in touch next time we have anything for you." The call ended with a decisive click.

Andy had been given the brush-off, no question. He huffed. Perhaps he should change his name. Disposable Mossbury certainly had a ring to it, although he wasn't convinced it was a good one.

However, he was sure his dismissal had nothing to do with William Wiseman or Onesta's concern for his welfare. Nor did it have much to do with Andy doing a bad job. He might be feeling disposable, but he had brought his A-game to this job. He always did.

So why was he out on his ear?

Was it because he suggested he might not be willing to go ploughing into the hotel if there was a police operation taking place? Or was it because he recognized the cop in the first place? Andy began to wonder if he had been given his marching orders so the plan could continue unabated, with a different pair of eyes behind the camera lens. An unquestioning pair of eyes who knew nothing about Jim Carello and his true line of work.

Andy ran a hand across his forehead, his gaze habitually scanning the area outside the hotel. If that was so, then William Wiseman must have even fewer scruples than Andy thought. Could getting some lewd photos be worth putting his ex-wife in that kind of potential danger?

He couldn't believe Mr. Wiseman would be that mercenary, couldn't see what it would achieve. As Andy shuffled up behind the wheel of his car, another possibility swam into his brain. What if the news about the cop hadn't made it that far? What if Onesta had made the decision without referring to his boss? Andy blew out his cheeks. If Onesta was going it alone, then he was playing a dangerous game from both ends.

Andy wondered if he should call the cops and tell them what he'd surmised. But what did he definitely know? A lot of suppositions about what might be taking place weren't facts. He wasn't sure about any of it. Perhaps it was a total coincidence that Jim Carello was outside The Valentine Retreat.

A car drew to a halt behind him, holding up a sea of traffic as the driver flashed his headlights repeatedly. Andy rolled his eyes; it was that idiot, Kenny Johns. Giving everyone a masterclass in how to subtly position your car for an undercover stakeout. If anyone *hadn't* seen him flashing his lights it would be a miracle.

Andy twisted the key in the ignition of his own car, indicating to pull out before Kenny decided to blow his horn for good measure. Onesta was scraping the bottom of the PI barrel. He must have been desperate to employ Kenny Johns. Andy eased out of the space, pulling on his seatbelt as he checked his rearview mirror.

He drove around the block a few times. He might sort out the rest of his laundry. Or he could head over to the Lucky Break to play a few games of pool with the boys. Grab himself a takeout or pizza afterward. Hawaiian, perhaps. Maybe a classic pepperoni with a stuffed crust. How about going wild and buying himself a twenty-dollar bottle of bourbon with which he could celebrate losing his job? If he was lucky and Jeremy's neighbors weren't having another all-night party above the room Andy was staying in, he might even get some sleep. It would be kinder on his spine than the Ford's front seat had proven to be.

He could phone his wife.

He should phone his wife. When Linda asked him to move out, it was supposed to be a temporary thing, a breathing space for them both. Time to reevaluate what was important in their lives. She had dressed up the request, making it sound like she was doing him a favor, like she was giving him the opportunity to break free—as if she thought that was what he wanted. After all, she'd said, he never spent any time with her and the kids, as he was always working.

He should phone her and tell her he didn't want to break free.

He needed to ask Linda why she thought he worked all the hours God sent. It wasn't because he had lost interest in being with her and the kids—quite the opposite. The real reason was he was scared shitless that one day his work would dry up, and they would run out of money. It almost happened when Rory was a toddler and the bank foreclosed on Andy's loan. He was amazed that Linda seemed to have forgotten how they'd almost lost the house. Everyone knew being a PI didn't get him particularly high up on the secure income leaderboard, as this evening had proved.

He should tell her the truth. He should tell her that he wanted, more than anything, to be with his family.

But what if he made the call and she told him they didn't want him back? That he might have become disposable to the only three people in the world he truly cared for?

Andy let out a deep breath. Perhaps he would wait until tomorrow to call. Another twenty-four hours couldn't hurt, in the grand scheme of things. A call like that was so important, it wouldn't do to rush into it and say the wrong thing.

Plus, he couldn't shift the feeling that had settled in his gut. He might not be on the Wiseman clock any longer, but the heavy weight squatting in Andy's belly as he circled the block wasn't about his home life. It wasn't even indigestion.

Something didn't sit right about the conversation he had with Don Onesta, and no matter how easy it would be for Andy to take the next left turn and leave The Valentine Retreat behind, that same something kept making him turn right.

Chapter Eighteen

Monday Early Evening

Jim lodged a hip more firmly against one of the tall vinyl-topped stools which lined the serving counter in the Tick Tock diner. He couldn't settle. He flipped his mobile over, swiped at it, and looked at the screen for about the sixth time in the last minute. The message was still at the top of his inbox. He turned it facedown again and drummed his fingers on the countertop.

"More coffee?" The waitress must have misinterpreted his action as a silent request for a top-up. She hovered her jug of coffee over his mug, which was still half full.

"No, thanks. I'm good."

The message was from Luther Jackson, a coded text which read *"Call Uncle Ted, Auntie Helen isn't well."* A clear instruction that he was to phone in, that Jackson needed to tell him something pertinent to his undercover operation which couldn't wait until the following day.

Jim should phone in. He wasn't even sure why he hadn't already done so. Except that he had all but confessed his attraction to Megan in his meeting with Jackson earlier. If he had sat brooding in his aquarium long enough, he might have convinced himself that Jim wasn't totally on his game. If he'd done that, it was possible he would pull the plug on the current operation and order Jim out.

It was also within the realms of possibility that he might have worked out, same as Jim had, that they could use the information he'd already got to investigate the "pillow-talk for robbery." With some cross-department cooperation, it would be easy to trace the robberies back to women who had stayed at the hotel. A few embarrassing conversations, and they'd have a link.

But they needed more than that. Hard evidence of Valentine's complicity in the robberies wasn't going to be enough. More than that, they had to know he'd ordered them.

Perhaps Jackson wanted Jim to hold fire, to keep Megan at arm's length. Maybe Jackson had spoken with the department lawyers. Once he was away from the aquarium, it had occurred to Jim that it wouldn't be ethical to use information he gleaned from Megan if it were gained under false pretenses. Jackson would know the same.

Nor would it be ethical to set Megan's ex-husband up as a target for Valentine's cronies without his prior knowledge and permission. Jackson was probably still smarting from any conversation he might have had with the suits.

But a lot of work had gone into setting Jim up at The Valentine Retreat, and he had just gained access to the inside track on what was really going on. He wanted to make the most of this chance to prove himself to Jackson, as well as the brass upstairs. Maybe even get himself on the radar for a promotion.

And while he was happy to renegotiate the purpose of his being at The Valentine Retreat, he wasn't prepared to leave. Not yet. And certainly not with an evening with Megan in the offing. Nothing short of an earthquake topping nine on the Richter Scale could stop him from spending time with her.

He picked up the phone and dialed Jackson's direct number. "Hi, it's me," he said.

"You took your time," Jackson said. He didn't suppress the irritation in his voice. "And don't spin me any garbage about not having signal."

"I had to wait until I was clear of the place before I called," Jim said. He hadn't been at the hotel since this morning, but he hoped Jackson might swallow that as an excuse.

"The thing is, Jim, the car you noticed parked across the street is a PI's car, as you thought."

"Okay." The news didn't surprise him, but why was this information important enough to prompt Chief Jackson to send him that text? "What's that got to do with me?"

"It's not so much what it's got to do with you, but rather what it's got to do with her. With Megan Wiseman, or Leadbetter, or whatever the hell she's calling herself. She's got a tail."

Jim frowned. Someone was following Megan.

"The tail phoned me."

"Why?" It wasn't as if the LAPD didn't encounter private investigators, but generally their paths only crossed when dispatch sent some uniforms out to deal with a suspicious loitering vehicle.

"He recognized you."

"Are you telling me my cover's blown in the hotel?"

"No, it's not that. This guy, Andy Mossbury, he saw you talking to his subject outside the hotel. He's put two and two together, and the guy has actually come up with four."

"What do you mean?"

"What was his phrase? He described the two of you as looking like you wanted to be closer than macaroni and cheese." Jackson laughed. "Anyway, his brief was to get photos of Megan with whoever she shacks up with at The Valentine Retreat. You, in other words."

"Shit." Jim ran a hand through his hair.

"Quite." Jackson paused. Jim could hear him breathing, then he said, "Thing is, this PI said he told his boss he thought you might be a cop, but he couldn't be sure. Anyway, he's off the job now. He wanted you to know that another PI's taken his place, and someone inside the hotel is supposed to tip the guy the wink when a good photo opportunity presents itself, if you get what I'm saying."

"Someone wants compromising photos of Megan," Jim said.

"In a nutshell, yes."

"Who?"

"Her ex."

"Why?"

"Christ, Jim. I don't know. You're messing with the rich and famous. Who the hell understands any of what they get up to?"

"Are you ordering me out?"

"I probably should." There was a pause. Perhaps Jackson was wrestling with his thoughts the same as Jim. "Do you want out?"

"No." The answer was out before he realized he'd spoken. But it was the truth. Even if Jackson fired Jim over the phone, there was no way he was leaving Megan alone in there, especially now. "Who is informing the PI from inside the hotel?"

"He didn't know. He wanted me to warn you that your quiet night in with Megan could turn into a threesome."

"Great." He took a mouthful from his mug and swallowed. The coffee had gone cold. "I really don't want to throw this operation. There must be another way." His mind clutched at different scenarios in its search for a one-size-fits-all solution to the problem. "What about this? I stick close enough to Megan to find out something useful to take to Valentine tomorrow morning, keep my cover and my goal intact. I can always make some shit up to tell him, if necessary. I have no intention of doing anything other than talking to Megan tonight, finding out a bit more about her, so there won't be any reason for the PI to barge into the place either."

"Jesus wept, Carello. If that's your technique, it's no wonder you're still single. Do you want me to phone your mommy and let her know you're going to be home late?"

"Harsh, Chief, even for you."

"Yeah, well. Some sex worker you're turning out to be. Next you'll be offering to plump pillows and read bedtime stories."

"There's nothing wrong with a plump pillow." Jim smiled as Jackson snorted a laugh.

"I appreciate you sticking with this, Jim. I want you to know that."

"Yeah, well. I've come this far. It seems pointless to throw it all away."

"I want you to phone in first thing tomorrow, let me know what's going on. Make sure you maintain your cover, no matter what. You know that's more important than anything else."

"Of course."

Jackson let out a long breath, then said, "Well, all right, then. If I have your assurance that you can handle it, then I guess that's good enough for me."

"I can handle it, you have my word," Jim said.

Chapter Nineteen
Monday Evening

The pianist was in full flow as Megan followed Jolie into the bar. His fingers moved across the keys with the kind of confidence only a seasoned professional possessed. The music he produced was quiet and understated, which was more than could be said for his shirt. The vibrant duck-egg blue and plum check of the fabric was highly visible under his beige linen suit, open at the neck and unapologetic.

Megan smiled. For the first time in such a long time, she felt a spike of anticipation about this evening. She glanced down, smoothing the fabric of her own shirt under her fingers. Another shirt and black trousers combo. Jolie had suggested Megan might extend her wardrobe, maybe go wild and buy a couple of dresses, but up until this evening it hadn't seemed important.

At least this shirt had a more feminine neckline than some of her others. The repeating pattern of gray birds on the wing contrasted with the cream fabric, and the whole thing plunged its way far enough to show off the long glittering string of tiny, mirrored beads she wore. Her only nod to jewelry on this trip.

"I see him," Jolie said, heading toward the far end of the bar.

Megan hung back as Jolie greeted Chris with enthusiasm. There was no sign of Jim. She checked her watch, then remembered they hadn't specified when they would meet. She pulled in a breath, wishing they had set a time so she would know if he had changed his mind. Allow her the chance to deal with the prickle of disappointment on her own terms.

The room was less populated this evening, the weekend buzz replaced by a more relaxed atmosphere. Serving staff were having a much easier time moving around, with trays held easily on an upturned hand as they ferried empty glasses to and collected fresh orders from the bartenders. Intimate groups of people sat at some of the low tables, visible through the waving fronds of the potted palms.

"Can I get you something?"

The bartender's question claimed Megan's attention. She ordered a lime and soda and thanked him when he placed the tall glass in front of her.

"On your tab?" he asked.

"Yes, please. Suite 69."

"Not a problem," he said, his smile bright and accompanied by an unexpected wink. He looked past her and nodded his acknowledgement to someone, then moved away.

"Hi."

There was no need to turn, she recognized the voice. "Hi, Jim," she said as he shrugged his way out of his leather jacket. She looked more closely at his face. "What did you do?"

Jim's hand traveled up, his fingers tracing over a small patch of damaged skin. "Would you believe me if I told you there were five of them, and I took them all down single-handed?"

"Um, no. Not really," she said, trying to appear serious, although she couldn't stop the corners of her mouth twitching.

"Damn." He grinned. "You're right. Cut myself shaving."

"Does it hurt?"

"It didn't, until I put aftershave on without thinking." He pulled a face then shrugged. "A bit of pain reminds me I'm still alive."

"Do you need reminding?" She kept her tone light, but it was a genuine question. She had spent months wondering if she was still alive.

"Not lately." He smiled at her, then waved a finger at the bartender, ordering himself a beer. "How did the sightseeing go?"

"Would you be offended if I told you we totally ignored your advice?"

He rolled his eyes. "Jeez. After all my hard work compiling that list, you just ignored it?"

Only a couple of days ago, a comment like that would have had her taking hold of the fingers of one hand in the other to stop the trembling. She had totally lost the ability to gauge what was a rational reaction. She'd learnt a long time ago that the British sense of sarcasm she'd grown up with had no place in William's world. If he made a comment like the one Jim just had, he would have meant it. Literally. He would have expected an apology, an explanation.

This evening, though, she took hold of her drink instead. She marveled at how the liquid hardly shook on its way to her mouth, the ice barely clinking against the wall of the glass. The look on Jim's face was enough to reassure her he was joking.

"Don't worry, your list is still on my phone. We might go to the observatory tomorrow if that makes you feel better."

"That wasn't even on my list."

She grinned. He took hold of his bottle of beer, waving away the glass. "So, did you have a good day not seeing the sights?"

~ * ~

When Jolie and Chris joined them a while later, Megan wished they hadn't. She wanted to continue to talk to Jim, to have his attention all to herself. To watch his brown eyes crinkle when he smiled, to observe the path of his fingers as they ran their way through his hair or eased the collar of his crisp blue shirt. To wonder when she'd moved close enough to be able to smell the subtle citrus of his aftershave.

The flash of something akin to annoyance passed across Jim's face, too, when the others approached. Or was that wishful thinking on her part?

Chris carried with him an opened bottle of champagne and a fistful of glasses. Jolie took one look at Megan's glass and rolled her eyes. "Time for a proper drink," she said, lifting it from her fingers and pushing it onto the bar. "We're going to find somewhere to sit. Come and join us."

It was a statement rather than an invitation. Megan trailed behind Jolie, and they weaved their way through the bar looking for an empty table.

"How did the audition go?" Megan asked Chris once they were seated around a table close to the pianist.

"Do you know, I think I nailed it." He poured champagne into the glasses and passed them around.

Megan didn't really want any, but she accepted it. Jim took his glass, setting it onto the table beside his bottle of beer.

Chris flashed her a brilliant smile. "To be honest, I'm perfect for the part. At last my agent seems to be coming up with proper leads."

It transpired the role was for that of a love interest for one of the established characters in the daytime drama *Daylight Dreams*. Chris bandied about names of actresses and directors, none of which Megan was familiar with. Whilst he talked, she smiled and nodded, her attention firmly on Jim as he drained the last of his beer. He tipped the bottle to check it was empty before lodging it back on the table.

"I have to keep everything crossed and hope I get a call back," Chris said.

"How long do you have to wait to find out?" Megan asked absently.

Jim shuffled his feet and leant across, brushing her wrist with his fingertips. "I'm going to get another beer," he said, "Do you want anything?"

She shook her head, hoping the shiver shooting up her spine hadn't been visible. Chris suggested Jim should get another bottle of champagne whilst he was up. She stayed completely still, her gaze tracking Jim as he headed for the bar, only realizing she was holding her breath when he was halfway across the room.

"The callbacks will be quick. I might even hear tomorrow." Chris continued to talk, but Megan wasn't listening.

As Jim chatted with the bartender, she wondered what it was about his easy manner and quick smile which had her feeling as if she'd always known him. How it could be that such an innocent touch from his fingertips had her nerve endings searing and her cheeks flushing with heat?

"Don't you think? Megan, are you even listening to me?" Jolie sounded irritated.

"Sorry, what?" She dragged her gaze away from Jim.

"I said we could take the rest of the champagne up to the suite and enjoy it there."

Megan frowned. "I don't know."

"Then we can relax properly." Jolie glanced at the pianist. "And we can get away from that racket."

Before Megan could reply, Jim returned to the table with two bottles, one of beer, one of champagne.

"We're all going to head up to the suite," Chris said.

"Oh. Okay." Jim hovered by the table, his gaze finding hers. "If you like?" He looked conflicted, as if he was expecting to retake his seat but now wasn't sure what to do.

"I don't mind," Megan said. "We could stay here if you'd rather?" She gestured to the empty chair.

"No way," Jolie said, climbing to her feet and pulling at Megan's arm. "Come on. It'll be fun."

Chris scooped up their glasses and headed for the foyer and the elevators. Jolie tugged at Megan until she stood. She glanced at Jim. He walked a way behind, an expression on his face which she found she couldn't read.

She resolved to have a single drink with Jim in the suite. Then she would suggest they call it a night and ask if she could see him again the following day. Allow him to escape, if that was what he wanted. She suspected his expression might be his attempt to hide how he felt at being put into this awkward position. That he wasn't comfortable with being asked up to their suite.

As the elevator sealed the four of them into its space, she

couldn't stop the ripple of anticipation which bubbled its way through her. The feeling was impossible to ignore. She didn't want this evening with him to end. But as much as she wanted him to be there, she wanted him to want to be there just as badly.

~ * ~

Jim stood awkwardly with a bottle in each hand, staring at his own reflection in the interior paneling of the elevator. This wasn't the plan. At least, this hadn't been his plan. He was supposed to be keeping things above board and visible. He should be staying in a public space with Megan to ensure the PI would have no reason to move in with his telescopic lens.

He glanced across at her. Not that he minded an invitation to her suite. There must be a way to negotiate through this. He hadn't noticed anyone taking more interest than he would expect in any of them while they had been in the bar, and no one tailed them to the elevator. Someone was watching, though, and it was unnerving not to know who it was.

He would stay for a single drink, try to find out a few pertinent facts with which he could construct something that sounded plausible enough to tell Valentine, then say he should leave. If he was lucky, perhaps Megan would agree to meet up the next day. He might suggest the diner again. Or offer himself as her personal tour guide for the day. The thought of the two of them walking around the Griffith Observatory together made him smile.

Chris was still talking about his audition. Jim supposed that actors probably needed to be self-absorbed, that their focus was primarily inwards. But Christ alive, was he ever going to stop with the minutiae about the scene he'd acted out? Did the rest of them really need to know how many times he'd practiced his lines in front of a mirror to perfect his expressions?

Jim wondered if Valentine had explained the "pillow talk for robbery" aspect of his business to Chris. How easy Chris was finding it to ask the women he was with about themselves and their lives, rather than telling them all about his. Although Jim reasoned that Chris would probably turn it into an acting role. Perhaps he already was. Perhaps that was all any of them were doing. Acting out a role. Jim certainly was. It wasn't as if he could be honest with Megan about who he was and why he was here, could he?

Chris and Jolie spilled out of the elevator as the doors opened, threading their way toward the suite. Jim hung back, allowing Megan to exit the space first. She turned before he had a chance to move.

"Please don't feel you have to stay," Megan said. "I know Jolie can be a bit forceful sometimes, and I don't want you to feel awkward. I can tell them you decided against it, if you like?"

"Do you want me to go?" The elevator doors began to close.

He stuck a foot against one of them and reached out to press the hold button, his action awkward with the bottle of champagne already clasped in his hand. She took the bottle from him, her fingers brushing his. Did she notice the touch?

"No. I don't," she said. "I felt you were a bit ambushed downstairs. That's all."

He smiled. "I wasn't ambushed. It's all good."

She nodded and took a step back, allowing him across the metal running strips embedded into the corporate carpeting. They walked along the hallway in silence. He couldn't think of a single thing to say. No flippant remark to get her to smile, no piece of trivia from his bottomless pit to impress her with. His fountain of knowledge seemed to have dried up, as had the roof of his mouth. He swigged at his beer as she ran her key card through the lock and opened the door to the suite.

"There you are. We're dying of thirst in here." Jolie took the champagne from Megan and set about opening it. "Too busy necking in the hallway, I suppose." She winked at Megan, who ignored her and went to the window.

Jolie filled a couple of glasses and picked up the empty two. "Do you mind if we take this?" She waved the bottle in their direction. Megan shook her head.

"No. You're welcome to it," Jim said, setting his beer on the table alongside the filled glasses. He didn't much like champagne at the best of times.

"Don't wait up," Jolie said, flashing a grin and skipping across to an open doorway. Her bedroom, Jim supposed, with Chris already inside it. Jolie closed the door with a decisive click.

Awkward.

He wandered across to the window, staring out at the city beside Megan.

"It's beautiful, isn't it," she said.

The city was a lot of things, but Jim had never considered it beautiful. "I suppose." The red taillights and bright headlights of the flow of traffic crisscrossed the block, the infinite squares of light coming from neighboring buildings, a mixture of office and residential blocks. A whole cacophony of life, from a single viewpoint.

Was it only two days since he'd been in this same spot, watching the same lights, when he thought she'd fallen asleep after her massage? Was it only two days ago that he thought his life was as complicated as it could get? He laughed.

"Are you okay?" she asked.

"I'm fine," he said, then realized his choice of word. He glanced at her, but she didn't seem to have noticed. "Do you want me to leave?"

"Do you want to leave?"

"No. Not really."

"Then don't." She smiled at him. Not a big enough smile to light up the gold flecks in her eyes, but a smile, nonetheless.

Chapter Twenty

Megan couldn't think of a single thing to say. She wandered to the table, picking up one of the glasses of champagne and the bottle of beer. She held the bottle out to Jim, but as he grasped it he inadvertently took hold of her fingers too.

He slid the bottle into his other hand and released his grip. "Sorry," he said.

How was she going to let him know that she wanted him to touch her? The weirdest thing in all of this was the more she wanted his touch, the further away the possibility seemed. Like a dragonfly on a pond—no sooner had you caught sight of it than it would flit and swerve and disappear, and the process of searching for it started all over again.

His gaze remained fixed on something outside the building, his fingers picking at the edge of the label on the bottle. His attention seemed to be a million miles away from her.

She took a deep breath. "Okay. Which one? Dire Straits or The Police?"

Jim nearly dropped his bottle, fumbling and catching it in time. "What?" He looked uncharacteristically ruffled by her question.

"Which band do you prefer: Dire Straits or The Police? I was wondering if your taste in eighties music is as impressive as your knowledge of it."

"Oh, right. I see what you mean." He downed a mouthful of beer.

"Are you stalling?" She edged closer. "Were you faking it with your answers last night?" She smiled to make sure he knew she was joking.

"Not at all." He looked at her, the tight lines around his eyes easing as his mouth crinkled into a smile. "It's a tough choice, that's all. It's not a decision I could make lightly. If you'd said Glass Tiger versus either of them, I could have answered in a heartbeat."

"But I didn't. The hardest choices are always the more

interesting ones, don't you think?" She held his gaze and, this time, he didn't look out through the window again. He stayed, with his full attention warming her face like bright summer sunshine. "So, which one is it?" she said, her voice cracking as she spoke.

"Dire Straits."

She nodded. "Okay. We have a winner."

"The right decision, do you think?"

"Who knows?" she said. "I don't think I could choose between them to be honest."

"So why did you ask?"

She noticed him inch closer to her. "I wanted to know which one you'd choose."

"Why?" He kept moving. He was close enough now for her to breathe in his citrus scent. Close enough to touch.

"I want to know more about you," she said. Plus, if he was talking, it gave her the excuse to look at him, but she didn't say that. "About what makes you tick."

"Would you mind if I said I want to know more about you too?" He reached out a hand, taking a strand of her hair and trailing it between his finger and thumb before allowing it to fall back against her shoulder.

"What do you want to know?" The distance between them was less than a single step. She shifted to bridge the gap, stopping just shy of him. She was tall, but at this proximity to him she still had to tip her head to maintain eye contact.

He ran a hand around the back of his neck, the braided bracelet he wore dipping in and out of the cuff of his shirt. On impulse, Megan took hold of his hand and guided it down until he wrapped it around her waist. Then he pulled her against him, the warmth of his body and the firmness of it hard against hers. She threaded her hand up until her fingers touched the side of his face, tracing their way across the unfamiliar terrain, gently avoiding the tiny patch of roughness where the skin was damaged.

She repeated her question, although this time she didn't manage much more than a whisper. "What do you want to know?"

The skin beneath her fingers shifted as he smiled. The ridges disappeared again just as quickly, his intense gaze fixed on her. The walnut brown of his eyes darkened and swirled into whirlpools of depth. "All of a sudden," he said, "I can't seem to think of a single thing to ask."

She slid her fingers until the smooth warmth of his skin gave way to the coarse sandpaper of the hair on the nape of his neck. She allowed her fingers to enjoy the texture. It was enough to stoke the fire which had begun to build inside her. He responded to her touch, the heat in her belly spiking when he let out a low, almost imperceptible moan. At last, his head dipped toward her, and his lips took control of hers. She closed her eyes, her other senses taking control of her brain.

His kiss was worth the wait. His hand traveled up from her waist, his fingers threading themselves through her hair and cupping the back of her head as the softness of his lips on hers made the heat spike inside her again. He pushed her until she ran out of floorspace, lodged against the wall beside the window. With her back against an unyielding surface, there was no denying the urgency with which he pressed himself against her, and she wanted more. She wanted his skin against hers, she wanted to block out the rest of the world, eradicate rational thought and go with what her body was telling her. No, it wasn't telling her—her body was screaming at her.

She needed to get his shirt off, but she still had her champagne in one hand. She shifted, wondering how to get the glass to the table without ruining the moment. He must have sensed her awkwardness and pulled back, lifting the glass from her hand. He reached across and lodged the glass and his own bottle onto the table. In his hurry to set both down, he caught the edge of the bottle, spinning it against the glass. Both cascaded onto the floor. The stem of the champagne glass smashed against the hardwood, a pool of alcohol trickling from the bottle and circling the pieces.

Jim muttered an oath. She grinned as he crouched and carefully picked out the glass. Taking the pieces across to the bin near her bedroom door, he dropped them in.

"I'll get a towel," he said.

Before she could suggest she should go rather than him, before he realized he would have to go through her bedroom to find a towel, he had already headed through the door.

"Everything all right out here?"

She hadn't noticed Chris standing in the doorway, naked apart from a towel drawn tightly around his waist. "We heard a crash."

"It's nothing. A glass broke, that's all." She attempted a smile. Still burning from the intensity of Jim's kiss, but with the sudden loss of his touch, her emotions flick-flacked inside her. "Jim's getting something to clear up the mess."

Chris ran a lazy hand through his hair. "You look nervous."

"Do I?" She was feeling a myriad of things, but nerves weren't one of them.

"A bit. Jolie said you haven't done anything like this before. It'll be fine."

"What do you mean?"

"No need to be anxious." He flashed her another wide smile. "Jim? He's a dead cert, babe. We all are." He pulled at the red braid wound around his wrist, waggling it between his fingers. It looked like the one she noticed Jim was wearing. "Satisfaction guaranteed." He winked, then disappeared back into Jolie's room.

Satisfaction guaranteed? He's a dead cert? What was that supposed to mean?

Megan perched on the scrolled end of one of the couches, waiting for Jim to return. She remained passive as he mopped up the liquid, folded the towel and discarded it.

He joined her and made a throwaway comment about being naturally clumsy, but she didn't smile. Her focus was on his wrist. She pulled at his sleeve, hooking her finger underneath the red braid and tugging his arm up until it lay between their lines of sight.

"What does this mean?" she asked.

"It means I work for the hotel," he said. "Why?"

~ * ~

Something had happened in the time he'd been gone, that much was clear. The fire he'd seen held within the flecks of gold in her eyes had evaporated, replaced by something much colder and harder.

"Please tell me the truth," she said. A wrinkle of a frown formed between her eyes. "I've stayed in a lot of hotels and I've never seen staff identified by something like that before." She glanced once more at the braid, then let go of it. "What does it mean?"

In a reflex action, Jim shuffled the braid out of sight again, then placed his palms flat against his thighs. He puffed out his cheeks. He couldn't see a positive way out of this without lying to her. And he'd learned a long time ago that lying to a woman tended to come back to bite you, sooner or later.

"Did you know this suite is booked under a red-braid package?" he said.

"I don't know anything about the booking. Jolie won our stay here in some competition she entered."

Jim frowned. "Are you sure?" The cost of the suite for the length of time they were booked in for was eye-watering, at least as far as he was concerned. He lived well on his detective's salary, but their stay wouldn't leave him much change from a month's wages. That was some competition prize.

"Of course I'm sure." She crossed her arms.

"What did Jolie tell you about this hotel?"

"How come you're suddenly asking *me* questions?" Her defiance was clear. "You still haven't answered mine."

"She didn't mention the red braid part of it?"

"No. She said we were having a few days in a swanky hotel. Please answer the question." She pointed to his wrist again. "Tell me what it means."

He sighed. As he'd suspected—and had desperately wished was the case—Megan was ignorant to the in-house benefits of their booking. Not that it helped him much. He was going to have to tell her the capacity in which he was employed by The Valentine Retreat, and he couldn't imagine she was going to like what he said.

Or maybe she wouldn't care either way. Maybe she simply wouldn't like having been kept out of the loop about it. Not that that would make him feel any better.

Either way, this evening was about to come to a crashing end. He was going to lose her. He had nothing to take to Valentine, and that would mean he would have nothing for Jackson either. Regardless of any of that, Jim wasn't going to lie to her.

He softened his tone as he said, "It means I am at your disposal. Completely and utterly. Whatever you want, I will give it to you. That's what it means."

He ran a hand through his hair as she processed his words. Watched the frown flick on and off like a switch.

"But that's room service," she said. "Or butler service. Is that what you mean?"

"No, Megan. I am here to give you anything you want. Personally." He emphasized the words, hoping he wouldn't have to spell it out any further.

The way she slowly began to shake her head and her disdainful expression were killing him. She'd grasped the full extent of what he was saying. "Anything? You mean, you talking to me, your attention, the kiss... That all comes with the room?"

He nodded.

"If you hadn't knocked the bottle? If we'd..." She cut the sentence short, her cheeks flaring with color as her gaze flicked across to her bedroom door. She took a breath. "That's included, too?"

He nodded again. This was turning into a complete screw up. Why hadn't he kept her in the bar, rather than coming up to her suite? Why had he kissed her? Some undercover officer he was. Unable, it seemed, to stick to the simplest of plans.

She messed with his head that was the problem. He couldn't think straight when she was around. It was difficult to think at all, when he was close to her all he wanted to do was soak her up, like an intoxicating sponge.

"After I go? When our stay is over, what then? You wave goodbye and move on to the next woman who happens to look your way?" Her voice was pinched and tight, and the color leaving her cheeks was replaced by a sheen of cold porcelain. She looked as if she had been carved from alabaster.

"In theory."

"What the fuck does that even mean, Jim?"

"Yes, Megan. I move onto the next guest. That's supposed to be how it works."

"Supposed to be?"

"I'm not sure I'll be able to do that when you leave."

"Why not, if it's your job?" She spat the words. He didn't blame her.

"Because they won't be you."

She gave a mirthless laugh. "I bet you say that to all the girls."

"If only I could make you believe that I really don't." Short of telling her about his real purpose at The Valentine Retreat and jeopardizing his career by revealing who he really was, he couldn't see how he was going to salvage anything from this moment.

Would she even care if he told her that he'd spent the entire time since he'd been in Valentine's employ avoiding getting too close to any of the guests? Or that he couldn't imagine anything he wanted to do less than move on to someone new once she left? He sighed in defeat.

"I want you to leave," she said, her expression nothing more than a mask. "I want you to get out. Now."

Chapter Twenty-One

Once he was gone, Megan leant against the suite door. What the hell had just happened? How had she managed to fall so completely for the wrong man—again? Perhaps she had "cosmos please kick me" running through her, like the words spun through a stick of seaside rock.

Maybe it was the universe's way of clarifying the position to her, once and for all, where living with cats in Connecticut was concerned. Perhaps she should start a house search in Bridgeport right now. Book up to visit an animal shelter soon, investigate sourcing a few feline buddies to keep her company through the long, lonely, beckoning years.

With the warmth of his lips still echoing on her own, she closed her eyes, balling her hands against them. It was hard to tell if she was going to scream or cry. Or do both. Goddamn it. She really liked Jim, had hoped to get to know more about him. In fact, screw the niceties, for once in her life she really wanted this guy and, no point denying it, she had been more than ready to take him to bed. Her feelings had become intense enough to push all her worries to one side, instead she was determined to enjoy his company regardless of the quagmire of her own life. Determined even to attempt to find a way to keep him in her life, to deal with William and whatever hand grenades he might throw to try to wreck things. She was desperate to find out if Jim might be the one to give her the happiness Jolie was always saying that she deserved.

Until she met Jim, she didn't think happiness remained a factor in her life. She wasn't even sure she wanted it. But time spent with him had given her a tiny taste of what she had been missing.

Right up until the part when he told her he was a…a what? A gigolo? A sex worker? A butler with benefits? She wasn't quite sure what kind of a label to put on him.

Striding over to the table, she lifted and drained the remaining glass in a single gulp. The champagne pricked at the back of her nose and stung her eyes, making them water. Megan slammed the glass down at the same time as there was a knock at the door.

Screwing one eye closed to peer through the viewfinder in the door, she saw Jim standing on the other side. He ran a hand through his hair as he waited, an uncomfortable expression on his face.

She yanked open the door and stared at him.

"I'm sorry," he said. "I left my jacket." He pointed to where it lay, over the back of the farthest couch.

"You'd better get it, then," she said, pulling the door open far enough to let him in.

"Thanks."

"I don't want your thanks," she said as he crossed the room and fetched the jacket, balling it up in his hands. "I don't want anything from you."

"Okay. I'm sorry. I'm going."

"I thought we'd already established that was what you were going to do."

He hovered in the doorway, not quite far enough out for her to close the door on him. "I don't want it to be like this."

"Why should I care what you want?" she said, the sting of disappointment impossible to hide. She went to push him, to try to shove the sense of desolation through the door with him, but he took hold of her arm. His grip was firm but not rough, his fingers warm against her skin.

"Please," he said. "There are things about me I need you to know so you can understand who I really am. Why I'm working here."

She yanked at her arm until he let her go, her voice rising in anger. "I can't imagine you could tell me anything which would make me understand why you've led me on like you have. I feel so stupid, Jim."

"You're anything but that, Megan. If I could explain, I think you might see things differently."

She should close the door in his face, banish him from her life before he caused her any further pain. But the bottom line was she didn't want to. She was standing close enough to breathe in the citrus scent of him again, she could see the red mark on the side of his face, she could reach out and touch him if she wanted to. And, God help her, she wanted to.

By his own admission he was already bought and paid for. She could do exactly what she liked with him. Perhaps she should ask him how it felt to be someone else's property. What it was like to belong to another human being for a while.

Except she already knew exactly how that went, didn't she?

William had bought and paid for her more times than she cared to consider, even though she wasn't aware of it, not to begin with. It was as if he still owned her, in ways that drilled further into her core than the financial agreement ensuring her brother's care. He still owned her ability to enjoy anything, he controlled her with the years of conditioning she hadn't realized were taking place until she was in so deep she'd almost drowned.

It was meeting Jim which had given Megan the impetus to start kicking her way back to the surface again, to swim away from the shipwreck rather than drown alongside the wreckage of her life. She owed him for allowing her to believe she might even find dry land one day. She owed him a chance to explain.

Anyway, there was no way she was interested in ownership. That much was definite.

Her shoulders dropped, and she stepped back from the door, letting him back into the suite. "You don't have to justify yourself to me," she said. "You barely know me. And we're all just trying to make it from one day to the next. I understand that better than you might think."

"There are things about who I am which I can't tell you, not right now." He took a step closer, his voice dropping until it was barely more than a whisper. "But I want you to know them. I'm desperate for you to know them. The thing is, working here is temporary. I'm pulling the plug on this job as soon as you leave this place. I've already decided that's what I'm going to do. If I told you I do something a million miles away from being an escort, that I did it before I came to work here and that I'll do it again once I leave, would you be able to believe me? If I told you I must be the only red-braid worker in this place who hasn't slept with any of the guests, would you be able to trust me? Then, after you leave this place we could meet up and have a proper conversation, and I'll explain it all to you."

She looked at him, so close to her now she had to tilt her head to study his face. She frowned. He hadn't balked from telling her what the red braid meant, so why was this information so difficult to vocalize? "Why can't you tell me now?"

Another step brought him closer, only inches away. He leant toward her ear and whispered, "If I could, I would." Agonized indecision crossed his face. He glanced away, up toward the ceiling, then back at her again. He shook his head, his shoulders slumping with a taint of defeat.

Megan reached out, framing his face with the palms of her hands. "Tell me."

He took a decisive breath, then said quietly, "My role here, this whole red-braid deal…you're an intelligent woman, Megan, think about it for a moment. Who might be interested in stopping this kind of skin trade?"

He bridged the final gap, moving right up against her as her brain whirred, and it dawned on her what he was saying. Her hand flew from his face to hers. "Are you trying to tell me you're a—" She couldn't finish her sentence because Jim placed his hand over her mouth.

"Sorry," he breathed, gently removing it. "I shouldn't have done that."

"You're a cop?" She mouthed the words.

"I shouldn't be telling you; it goes against *everything*… My boss is going to bust me right back down to traffic if he ever finds out. But I need you to know. I want you to know who I really am. What I really am."

"You're here undercover?"

"Yeah." He pressed his fingers up to his lips, shaking his head, before he glanced around the room. He touched his ears. Was he worried the room might be bugged? This was too much to take in.

"I need you to know this place isn't a good place to be. It's rotten to the core. Will you take your friend and go home? Tomorrow?" His lips were still millimeters from her ear. "Then we could meet. Start again, and maybe do this for real? If you want to."

He was so close to her she was finding it harder and harder to concentrate on what he was saying. Amidst his revelations, which she was struggling to get her brain around, something else kept bubbling to the surface. It was the reason she'd been so upset by his explanation of what the red braid meant, why she'd opened the door to him again so he could fetch his jacket rather than getting it for him. This feeling was the reason his voice, so low and quiet in her ear, was filling every inch of her consciousness.

"I'll gladly leave this place." Unable to ignore the feeling any longer, she stood on tiptoes to get her lips as close to his ear as she could. "I'll go home tomorrow if you promise me one thing."

"Anything."

"Promise to take me to the diner before I leave?"

"Of course I will. What time?"

She held her breath for a moment. Logic suggested she shouldn't do this, but there was no way that sentiment could compete with what bubbled around it like hot lava. "Why don't we decide in the morning?"

Layers of sensibility scattered, like bright pinpoints of curling flame when dry leaves are thrown onto a bonfire, until all that remains is the pure intensity of the fire.

Linking her arms around his neck, she said, "I think you should stay. I want you to stay."

Her fingers sought out the hair on the back of his neck. There was something about touching him there. The heat was instant, building inside her more rapidly than before, made all the more intense when he took hold of her. On tiptoes, she brushed his lips with hers, gratified when he pulled her against himself even more tightly and gave a low groan. This time he kissed her with an intensity which took her breath away.

Like before, a single thought pierced its way through the technicolor waves of heat which enveloped her. There were too many clothes. Desperate to feel his skin against hers, she fumbled with his shirt collar, easing her hands around until they rested against the ridges of his collarbones. Reaching for the first button on his shirt, she fiddled with it until it released. Down to the next one, then the next, her fingers fumbling and trembling as she fought to undo them.

Once she'd prized the two sides of the shirt apart, she paused. Unsure if it was his sharp intake of breath at her touch, or the firmness of the lines of muscles under her fingertips, something initiated another wave of heat passing through her body. The exact cause didn't matter, all that mattered was the fire tracking its way out from the base of her stomach, spreading and intensifying. A massive firework.

As she pulled his shirt free from the waistband of his chinos, she realized there was another goddamn button. Abruptly, he stopped kissing her, moving his head back to look at her. His eyelids heavy, his breathing fast as he stared at her.

"We should stop," he said. "We shouldn't do this. You don't understand."

Ignoring him, she continued to push at the shirt, trying to slide it from his shoulders, desperate to separate fabric from skin. "Take it off."

She heard her own words as if they had been spoken by someone else, impatient as he undid the final button and allowed the shirt to slide to the floor, where it joined his jacket. He stood motionless, and all she could do was stare at him. Stare at the upper half of his body, the muscles defined and clear, just bulky enough to be totally and utterly sexy. Waiting to be touched, to be kissed.

How she wanted to touch him, all of him. Megan had never before been so physically attracted to a man, the intensity of the feeling riding a fine line between heat and an inferno.

She smiled at him, and he smiled back. The deliciousness of knowing what they both wanted to happen next, but with the anticipation of it all still to come.

"Take mine off," she said. She needed his hands on her body, needed his skin against hers.

Still, she surprised herself with her own words, with the huskiness of her own voice. She was never this bold, never had been before. She was so very turned on, it was as if Jim was surrounded by a halo of technicolored light and everything else in the room paled away in hues of gray.

"Are you sure?" he said as his fingers reached up to her shoulders. In reply, she took hold of his hand and brought his fingers to the silk edges of the V-neckline, tracing them down to the top button, nestled right between her breasts. She didn't speak; instead she pressed his fingers against the buttons.

Her hands dropped to her side as he undid the first button, her gaze traveling back up to his. "Faster," she said. "Do it faster. Please, Jim…"

He loosened the next button, then the next, his breathing rapid. Now it was his turn to stare at her as she wiggled her shoulders free of the silk and dropped it. The little gray birds on the fabric momentarily took flight before they settled onto the floor.

She fought to control her breathing as Jim ran his fingers across her belly, tracing a path up until they hit the edge of her bra. Even through the delicate lace every touch was so intense it was almost painful. He threaded his way up, looping fingers beneath the straps, her shrugs loosening them and his fingers tugging until they fell away.

Her own hands traveled around to her back, fumbling for the clasp, shedding the fabric. She gasped as his mouth found its way around one nipple and then the other. Every touch was red-hot, every inch of her body was ready for him, desperate for him.

"Take me to bed," she whispered.

He leant down, scooping her up behind her knees. With his other arm strong around her back, he carried her into the bedroom.

Chapter Twenty-Two

Tuesday Morning

Andy Mossbury woke to the sound of a garbage truck upending a dumpster, the contents rattling and cascading into the belly of the vehicle. The whining of the mechanical arms lowering the dumpster back down was timed perfectly to him stretching his own arms as far above his head as he could manage in the confines of his car.

He cranked the seat back into an upright position and looked around. Not much to see. The view hadn't changed since he drew up on the side of the street bordering The Valentine Retreat the previous evening. He'd continued to circle the hotel until hunger got the better of him, and he'd slammed his car into a space, heading to an all-night supermarket to stock up on supplies.

After he'd eaten it seemed futile to drive anywhere else, so he settled in for the night. By the time he'd woken one thing was sure. Whether he was being paid or not, he only had a limited number of nights left in him for sleeping in a car. Especially a car as filthy as this one. He wondered how long it would take to get it properly valeted.

Perhaps he should get it done before he phoned his wife. He could really impress her with a clean car. He could drop it in at Dan's Autos, around the corner from the family home.

He took a moment to chuckle to himself. Like that was going to happen. Filling a black bin liner was about as close to a valet as this car was likely to get, no point trying to act all classy.

Whether or not he cleaned the car out, though, there was no getting away from the fact something had to change, and soon.

Andy squirted some breath freshener into his mouth, then checked his reflection in the rear-view mirror. If he was being critical, the beard was beginning to take on a hobo edge to it. He should find a washroom later today and sort it out. Right now, though, coffee was the priority.

The air outside hadn't yet absorbed much warmth from the rays of a sun only just peeking out from behind the buildings, so Andy grabbed his sports jacket, ramming his wallet into a pocket. He felt around for his mobile, finding it lodged between his seat and the central console of the car.

He slipped that into another pocket and climbed from his seat, which complained at the injustice of its overuse with a squeak almost as loud as his own grunt of discomfort.

He slid one arm then the other into the jacket, levering it up and slamming the door as he moved tentatively along the sidewalk. It took a few strides to check whether he had retained proper use of both of his legs. He didn't get much further before his phone rang. Onesta's office.

Andy ran a hand up his sleeve to check his watch. Either Onesta had taken some kind of an overtime-enhancing drug, or he had strong-armed Rhonda into working early.

"Yes," he said, keeping his tone light in case it was Rhonda.

"Where are you?"

It wasn't Rhonda. It was Onesta, and he sounded pissed.

"I'm in Hawaii. Toes in the pool, pina colada in one hand. Why?" Andy headed along the sidewalk toward the deli café, hoping it would be open.

"Kenny Johns said he saw your car parked across the block from The Valentine Retreat. What the hell are you playing at?"

"Why does it matter where I am? I'm not on Wiseman's books any longer. Last time I checked this was still a free country. That means that even people like me can go where they like."

"It's Mr. Wiseman to you."

"Of course it is." Andy waited at the stop sign, willing the red to turn to green. Coffee was occupying an increasing proportion of his conscious thought.

"I've been up all night waiting to hear something from Johns." Onesta paused. Andy could hear his breathing—tight and sharp, through his nose—his anger barely suppressed. "It's been a very trying night. We were hoping to have something to take to Mr. Wiseman by this morning, but there's been no word from our source inside the hotel."

"Okay." He wasn't altogether sure why Onesta was telling him this. "And what about the cop?"

"Andy, I want you to back off and go home. I don't want you anywhere near the hotel. We're pulling the plug on the whole thing and will reassess the situation once everyone has had some sleep." There was a pause in which he decided he wouldn't tell him that he'd slept quite well before Onesta said, "Did you hear me?"

"I heard you."

"Just go home, Andy. If you want to be paid, forget about this job. And forget you ever saw that cop."

Onesta ended the call, and Andy glanced around, realizing he had missed his opportunity to cross the street; the hand was red again. There was something in Don's voice which Andy had heard once before, when things hadn't gone how he had planned.

His words then had been sharp, his tone clipped, the anger barely under wraps. This was him lashing out, at least as far as he was able to in his buttoned-up world.

It might have been better for everyone concerned back then if the man had been able to go out and find someone to punch. He sounded like he wanted to punch someone again this morning, but that wasn't his style. His style was far less straightforward, far more at home hiding in the dark corners with the monsters.

No, Onesta was much more likely to do something under the radar to relieve his frustration, and the way he had been so keen for Andy to forget about having seen Jim Carello made Andy's mouth go dry.

Surely it was Andy's twisted thought process that made him wonder whether Onesta's next move might be to throw the cop to the wolves? It couldn't be anything more than his overactive imagination. Could it?

He suddenly wished he hadn't mentioned Jim Carello at all, except he had no real choice. There was no way to avoid disclosing anything which was relevant to the job, Andy was well aware of what Onesta was like when important information was withheld from him. He had simply been trying to shortcut the fallout which would have occurred a bit further down the line in any case, but now he wasn't so sure he should have done it.

Furnished with a takeaway coffee and a breakfast muffin, he headed back to his car. Kenny John's car was conspicuous by its absence, so Andy lodged his provisions on his dashboard and fired up the engine.

He pushed his way out into the traffic, rounded the corner, and slid his car neatly into the gap. Years spent behind the wheel ensured he was a master of parallel parking. In fact, he could park his car pretty much anywhere, and quickly.

He peeled down the edge of the muffin wrapping and took a bite. Perhaps he should stay put for a while longer. He might see the cop and be able to explain the situation.

Perhaps he could give Rhonda a call, ask her to find out the name and the number of the informant inside the hotel. Better still, she could get him Megan's number.

Then Andy could call her directly and ask to speak to Jim. Perhaps he could call Chief Jackson again, make an even greater fool of himself by spilling his ludicrous suppositions all over the man.

Andy sipped his coffee. Thinking about how to phrase his worries in a way which would sound plausible to a chief of police was enough to convince him he was clutching at straws.

While he finished his muffin, he would think about the situation logically and then decide what to do.

Chapter Twenty-Three

Megan stayed quiet and still. Jim was still asleep, one arm draped across her waist. Warm and richly tanned, it contrasted starkly against her pale skin. She'd been awake for a while, taking the opportunity to study him. Face down, with his other arm spread-eagled across his side of the bed, the muscles in his back were relaxed but still defined as he lay there. She focused on the calmness of his rhythmical breathing, closing her eyes as she listened.

Behind the seclusion of her eyelids, her mind wandered back to the previous night. She couldn't help herself. There weren't many things she had experienced over the last few years that she wanted to relive, but that was without doubt one of them.

Early on with William she thought the sex had been great. It should have been if the number of women he'd bedded was anything to go by.

Turned out, what she believed was great sex with him was nothing more than the climb up to the first drop on a rollercoaster of a ride. Megan couldn't remember the last time she'd been as out of control as she was with Jim. It was beginning to sink in that she didn't think she'd ever experienced anything quite like that before.

Just when she assumed the sensations couldn't get any more intense, she discovered another layer of heat and fire and want, then another, until the world exploded into shards of gloriously shimmering light. Thinking about it was enough to make her want to do it all over again.

She shuffled over and opened her eyes. Her movement woke him. The muscles in his back and neck stiffened as he stirred. His face was creased from the folds in the sheets, the lines changing as his expression shifted from sleep to consciousness.

"Thank God," he said, running a hand through his hair.

"What for?"

"I thought it was all a dream, but you're real. You're here."

"I'm definitely here," she said.

"How are you feeling?"

"Oh, I'm fine." She buried her face into the pillow so he didn't see the grin she couldn't stop.

"Only fine?" He slid an arm around her waist and pulled her toward him. "I think we should aim for something more impressive than fine."

She wrapped her arms around the tops of his shoulders, her fingers revisiting the short hair on the back of his head. "Like what?"

"How about sensational?"

Sensational sounded good. And achievable, especially when she pressed herself against him. The effect of his body on hers was instantaneous.

There were no words for a while.

She wanted to stop time. She wished she could hold on to these moments somehow. Find a way to capture them and cork them in a bottle, shining and bright. Could she keep Jim in her life? Could they work? Was it even what Jim wanted?

There was no way she could move on with a new man without interference from William; that was a certainty. Now was not the time for that man to creep back into the forefront of her brain. Now wasn't the time for thinking about anything except the way Jim was making her whole existence spin.

Eventually, breathless and covered in a sheen of sweat, they lay quietly again.

"Would you still like to go to the diner for breakfast?" he asked.

She touched the rough texture of his stubble. "I'd like to stay right here, to be honest. We could order room service."

"We could." He lowered his voice. "But I want to talk to you, properly, about this place and getting you away from it, and I can't do that here."

She hadn't forgotten the revelations of the previous evening, one coming so fast on the heels of the other they'd made Megan's head spin. As she lay in his arms, she knew she would have taken him to bed without hesitation before he told her about the red braid. When she'd found out what it meant she'd felt such anger, intense and jagged like a serrated knife.

But this morning she realized the anger was about more than his role in the hotel. It had a lot to do with discovering she had been misled, that she was on the back foot. That somehow she was stupid not to have known.

William did that to her all the time. Suggested he'd told her things and she'd forgotten about them, when he had done no such thing. Insisting she knew about functions and being angry with her for not being ready on time, when he hadn't even mentioned them. Making her believe she was stupid, inadequate, in need of his confirmation on even the most basic of facts.

The thing was, Megan wasn't sure that taking Jim to bed had anything to do with finding out he was a police officer, either. She might well have done it even if she'd known about the red braid right from the start. It was his honesty she valued, over and above his profession.

"Okay," she said. "The diner it is."

"Good," Jim said. He traced the side of her face, his fingers brushing her neck, feathering their way down her arm. "That's really good."

Neither of them moved.

Megan allowed her gaze to flow across his body, touching a star-shaped, ragged scar near his left hip. She'd seen it the night before but had been too preoccupied to mention it. "What's this from?"

"A .22 bullet," he whispered, tickling his lips against her ear. "Line of duty."

"Oh my god. Really?" He'd been shot. She supposed she shouldn't be completely surprised; he was a cop after all.

"No big deal. My gun was bigger."

The soft warmth of his breath in her ear was driving her wild all over again. There was another mark, this one below his left arm. "And this?"

"Kid with a knife. I wasn't wearing my vest. Stupid mistake." The roughness of his stubble scratched her cheek.

She'd noticed one more. "This one?" A gouge to one side of his sternum, almost hidden by the wiry hair on his chest.

"My brother, with a sharp stick, when I was about seven. Pure accident, that one." He grinned. "Although it's still a bit sore. Any chance you might kiss it better?"

"I'll see what I can do," she said.

~ * ~

A while later, her fingers laced between his, Jim and Megan headed for the Tick Tock diner.

As they walked, he pulled his mobile from a pocket. "I said I'd check in this morning. Would you mind if I make a call?"

"Of course not," she said.

He squeezed her fingers before he let go and dialed a number. He put the phone to his ear, retaking her hand in his free one as he waited for Jackson to pick up. It only took a couple of rings before he heard the chief's voice.

"Jim. Are you okay?"

"I'm good, everything's fine," Jim said. He glanced at Megan and was gratified by the obvious amusement in her sideways glance.

"Any sign of the PI?"

"No, there was no sign of anyone."

"You sound very sure about that. You plumped her pillows then left, did you? Stayed on point all night polishing your armor?"

"Not exactly." He didn't elaborate.

"Well, I hope you had a better night than I did. I spent mine checking my pulse. Raced all night."

As did mine, Jim thought. "Too much coffee?"

"Is there such a thing?"

"You should get it checked out."

"Yeah. Tuesday after hell freezes over, next time I get a day off. I think we can assume the PI kept to his side of the bargain, though, and that your cover is secure."

"Yeah. About that…" There was no point keeping it from the chief. He'd find out sooner or later and, in Jim's experience, sooner was usually less painful. He held his breath for a second, then said, "I told Megan."

Jim held the phone away from his ear as the chief's voice escalated somewhere near the pitch of a bat. "You did what?"

"I know what you said, but it couldn't be avoided. It's all going to work out."

He was about to say something else, try to clarify the importance of Megan understanding it all, but he didn't get the chance. He caught the words mid-breath and turned them into a frustrated exhalation as Jackson berated him for his stupidity.

"It's under control, Chief, I promise."

"You can't begin to understand the position you've put us all in, Jim."

"I'll tell the brass it was all my doing. It's not your fault I didn't stick to the plan. They can bust me back down to traffic if they like. But it's all going to work out perfectly."

The phone came away from his ear again, and he shook his head as the tirade continued.

"No. It isn't going to work out perfectly, Jim," the chief said. "You've involved a member of the public. How stupid can you be? Never mind traffic. You'll be lucky to hold onto any role in the force at this rate."

"I think you're overreacting."

"Do you? Do you really? At this point I don't much care what you think. I'm officially pulling the op, Jim. I want you to come in. Now. Do you hear me?"

"I hear you, Chief. I'll see Megan away from this place then I'll come in."

"You better had."

The call ended with an abrupt click. Jim pulled in a deep breath.

"How do you fancy dating a traffic cop?" he said, eyebrows raised.

"You think I want to date you?" she said, her face ramrod straight.

He pocketed the phone and held open the diner door, willing her to do or say something to confirm that she was only joking and she wanted nothing more than to date him.

And, if possible, move in with him. Today. "Shall we find a table?"

They headed for the same booth they'd occupied the previous morning. She slid along the banquette, shedding her jacket as she did so. She smiled as a waitress appeared and gave them both some coffee.

Then she looked at him, her expression taking on a serious edge. "I was only messing around. About dating you, I mean. The thing is, Jim, knowing me is complicated. More complicated than you might imagine."

She was being followed by a PI on the orders of her ex-husband, her stay in a luxury hotel supposedly a prize her friend had won in some competition. She didn't know anything about the kind of place she was staying in, but her friend clearly did.

He'd already worked out there was more to Megan and her being at The Valentine Retreat than met the eye. There were so many questions he wanted to ask. But not right now.

"Who isn't?" he said. "I've just gone from career junkie cop to— well, I'm not sure—potential security guard?" He plucked at the worst kind of downgrade he could imagine. The thing you ended up doing when you burnt out as a cop or faced down one too many bullets.

It was meant to be a joke, but she didn't laugh. "It's my fault, isn't it? You're in trouble because of me?"

He took her hand. "If it means I get to be with you, I'll take trouble every day of the week, Megan."

"That's a cheesy line." She rolled her eyes. His shoulders relaxed when he told her he had a whole arsenal of cheesiness in his bottomless pit and she began to laugh. "You can get medication for that."

The waitress appeared, and they ordered breakfast. The same

choices as the previous day. Whilst they waited for the food to arrive, Jim seized the moment and dodged out of the diner to run to the florist along the street, returning with a fistful of purple flowers wrapped with a bow.

He crossed paths with a bearded middle-aged man on his way back to the booth. Their eyes met for a second or two, but Jim's attention didn't linger on the guy. He was too busy watching for Megan's reaction to the flowers.

When she saw the daisies then smiled at him, his grip on reality slipped all over again.

Chapter Twenty-Four

Andy couldn't stop the corners of his whiskery middle-years mouth from taking an upwards turn at the expression on Megan's face when the cop retook his seat in the booth.

It wasn't for the flowers themselves. Of that he was certain. An ordinary-looking bunch of huge purple daisies mixed in with some greenery. One of those big florist's bows holding the stalks together. Hardly earth-shattering, especially for a woman who had experienced the kind of lavish flower arrangements that someone like William Wiseman threw around as if they were confetti.

No, the expression on her face was for the bearer of the flowers. Lucky bastard.

Andy had been on their tail from The Valentine Retreat. He was out of his car almost before they'd made it down the front steps of the hotel. His car door shut and locked even before they crossed the street, so deeply focused on one another they didn't notice the horns blaring at them as they dodged traffic.

He had been right about them knowing one another. From the way they were holding hands, Andy gauged that the two of them had enjoyed a much more pleasant night than him. There was a new sense of familiarity between them which hadn't been there the previous day.

He pulled the waistband of his trousers up, tightening his belt a notch as he set off along the street. Was it possible that he'd lost a few pounds overnight? He really needed to get a grip on his eating habits. The TV experts proclaimed he should only eat colorful things. Cut back on the beige of processed foods and carbohydrates. Of course those were the things Andy liked. If ever there was someone who felt right at home with beige, it was him.

As Megan and the cop rounded a corner, Andy stopped at the turn for a few seconds. He didn't think it likely Megan would recognize him, although he knew from experience that people were often better at clocking faces they recognized than they thought. It was a subconscious behavior people often did their best to ignore, but it was still ingrained in everybody.

Andy reckoned it was a prehistoric thing, from when recognizing friend or foe meant the difference between survival and being beaten over the head with a club.

He'd learned not to take anything for granted, so he made sure he wasn't anywhere near either Megan or the cop's line of sight as they walked along. He wasn't even sure why he was still following Megan. She was with Jim and everything looked hunky-dory. It was possible they were going somewhere for breakfast.

If that was the case, he could grab a snack to add to the muffin he'd demolished earlier. He might even get something colorful or leafy. The thought made him laugh.

Perhaps he would have a quick word with the cop, too, if the opportunity presented itself.

The cop pulled his phone out, placed a call, and took Megan's hand again while he held his conversation. She glanced up at him every few strides. They couldn't seem to get enough of one another. Andy had to take his metaphorical hat off to the guy because she was a seriously good-looking woman, with legs that pretty much went right up to her armpits.

Now he was seated at a table, watching Megan's face light up at Jim's return with the flowers. It occurred to Andy that he should back off. This was no longer something he was being employed to do, which made his invasion into the couple's privacy even more blatant. His own worries about Onesta seemed to be unfounded.

Instead, there was the distinct possibility that he was still here, trailing after this woman so doggedly to avoid doing the thing he wanted to do, but feared the result of doing more than anything else.

Andy shuffled on his seat. Disheveled, unwashed, and with his mouth resembling the bottom of a neglected bird's cage, he decided he couldn't go on like this any longer. Wanting to be the man walking along the street hand-in-hand with the one he loved might be a touch ambitious. He couldn't remember the last time he held his wife's hand.

To be honest, he couldn't remember the last time they'd done anything much except have badly suppressed arguments, keeping the anger low enough so the kids didn't hear them. There was no question that those kids meant everything to him, though, and he did still love her. That was a fact.

He recognized that was why he was crashing on his friend's futon, why he hadn't found a crummy studio apartment of his own to move into. Because that would have been like admitting this was a proper separation, not just their latest bust-up.

It would signal the beginning of the end rather than a bump in the road, and he wasn't willing to accept that. He'd given himself long enough to think about what he wanted, and he wanted to reclaim his family, whatever it took.

Maybe he would visit the florist's shop and get his own bunch of purple daisies to present to Linda. Or perhaps he should stop procrastinating, grow a pair, and get his life back on track.

~ * ~

Megan tucked her fork onto the plate. The pancakes had been just as good as the day before, the bacon crisped to perfection, the hint of maple syrup enough to lift the whole thing. Simple and very tasty.

She hadn't eaten it all, but she'd enjoyed it—an experience she thought she'd forgotten to associate with food. Jim hadn't finished his, either. He was pushing it around the plate.

"Don't you like it?" she said, her fingers curling around her mug.

He set his cutlery down with a rueful look of regret. "It's not that. I don't seem to have much of an appetite right now." He grinned at her. "I was going to say, 'not for food, anyway,' but that's another line straight from the cheese drawer, isn't it?"

"Oh my god. Totally cheese-tastic. You seriously need to work on your technique," she said.

"That's what my boss said too." The grin disappeared, his eyebrows knitting together.

"Will you be able to sort things out with him?"

"The chief?" He nodded. "Sure. I'll smooth things over with him in no time. He gets worked up far too easily. I think the guy might be in danger of developing an ulcer."

Jim was making light of the situation, but his expression didn't quite match up with his words.

"He must worry about you, though," she said.

"How do you mean?"

"Well, if you're undercover that has to mean you don't want the people you're working with to know you're a cop. And last night you told me. I'm assuming you shouldn't have and that's why you're in trouble with him today."

"That about covers it. But I had to tell you. I needed you to understand who I am."

"I'm glad you did, but your boss isn't looking at it from that perspective, is he? What would happen if the people who run The Valentine Retreat find out who you really are?"

He shook his head, brushing away her concern. "There's no way for them to find out, and now I'm off the job. Chief Jackson pulled the plug on the operation. I'll go back one last time to quit then head to the precinct and face the music." He closed a hand over hers. "That's not important, though. What's important to me is knowing that you're going to check out, like you said you would. Especially if I'm not around to keep an eye out for you."

"You make it sound like someone's after me," she said. She smiled, but he didn't smile back.

"It's not that." He paused, then said, "Megan, how well do you know Jolie?"

"Why?"

"Do you trust her?"

Megan pulled her hand away from his. "That's an odd question. Of course I do. I've known her since school. Why?"

"Your stay at The Valentine Retreat... You said she won it in a competition?"

"Yes, she's always entering them, but she never normally wins much. She was so excited about this and insisted I should be the one to come with her. To be honest, it wasn't something I was desperate to do. When I was still with my ex we regularly stayed in luxury hotels. I'm done with that." She bit her lip. William had forced his way into her thoughts. She shoved him out again. "Why are you asking about Jolie?"

"Do you remember which competition she won? Did she tell you?"

"No. She waved an email under my nose. I wasn't paying much attention. Why?"

He shook his head. "Ignore me. Sorry, it doesn't matter. I just know I'll be a lot happier once I know you and your friend are away from that hotel."

"I'm not sure she's going to be so keen to leave."

He ran a hand through his hair. "Will you persuade her? Listen, Megan, I know I'm asking a hell of a lot, but I'm serious when I say The Valentine Retreat isn't a good place to be."

Megan didn't get the chance to reply. Jim's phone rang, an insistent monotone bell. His shoulders stiffened.

"It's the hotel," he said as he answered the call.

The gist of the conversation was enough for her to slide her arms into her jacket and prepare to leave the diner. She glanced around for the waitress and asked for the check.

"I'd better get going," Jim said, pocketing the phone. "Valentine wants to see me. Hopefully I can combine the meeting with telling him I quit. Will you walk back with me?"

"Sure," she said. "I think I'll phone Jolie and see what she's doing." The expression on Jim's face made her add, "Don't worry, I'll persuade her to check out with me today. Satisfied?"

On the corner before the hotel, Jim tugged her to a stop. "Will you call and let me know when you're away from this place?"

She nodded. "Will you do the same?"

"Try and stop me," he said.

Chapter Twenty-Five

Jim left Megan on the corner of the street and headed for the staff entrance of the hotel. He shoved his hands deep into his jacket pockets. Nothing like as good as having Megan's hand in his, but it wouldn't be long until he planned to see her again. Once they were both away from The Valentine Retreat, he would ask her out on a proper date.

Telling her the extent of the activities taking place in the hotel, and her potential role in it, would have to wait. As would trying to work out how to explain to her that he knew she was being followed on the orders of her ex-husband. That he was privy to the reason too.

What wasn't clear was why her ex would want those kinds of photos of her.

The even bigger question was why they hadn't been visited at some point during the night by a PI with a camera. What had happened to the informant who was supposed to tip off the PI? He wondered what had prevented them from going through with their role in whatever was happening to Megan. Whoever it was, they must have known he went into her suite and hadn't come back out.

Jim stayed awake long after Megan drifted off to sleep the previous evening. He'd fetched their discarded clothes from the shared area of the suite, tiptoeing around like a teenager trying not to wake his girlfriend's parents. Aware that he'd dropped himself in the shit in his professional life and placed Megan slap-bang in the center of whatever her ex was trying to work in one fell swoop weighed heavily.

He finally drifted off to sleep in the early hours, once he was sure the rest of the world had slipped into the oblivion of the night.

There was plenty which didn't sit right about this whole thing, not least his suspicion of Jolie's role in all this. The competition win didn't seem plausible to him.

But Jim had only just met Megan; it was hardly the time to accuse her best friend of lying to her.

And about what? Jim wasn't sure. Best keep a lid on that line of inquiry, for now at least.

He needed to keep his wits about him for this meeting with Valentine. He needed to think about it, to focus. Valentine would want to know what he found out about Megan's ex-husband. Perhaps he should tell him he'd struck out, that he'd failed miserably in his task. Maybe Valentine would fire him on the spot. Problem solved.

Or he could take pieces from his conversations with Megan and create something interesting enough to persuade Valentine that Jim was a genuine employee, but with sufficient wool in the detail to ensure Valentine would want Jim to find out more.

Valentine wouldn't know that Megan was planning on checking out of the hotel early, not until she'd done it. That way, Jim could be sure that Megan would be safely away, and he could then disappear into the ether. Jim "Carenso" could evaporate, another insignificant Los Angeles resident lost without trace.

Megan had talked about art before Jolie and Chris crashed their conversation the previous evening, about the collection she had built up and left behind when she left William. Jim strained to remember the names of some of the artists she mentioned. He could possibly use them as bait.

He took the alleyway, moving quickly past the open kitchen doors, hearing the familiar yells of the aggressive chef resonating from the belly of the building. It didn't matter what time of the day he went past those doors, the kitchen always seemed busy and the chef was always angry about something, ripping into some poor schmuck or other.

He punched the access code into the staff door lock, then made for the elevator to take him up to Valentine's office.

Jim could understand why Anthony Valentine chose an upper floor for his office. The views from up there were exceptional, there was no denying it. He stood calmly in the elevator, convinced Valentine would already be aware he was on his way up.

The discrete camera in the top corner of that metal box would make sure of that. Jim did his best to appear confident and relaxed. He needed to play his part, now more than ever. See this role through to the end.

The elevator pinged, and he strode out, heading for the secretary's desk.

She greeted him with a smile. "Take a seat, Mr. Carenso. I'll phone through and let Mr. Valentine know you're here."

He settled in one of the chairs near the doors to the inner office. Almost as soon as he felt the squash of the soft leather he was climbing back out again, placing his phone onto the secretary's desk. This time, as before, Benny was ready to frisk him.

Jim raised his arms and stared past the guy's left shoulder, concentrating on keeping his heart rate steady. Eventually Benny finished and gestured him toward the desk. Benny retreated into his normal glazed expression, staring into the middle distance. A look which didn't focus on anything, but which Jim reckoned probably didn't miss much.

"Thank you for coming in," Valentine said. "I'm pleased you could make yourself available for this meeting. I hope I didn't drag you away from anything important?"

"No, nothing much, Mr. Valentine. I was getting some breakfast, that's all."

"Don't underestimate the benefits of a good breakfast. Most important meal of the day, isn't that right, Benny?"

"Absolutely right, boss." Benny sounded like a gravel grading machine.

"But I've been hoping you might have something for me, something as important as breakfast, maybe even more so. I've been on tenterhooks to discover whether you charmed your way into the ex-Mrs. Wiseman's good books last night. I hear reports that things looked favorable when you left the bar. Did you have a worthwhile night?"

Jim tried to remain as emotionless as Benny seemed to be, but he couldn't help his eyes narrowing. The man was vile. He wanted to sail across the desk and punch him so hard his teeth rattled. Instead, he did his best to relax his face, shuffling his weight from one foot to the other as he made a final decision on what he would say.

"Well," he said. "I see what you mean about getting women to talk about stuff. She couldn't wait to tell me how awful her husband was to her." Jim hated every word leaving his mouth, but Valentine was leaning forward in his chair, steepling his fingers together in anticipation. "It was so much easier than I thought it would be. I mean, a couple of glasses of champagne, a bit of sweet talking, and she was putty in my hands. You were so right, Mr. Valentine."

"What did I tell you, Jim? Women just love to talk. Let's cut to the chase, let's get to the nub of the matter, as it were. What did she reveal, before you got to her nub?"

Jim could hear Benny's wheezy laugh from somewhere behind him. Never in his career as a police officer had he wanted to nail two people as badly as he wanted these individuals.

He took a deep breath. "It seems Megan persuaded her husband to invest in fine art. She has an interest in that kind of thing."

"Fine art, eh?" Valentine glanced at Benny. "Did she name any pieces? Let you in on where they are hung or stored? Any precise property details?"

"She said something about a gallery in his beach house. In Malibu, I think." Jim imagined someone like William Wiseman probably would own a beach house, so it seemed plausible. "And she was talking about her favorite painting, by someone called Degas. Would that be right? I don't know much about art, I'm afraid."

"No need to apologize, Jim. We can't know everything, can we?" Valentine beckoned for Jim to sit down. "Before you say anything else, give me a second, will you?"

"Of course, Mr. Valentine." Jim slid into another leather chair.

Valentine glanced at Benny again, then reached into his inside jacket pocket, his hand fixing around something. Jim's heart rate leapt a notch. What was Valentine pulling out?

When his fingers reappeared, they were wrapped around nothing more sinister than a key on a chain. Jim concentrated on his breathing, the surge of adrenalin seeping back down to an acceptable level.

Valentine unlocked a desk drawer, replacing the key in his pocket. From the drawer he extracted a black notebook. With almost reverential care, he leafed through the book for a few moments, then picked up a pen and began to write something onto one of the pages. "Degas, you say?"

"Yeah, I think that's what she said."

Valentine made another note. He glanced up. "Where one Degas resides, I'll bet there are a whole heap of other art gems to keep it company. Does the ex-Mrs. Wiseman seem the kind of woman to know her Degas from her Matisse?"

Jim frowned. "Do you mean does she know about art?"

"That's precisely what I mean."

"I guess so, yes," Jim said.

"And William Wiseman has kept hold of these beauties, has he?"

"As far as Megan knew."

Valentine smiled, a perfect row of white. "It's not often that one of my employees has the presence of mind to gather such valuable information on a first assignment. I'm impressed, Jim. Is there more?"

The pen hovered over the page, Valentine's perfectly manicured fingers splayed as he held open the book. Jim was desperate to know what was written on those pages. What else would tempt Valentine to put pen to paper.

He tested his theory by saying, "I only found out a bit more, Mr. Valentine. She did say her ex-husband got angry with the firm providing the security system because the alarms kept going off when the cleaners were working."

Jim knew all about what could happen if security systems were only operational when properties were empty. He'd attended several robberies gone wrong, when the homeowners had come across the burglary while it was in progress.

Fatalities were not uncommon when this happened, which was why security providers far preferred the alarms to be operational around the clock. He did his best to look clueless for Valentine's benefit.

"The trials and tribulations of the rich and famous, Jim," Valentine said.

Jim smiled. "Absolutely. Must be dreadful for them."

Valentine chuckled. "So you're telling me the security alarms are active 24/7." The pen scribbled more notes.

"I suppose. Anyway, the only other bit of information was the initials of the security firm providing the system. Would that be of any use to you?"

Valentine looked up sharply, his pen hovering again. "That kind of information is absolutely solid gold, Jim. As good as money under the mattress. We will be having a conversation about paying off your debts if this information pans out. Most definitely."

Jim took the initials of a well-known security firm, changed them slightly, and said, "It was K and D, at least I'm pretty sure that's what she said. Could that be right?"

"Possibly. We can look into that." Valentine made another note. He shook his head, then said, "I can understand the need for these security systems, but I've always thought them to be a terrible invasion of privacy." He waved a hand around. "For example, I wouldn't dream of having cameras in here."

"I could try to find out some more about the paintings, if you like?" Jim said. "And the company name too. Megan's staying another couple of nights, I believe." There was no need for Valentine to know Megan's plans to check out early.

"That would be wonderful, but remember, subtlety is king. We don't want to scare the rabbit before we have the noose around her neck, do we?" Valentine made a few more notes, then closed the book with a decisive snap, sliding it carefully back into the drawer.

If Jim could get his hands on that book, it might hold the proof they needed to connect Valentine to robberies that had already taken place. Including the Branscombe death. That kind of a score could get him firmly back into everyone's good graces. And who knew what else was contained within its pages? In that split second, Jim made a decision.

"I want you to know how impressed I am, Jim. I have a feeling we're going to make a first-class team." Valentine stood and moved around the desk, indicating the meeting was at an end. "I haven't forgotten my promise to you, either. We'll get those pesky debts of yours sorted out in the very near future. Sound good?"

"That sounds fantastic, Mr. Valentine. Thank you."

Jim needed to get a look at that book. He had to stay in his role for a little while longer. As he shuffled himself from the seat, his fingers dipped into a pocket. He pulled out his red braid and dropped it underneath the desk, pushing it out of sight with his foot.

Whatever he'd said to Chief Jackson and Megan, getting out of The Valentine Retreat would have to wait a while longer.

Chapter Twenty-Six

They must have passed one another in the lobby, Anthony thought as Chris entered the lift moments after Jim vacated it. He watched Chris jiggling from one foot to the other. While the elevator rose through the building, Chris used the edge of his cuff to wipe at his nose. Anthony wondered if the boy had snorted the cocaine on the premises or whether he'd done it before he arrived.

Anthony didn't actively encourage drug use; if it got out of hand it tended to invite unwanted attention from the authorities. As long as whatever they did had no impact on their work in the hotel he chose not to interfere.

Sometimes, he'd decided, it could be argued it enhanced their performance. Whatever people needed to get them through the day—or night—was none of his business, unless it affected his business.

As the floor indicator pinged, Anthony slid closed the bottom drawer on his desk, hiding the monitor set within it. What in the hell did the wannabe Brad Pitt want this morning? After an exceptionally good meeting with Jim, Anthony was still in the afterglow of excitement. The last thing he wanted was to have to listen to Chris prattling on. He needed to get a hold of Harry Wendover, his go-to guy for security systems, then he wanted the team to start checking property details for the illustrious William Wiseman.

His phone rang. Picking up the receiver he barked, "Send him in Theresa, but tell him I've only got five minutes."

Benny took a step nearer the office doors, but Anthony waved him back against the wall. There was no need to waste precious time patting Chris down. Seconds later the door swung open and Chris appeared, flashing Anthony a huge smile.

"Thank you for seeing me, Mr. Valentine. I know how busy you are."

Anthony resisted the urge to point to an unspecified place on his nose and tell Chris he'd missed a bit. Instead, he said, "What can I do for you? I must warn you I'm very short on time, but I am keen to stay in the loop with all my valued employees. What do you have for me?"

Chris shoved himself into a chair, leaning forward with an enthusiasm he couldn't seem to contain. Anthony bit his tongue to ensure he didn't say anything about waiting for an invitation to be seated.

Perhaps he did have some useful information. Anthony was on a roll this morning, and Chris had spent the night in the same suite as Jim.

"Is it something to do with the Wiseman woman?" He held up a hand before Chris could speak. "Hold on a minute, before you tell me."

Reaching into the top drawer of his desk, and gently extracting the black notebook, he leafed through the pages until he found the one on which he'd written earlier.

Carefully sliding a narrow strip of clear plastic held within the pages to one side, he picked up a pen, then fixed his gaze on Chris. "What is it?"

"Oh, well, it's not really directly about Megan Wiseman," Chris said, his smile wavering slightly as Anthony frowned. "I mean, I expect you already know that Jim scored with her last night. I saw him on his way downstairs just now."

Anthony narrowed his eyes. He flicked the book shut, placing it back into its position between the pencils and the Smith and Wesson, lining it up precisely before he slid the drawer closed. "Why exactly are you here, then, Chris? As you said, I am a busy man."

"I wanted to tell you, well assure you really, that I'm completely committed to this job here at The Valentine Retreat. The exciting news is I've had a callback to an audition this afternoon, for a part in a TV show."

The grin was back, his all-American face tanned and flawless, not unlike something you'd see on a billboard advertising gum, or hair products, or condoms. Fleetingly, Anthony wondered what he'd look like in twenty years' time if he kept going with the hard drugs.

A moment of silence passed. It would appear he was expecting a reaction, an expression of Anthony's admiration at his achievement. Anthony remained motionless.

"The schedule would be tough, but my job here is an integral part of my life. Even if I get the part, I won't let it interfere with what I do here." He grinned again. "After all, I'd be mad to give this up, wouldn't I?"

Did the boy have no brains at all? Maybe they'd already been turned into a narcotic mush. He was about to suggest that Chris had better prioritize The Valentine Retreat above anything else when hysterical screaming from the outer office took everyone's attention.

Benny ran, throwing the office doors open as he reached beneath his suit jacket. Anthony hung back in case there was a need for Benny to utilize his weapon. When he heard nothing sinister, he stepped into the outer office. Benny had draped an arm around Theresa's shoulders, who in turn was pointing to the wall behind her desk, a horrified expression on her face.

Anthony looked at the wall. "Holy Christ. It's only a spider, Theresa," he said. "Deal with it, would you, Benny?"

Benny nodded, clambering onto the desk chair, a folded newspaper in his hand. He stretched up, reaching toward a sizeable spider, which had taken up residence about ten feet up on the wall. At some point Chris joined them. Anthony could hear his footsteps on the wooden flooring behind him.

On the chair, Benny did his best to balance as he slapped at the arachnid with the newspaper. The spider curled at the impact, dropping to the floor. Theresa screamed again. Benny climbed down, no mean feat for such a big man on a swivel-chair. He stepped on the spider for good measure, then flicked it onto the end of the rolled-up newspaper and into the trash basket.

Theresa shuddered. "Thanks, Benny. You know how I hate spiders."

"No problem, Theresa. It won't be worrying you no longer," Benny said, his voice low and gruff as he tossed the newspaper on top of the spider.

Anthony eyed Chris. "Well, we've got things to do, so unless there was anything else?"

"No, there's nothing else. Thank you, Mr. Valentine. I'd better get ready for the audition."

If he was waiting for Anthony to wish him good luck, he was in for a test of his patience. "Whatever," Anthony said, under his breath.

~ * ~

Jim hung around in the downstairs staff area, near the soft drink vending machine, with a view of Valentine's private elevator. How long could he wait, hoping Valentine and Benny might go somewhere? How quickly could he get into the desk drawer? Jim supposed he could force the drawer open, if necessary, but that would make noise and draw attention.

He located the closest fire alarm; maybe pulling that might give him the distraction required to get back into that office unnoticed. Or would Valentine take the book with him if he thought the hotel was in danger of burning to the ground?

Valentine's elevator pinged, the doors sliding open. Jim held his breath, then expelled it as Chris exited the space. He pretended to fiddle with the vending machine.

"You still here?" Chris said. "This place must be growing on you."

"Yeah, well, I think I'm getting into my groove at last."

Chris laughed. "You got that right if last night was anything to go by. You certainly turned her around. She was like a deer caught in headlights when I spoke to her."

"When you spoke to her?" Jim frowned. "What do you mean?"

"When you broke that glass, we heard the noise. Jolie wanted me to check you were okay. Megan looked like she was about to bolt, so I told her to chill out, that you were as good as in the bag."

Chris threw a huge smile in Jim's direction and continued to speak, which was probably just as well. Jim didn't trust himself to keep a lid on what he wanted to say at that moment. It certainly explained Megan's sudden coolness the previous evening.

Insensitivity seemed to be another of Chris's top ten characteristics. Jim imagined it might even give the guy's narcissism a run for its money.

Chris clearly didn't notice the hardening of Jim's jawline. "It was a bit weird, actually, because Jolie seemed more interested in what the two of you were getting up to. I couldn't get her to relax at all. Gave up in the end and left her to it. Anyway, I can't hang around too much longer, I got my callback for *Daylight Dreams*. I think I've got it nailed. This round is going to be more of a formality." He shrugged. "If they want me to jump through the hoops, that's fine by me. We all do what we've got to do, don't we, to get where we want to be."

"I suppose we do," Jim said. Chris wasn't wrong about that.

"I'm going to grab something to eat then get going."

Jim stared past Chris, his eyes widening. Valentine, accompanied by Benny, was exiting the lift, moving sharply in the opposite direction toward the main body of the hotel.

This could be the chance he was waiting for. "Good luck, Chris. I'll catch you later."

Jim held his hand up, spinning away from Chris before he could say anything else.

He shot across to the elevator, punching the floor number to take him to Valentine's office. Jim's heart was thumping again. The elevator doors parted, sliding silently to reveal a familiar scene.

The secretary was speaking on the landline, one hand holding the receiver, the other hand in front of her as she mimed something with a waggle of her fingers. "It was the biggest one I've ever seen... No, I know... And you know how much I hate them... Yes, I screamed when I saw it... Don't laugh at me, Kathy."

Jim approached her desk, an apologetic smile on his face.

"Hold on a second, there's someone here." She put her hand over the phone. "Can I help you, Mr. Carenso?"

"I hope so," he said. "I'm such an idiot. I think I must have dropped my braid in Mr. Valentine's office." He didn't need to put on an act; his heated cheeks flushed without any prompting. "I'm so embarrassed. I don't want him to know I've been so careless with it. I'm sure you understand."

The secretary was clearly conflicted. She glanced at the phone, then at Valentine's office doors, and bit her lip. "Mr. Valentine isn't here right now. I'm not supposed to let anyone go in there when he's not here."

"Would you be able to go in and get it for me, then? I've searched everywhere else; it has to be in there." Jim hoped the lure of her phone conversation would keep her where she was. "Or I could run in and get it. I won't be long."

Eventually she smiled at him. "Well, just this once. I'm sure it'll be fine. Go on in, Mr. Carenso."

He grinned at her as her attention was reclaimed by her call, and she continued to tell her story. Jim slid the office door wide enough to allow himself entry.

Once inside, he grabbed the braid from under the desk and tried to ignore the thumping of his heart as he rounded the piece of furniture and pulled at the drawer. It was locked. Damn it. Too much to expect it to be otherwise, he supposed.

Jim checked out the lock. Breaking and entering wasn't exactly a course offered at the academy, but he'd picked up a trick or two in the intervening years. He reached into a pocket and extracted the small bundle of tools he kept in his wallet.

A few moments later, he wiped the sweat from his upper lip and offered a silent prayer of thanks when the drawer slid gently toward him.

He eased it fully open, noticing the handgun and a box of .38 ammunition. The black notebook was front and center of the drawer. Jim fought to keep his breathing under control as he picked up the book. Much faster to pocket it and get out, but as a source of evidence, it would be better to find it in situ.

He scanned the pages. It was full of dates, figures, initials, and codes. On one page was a list of types of cuts of diamonds, with tally marks beside each one.

Jim snapped photos of some of the pages containing dates, then heard movement outside the office. He shoved the notebook back into place and slid the drawer closed, locking it before he crossed the room and pushed the door open to find the secretary ending her call.

He waved his braid at her. "I found it, thank God," he said as he headed for the elevator without glancing back.

Chapter Twenty-Seven

Megan found Jolie in their suite. "I need to talk to you," she said.

Jolie dropped the magazine she was browsing onto the couch. "From the look on your face I think I can guess what about."

"Can you? Go on then." Megan folded her arms.

Jolie grimaced. "You're angry with me about the red-braid thing, aren't you?"

"You thought I wouldn't be?"

"Why do you think I didn't tell you?" Jolie shrugged. "It was supposed to be a bit of fun, that's all."

"A bit of fun? They're not much more than prostitutes, Jolie. Or doesn't that concern you?"

"It didn't seem to bother you too much last night." Jolie tried for a cheeky grin, but it slid away as she looked at Megan's expression.

"That was—" She was about to say it was different.

That she hadn't slept with Jim because he was included in the cost of the room. However, in Jolie's eyes, he was nothing more than another one of The Valentine Retreat's employees.

Megan turned to the window. "I want to go home. I'm going to check out, and I want you to come with me."

Once they were away from this place, she would explain. She would tell her who Jim really was, what The Valentine Retreat really was.

"Are you okay?" Jolie sounded concerned. She came to stand beside her at the window. "He didn't hurt you, did he?" Her voice faltered. "It was just supposed to be fun," she added quietly.

"No, he didn't hurt me. Far from it. Doesn't change the fact you should have told me." Megan glanced at her friend. "Is that what's been worrying you? Keeping the true identity of this place from me? Was that why you took that elephant?"

Jolie shook her head and fixed her gaze on the view, the skin between her eyes pinching together and releasing. Megan wondered how long it would take for Jolie to tell her the truth.

"I'm going to pack," Megan said, heading for her room.

"Megan?"

"What?" She turned in time to see Jolie wiping at an eye.

"I love you. You know that, right?"

"I know. And I love you. I'd never have made it this far if it weren't for you. Let's get out of this place and forget this ever happened."

Maybe Jolie would open up to her once they were home. Now certainly wasn't the time to tell her that, in fact, the last thing she planned to do was forget the last few days had happened. That she was hoping the last few days might just signal the start of all the other days of her life yet to come.

~ * ~

Back in his office, Anthony's fingers felt for the handle on the central drawer in his desk, tugging habitually to check it was locked. He sighed. He wasn't sure why he checked. He had locked it; he knew he had. Not that it didn't prey on his mind; the contents of that drawer were about the only Achilles heel Anthony possessed.

He supposed it might be more sensible to keep the notebook in the floor safe, but he enjoyed the simple pleasure of leafing through its pages while he sat at his desk. He didn't want to have to mess around moving furniture and punching in the code every time he wanted to add something to a page.

In a perfect world, he would keep it in the safe. But perfection was a tough gig to maintain, both on a personal and a planetary level. Something to be strived for, not necessarily achieved.

Anyway, where would he be without other peoples' weaknesses and flaws? Other people's failures with their personal lives, their lack of discretion, their neediness. Much less wealthy, that was for sure.

There were few people to whom he had ever vocalized these thoughts. No, scratch that, there was only one person. And that person wasn't even in the country right now. So it was beneficial that things at The Valentine Retreat seemed positive. Particularly considering the fiasco at Sunset Heights a few months ago. It wasn't that Anthony had regrets about the Branscombe death. In his view, it was simply collateral damage.

But it was collateral damage that he didn't want linked to him in any way. To mitigate the situation, he had ordered a total cessation of that part of his business in the intervening months, in the hope that the heat would dissipate and the police would lose interest in their follow-up investigations.

William Wiseman's ex-wife in the hotel and Jim's remarkable success in his first assignment signaled the rebirth of that side of Anthony's business. A rapid meeting with Harry Wendover had set things in motion where locating Wiseman's properties was concerned. Getting ahead of the game in preparation for whatever further information Jim might harvest this evening.

The phone on his desk rang. "Yes, Theresa, what is it?"

"I have a call for you, Mr. Valentine, but the caller won't give his name. He does say he has some valuable information for you, though. Shall I put him through?"

Anthony held the handset gently against his face. So far, the day had been kind to him. He was feeling benevolent. It was entirely possible the information he was about to receive could prove useful. You never knew what was around the corner. "Go ahead."

There was a click and a moment of static before Anthony introduced himself. "How can I help you?"

"Am I speaking directly to Anthony Valentine?"

The voice on the other end of the line was well-spoken. Educated. Precise. "Yes, you are."

"I have some information for you. I thought you would like to know you currently have a member of the LAPD working undercover at The Valentine Retreat."

The handset slipped through his fingers. He grabbed at it, gesturing for Benny to come to the desk. The big man unfolded his arms and was across the room in a matter of seconds.

Anthony flicked the call onto speakerphone, trying to keep the tone of his voice level. "Well, that is of great interest to me. It goes without saying that I have the greatest respect for law enforcement. However, I am at a loss to know in what capacity an officer has been placed in my hotel. Could you enlighten me?"

Anthony had to remain calm. This could be nothing more than a needle from one of his rivals, trying to upset the smooth running of the hotel. Or it could be for real.

"I'm afraid I have no specifics. I do know this officer is a young man, and I have been made aware that he may be one of your special employees. Whatever that might mean."

He wished he could reach down the phone, get hold of this asshole by the throat, and squeeze the information out of him. Benny was staring at him, confusion written all over his face. It didn't take a genius to work out which obscenities he was mouthing.

Anthony shook his head at Benny and said, "All of my

employees are important to me, I can assure you of that. I would be interested to learn the name of this hard-working member of the police force, to thank him personally. I imagine that was the reason for your call?"

He phrased the last sentence as if it were a question, although there was little chance anyone would be phoning him to tell him about an undercover cop on his premises if their intention toward said cop were favorable.

There was a pause. "Unfortunately, I don't have his name."

That was as useful as a hole in the head. "May I have your name?"

The silence greeting his question made Anthony aware he was unlikely to receive an answer. A loud click heralded the end of the call.

"What the fuck?" Benny said, his voice loud and agitated. "An undercover pig here? What the actual fuck?"

"Benny, no need for language," Anthony said, although he agreed wholeheartedly with the sentiment. He took a breath, allowing the air to invade every corner of his lungs before he pushed it out again. A trick he'd learned to give the mind an opportunity to override the emotions. "Let me take a moment to think about this. If we are to believe the caller was telling the truth, we need to think logically. I think we can assume this man is one of our recently employed red-braid workers. But why send an LAPD officer in undercover now?"

Anthony thought he'd paid off enough of the lower-ranking city officials to allow The Valentine Retreat to hoist its sails and sally forth on the high seas without too much uninvited interest. Clearly he hadn't paid them enough. Or perhaps he hadn't paid the right people. A problem for a different day.

At this moment, it would be more productive to think about who the undercover agent was, rather than the why. Most of his red-braid workers had been at the hotel for at least six months. If any of them were cops, he would surely know about it already.

That left the two men employed over the last few months: Chris Kimble and Jim Carenso. Damn it to hell, he liked Jim Carenso. He'd started to imagine him to be someone Anthony could build a great working relationship with. He'd already brought him golden information about Wiseman. Surely a cop wouldn't do that? It would be against some ethical code or other, no doubt.

Or maybe it was a ruse to throw Anthony off the scent.

He shook his head. He couldn't believe it, not in all honesty. No, he didn't think it would be Jim.

That left Chris Kimble. While Anthony didn't particularly like the guy, he had identified Wiseman's ex-wife. And he appeared to take drugs, most likely cocaine. Cops got tested for that kind of thing, didn't they? Then there was all that nonsense about acting. Why bother making your cover so complicated?

Either he was a wannabe actor looking for something to tide him over while he waited for his big break, or he was a far better actor than Valentine had given him credit for, the irritating demeanor and assumption of drug use all a clever bluff to throw suspicion elsewhere.

Anthony thumped his fists on his desk. Why was nothing ever simple? One step forward, two back.

"Can I get you something, boss?" Benny said. "Coffee? A shot of bourbon?"

"A crystal ball?" Anthony said, unable to keep the bitter tone from his voice. "A truth serum?"

Benny pushed at the sleeves of his suit. "I can always find out who it is, boss, just say the word."

Anthony shook his head. "No. Let's not visit last resorts first, Benny. It may not be as much of a problem as I fear." He forced his hands to relax. "Naturally, I'll have to fire Carenso and Kimble, but that might be all the action that's required."

There was no way either Jim or Chris could have any physical evidence against the hotel, he was sure of that. Even if he had just brought Jim into the fold on the information gathering side of his role, it could all be denied. He would simply say the guy had misinterpreted the whole thing; he'd grasped the wrong end of the stick.

Neither Jim nor Chris could have anything concrete on a single thing discussed in this office. Anthony had the whole thing set up to ensure plausible deniability, should the worst happen.

A thought flashed into his mind, followed by a frown scudding across his face like a dark cloud. He reached into his pocket and extracted the key, unlocking the top drawer of his desk and sliding it open. Maybe he should check the Achilles heel, to be sure.

His eyes narrowed. His black notebook was there in the drawer, between his Smith and Wesson and the box of pencils. However, to Anthony's eye, it seemed further back in the space than he had placed it. He glanced at Benny, but there was no way his enforcer could have peeked in the drawer. He hadn't left Anthony's side all morning.

Maybe the book had simply shifted when he shut the drawer earlier. Maybe this talk of undercover cops was sending his neurotic-meter into overdrive.

One way to be sure. Anthony lifted the notebook from the drawer and leafed through it with extreme care. The thin strip of clear plastic, which acted as a bookmark as well as a tamper detection device, was nowhere to be seen. It wasn't between the pages Anthony had written on earlier. It wasn't anywhere in the book.

He glanced around, his gaze traveling across his desk and onto the floor. Difficult to see anything against the polish of the parquet flooring. Anthony closed the notebook and got down onto his hands and knees, casting around until, at last, there it was. Wedged under one of the wheels of his desk chair.

Someone had looked in his notebook. No question.

So much as a hint of that level of invasion of his privacy would have been enough to make his blood pressure rocket on a normal day. Couple that with the news about an undercover cop? There was a colloquialism for it, if he could remember it. Oh yes—this shit just got real.

He climbed to his feet, gratified to see Benny's incredulous expression. "Are you okay, boss?"

"No. I'm fucking well not okay, Benny." He picked up his phone. "Theresa?" he barked. "Get the hell in here, right now."

The office door opened, and Theresa poked her head through the gap, her eyes wide with concern, possibly even fear. "Is everything okay, Mr. Valentine?" She took a few steps into the room, then changed her mind and stopped. Something to do with the mask of anger which currently resided in place of his face, Anthony imagined.

"No, Theresa, it is not. Someone has been in my desk."

"It's not me, Mr. Valentine." She backed away. Not the bravest female Anthony had ever come across, by a long chalk.

Then it struck him. When Theresa had taken their attention earlier with the screaming and the spider, he had been meeting with Chris Kimble. And he'd taken the book out of the drawer when he thought Chris had something pertinent to tell him. Chris had seen the book.

Anthony strained his memory, and with a gasp remembered he left the room to find out what all the fuss was about *before* he'd locked the drawer. Not only that, but Chris hadn't come straight out of the office when Benny was dealing with Spidergate. He came out a while later. Plenty of time to open the drawer and rifle through the book. Opportunistic—and ballsy—but completely possible.

Anthony found himself becoming convinced the cop had to be Chris Kimble. He was the only one who had spent time alone in the office. Foolishly, Anthony had left the drawer open for those few minutes…

There could be no question. They needed to extract Chris from circulation and find out for sure, before he had the chance to take any of the information from the notebook to anyone else.

Perhaps that was what all the guff about an audition was about, a way to cover his true destination: a local police station. They needed to act decisively. He was about to give Benny the relevant instructions when Theresa made a strangled sort of a noise.

"Oh, Mr. Valentine?" she said.

"Yes?" Make it good, he thought, we haven't got time to waste.

She bit her lip. "Perhaps I shouldn't have let him, but he was only in here for a few seconds. I was in the middle of something. I didn't think it would hurt. He realized he'd dropped his red braid in here, you see, and he didn't want you to be cross about his carelessness."

How did the girl not realize she'd missed out the vital piece of information? "Who, Theresa? Who came in here unattended?"

"Oh, sorry. Yes. It was Jim. Jim Carenso."

Chapter Twenty-Eight

Megan packed the last of her belongings, folding the cream shirt from the previous evening and tucking it into her bag. Her hands stayed against the softness of the fabric for a moment as her mind slipped back to the sensation of Jim undoing its buttons. Not long to wait before he would be undoing them again, she hoped.

At the thought of it, heat rushed through her body like a tidal wave. Clearing her throat, she reached for another piece of clothing to place on top of the shirt, hiding it from view.

There was no doubt she couldn't wait to get away from this place. Already imagining Jolie's reaction once she got to tell her who Jim really was, weighing up how much of the previous evening she might share with her best friend, how best to illustrate the emotions this man stirred up inside her.

Without question, she was going to need Jolie's support. Explaining to Jim what it would mean if he was serious about being involved with her wasn't going to be easy. He would have to endure the scrutiny of William's lawyers, and he would probably have to tolerate his family and friends being tailed, their past lives being put under the microscope. It might well make Jim want to turn and run.

And Megan couldn't forget her brother in all this. She had to navigate a path which would allow his care to continue to be provided for. That would be the really tricky bit—trying to be compliant enough for William to even want to continue to pay for Craig.

The heat from a moment ago dissipated, replaced by a cold knot in her stomach. She was going to need Jolie more than ever, to lean against her whilst she tried to navigate a path through the days to come.

Zipping her bag closed, she glanced around to check she'd packed everything. Her gaze fell on Jim's flowers. Still fresh and beautiful in a vase on her dressing table. Would it be ridiculous to take them home with her? She decided she didn't care; there was no way she was going to leave them behind. Shaking the worst of the water from the stalks, she fastened the ribbon around the bundle as best she could and carried everything through to the living area of the suite.

Ten minutes later, Megan and Jolie headed away from the elevator for the final time and took the corridor leading to the wide sweeping steps into the hotel's foyer. Megan's gaze strayed to the elaborate coving and wallpapering, the cornicing and ceiling roses whose chains cascaded into candelabras from above. This was a modern high-rise block, the plasterwork a pure expression of wealth and opulence with a sole aim. To impress the guests.

But she supposed the candelabras fitted in well enough with the rest of the overblown décor.

At the desk, they were greeted by "Madison," whose brass nameplate seemed to catch fire on one corner every time it reflected light, her red lips an almost perfect match for the scarlet of the hotel livery. There was a definite cabin-crew vibe to the neat, pinched skirt suit she wore.

"We're checking out," Megan said, sliding her key card across the desk. Jolie produced hers. "Suite 69."

"Of course, ladies." Madison punched a few details into her computer, frowning as she looked at the screen. "The invoice for your stay is already taken care of, but you appear to be checking out early. Has there been a problem? Is there anything we can do to help?" Her frown remained in place, her focus flicking from Jolie to Megan.

"No. There's no problem," Megan said, "We need to get home, that's all."

"Because here at The Valentine Retreat, we pride ourselves on the highest standards of service, on knowing that each and every guest has a wonderful time. Has everything met your expectations?"

Megan's stay had been anything but what she had been expecting, not that she was going to tell Madison. "Everything has been fine, thank you. This is certainly a remarkable place."

Madison seemed placated by the response. She nodded and smiled. "I need to make a phone call before I finalize your departure. It's protocol, nothing more. Would you mind?"

Megan shook her head. "No. Please carry on and do whatever you need to."

~ * ~

Anthony picked up the phone again. It had been red hot since the news had broken about the undercover cop. There were a lot of wheels to set into motion.

"Mr. Valentine, Madison's calling up from reception. A couple of guests are checking out early. Shall I put her through?"

"Yes, Theresa," Anthony said. What the hell had gone wrong now? The phone clicked as the call came through. "Hello, Madison. What's the problem?"

"There's no problem, Mr. Valentine. I know you like to be kept informed if anyone leaves early, but they've enjoyed their stay."

Anthony relaxed; he didn't need another fire to fight. "Well, thank you for your attention to detail, Madison. Out of interest, who are the guests?" If it wasn't anyone important and he didn't need to smooth any ruffled feathers, then he would stay put. He had enough to deal with.

"Just a second." Anthony could hear Madison tapping on the computer. "Megan Leadbetter and Jolie Walsh. Suite 69."

Anthony's grip tightened on the handset. He became aware of the rushing sound of blood through his ears as he made the connection. Was it a coincidence they were leaving early? Or were they somehow in on the whole undercover cop deal?

"Madison." Anthony was thinking fast. "Please keep those ladies in reception for a while. I'd love to come down and wish them a pleasant journey. I think that might be a nice touch, don't you?"

"Sounds wonderful, Mr. Valentine."

"Get them some coffee. Perhaps ask them to complete the hotel satisfaction questionnaire." A document designed to delay unhappy guests long enough for Anthony to reach and sweet-talk them, the completed data erased moments after the guests left the hotel.

Moments after ending the call, Anthony dialed out, drumming his fingers against his desk as he waited for Benny to pick up.

"Boss?" Benny's gruff tone filled Anthony's ear.

"How's it going?"

"Smooth as silk. We've already located Chris Kimble. He wasn't happy, said he was on his way to an audition, so we had to encourage him to stay. He's still unconscious."

Anthony enjoyed these moments far less than Benny seemed to. But then, that was what Benny was employed for. To deal with the difficult end of things. To find out information from people unwilling to share and take care of the problems that wouldn't go away anyhow else.

"And Carenso?"

"Still in the hotel, by all accounts. We'll find him, boss."

"We have a further complication."

"Shoot."

"The women. Megan Wiseman and her friend are checking out. Right now."

"Is there a connection?"

"I don't know." Rarely did Anthony feel the need for someone other than himself to make a decision, but now was one of those moments. "It's possible."

"Do you want me to do a full clean?"

Anthony paused. A full clean. Was that what he really wanted? He'd already sanctioned Benny to take Jim Carenso and Chris Kimble to The Farm. Extract whatever information was possible, find out which one was the cop, what they'd seen in the notebook, and if the information had made it any further than their own eyes. The trip to The Farm was only ever one way. It was a guarantee the specific problem would disappear for good. He also needed to know if the fire had spread and whether he would have to make his beloved notebook disappear too.

But taking the women? Maybe he should allow them to check out, go on their way. To get on with their lives. Chances were, they wouldn't give Jim or Chris another thought. Their stay at The Valentine Retreat would be nothing more than a bit of unencumbered fun.

The thing was, Anthony didn't like to take chances. Chances were for gamblers, and gamblers were usually out of control. Anthony loathed the feeling of being out of control. His actions were taken for precisely the opposite reason, to remain in control.

The blood rushed through his ears, as loud as Niagara Falls. He needed to stop dicking about and decide—time was slick.

"They're at reception," he said, his voice sounding leaden. It felt difficult to operate his tongue. "I'm going down to meet them. I'll offer them a ride to wherever they need to go. Keep them talking for a bit. I think the ride needs to be our minivan. You know what I'm saying." He couldn't bring himself to say the words, but he didn't need to. Benny would understand.

"Absolutely. Boss, I've just thought of something." Benny let out a wheezy laugh, before he continued. "The plus side is, they've already packed all their stuff for us…"

Anthony ran a hand across his forehead. "Get that van out front, do you hear me, as soon as you've found Carenso."

The wheezing laugh stopped, the gravel reasserting itself. "No problem, boss. We'll be ready when you are. We'll gather all the trash into one can and get rid of it for you. Nice and neat and tidy."

Chapter Twenty-Nine

Jim pocketed his phone and zipped his jacket, pressing the flush button as he left the stall. The staff restroom was as good a place as any to find the privacy needed to send Chief Jackson some copies of the photographs he'd taken in Valentine's office. He'd followed them up with a brief explanatory text message.

For appearance's sake, he washed his hands then headed for the door. It swung open before he had a chance to reach for the handle, his way blocked by a solid presence.

"Shit, man, you startled me," Richie said.

"Sorry," Jim said, swallowing the golf ball of apprehension Richie's sudden arrival had triggered. He shuffled to one side to allow him access to the room.

Richie seemed in no hurry to move. "So, you think any more about what I was talking about the other day? Got any requirements, any requests?" He patted a pocket. "Fully stocked, man. Just say the word."

"That's good to know," Jim said.

The last thing he needed right now was a discussion about drugs. He wanted to get The Valentine Retreat as far behind him as he could. He was preoccupied with his thoughts. This new piece of evidence, the notebook, could be enough to get him back on track with the chief.

"I'm great right now, though." He reached for the door, pulling it as far open as it would go. "I'll be sure to come to you if anything changes, okay?"

After what seemed like an interminable amount of time, the huge man fisted his hand and held it out. Jim bumped it with his own.

"My man," Richie said, nodding to a silent beat as he strode past Jim into the restroom. "Later."

"Later," Jim said under his breath, heading along the corridor with a building sense of urgency.

The staff exit lay up ahead, a mere twenty yards away. He fought to control his breathing. He wanted to run, but logic told him no one knew he'd looked in the notebook. Nothing had changed for anyone but him. He needed to calm down, get out of the building without drawing any attention to himself, then jump into a cab.

He forced himself to breathe out slowly, his hand extended to push open the staff door. He was almost there…

"Jim Carenso."

A gruff voice sounded from the other end of the corridor. Resisting the urge to acknowledge whoever was calling to him, he kept his gaze front and center, pretending he hadn't heard. His hand touched the door as the voice called his name again, louder this time, and closer. Whoever it was, they were travelling fast, coming his way. Jim pushed open the door, turning to grab a glance as he headed for the alleyway. It was Benny. He thought he recognized the voice. Not good.

He shot through the door as Benny shouted, "Jim Carenso, stop right there. Mr. Valentine wants a word with you."

Jim disappeared from his sight, down the alleyway. A black minivan blocked the end of the alley, a couple of heavy-looking suited men flanking it, facing the street beyond. Not good. Not good at all.

He could hear Benny exiting the staff door behind him, the slam of the emergency bar against the wood. Jim darted to the rotting side wall between some bins, pulling out his phone as he searched the wall for a suitable gap in the brickwork to hide it. The last thing he wanted was to have that—complete with the photos of the notebook—found on his person.

Once he'd rammed the phone into a large enough gap, checking it was wedged out of sight, he pulled out his lock picks, tossing them behind a pile of cardboard. Back into the center of the alley in the nick of time, he saw Benny in his peripheral vision, closing in on him.

"Jim Carenso. Stand still."

His tone slowed Jim's pace; the creeping fear associated with recognizing the increased confidence behind Benny's words took control. Jim already knew what he would see when he turned. Standing square on to him, Benny held a gun, its barrel pointed directly at Jim's chest. One look was enough to tell him Benny was no stranger to handling that revolver.

Clattering from the kitchen area made Jim swivel. The doors flung open, the ever-angry chef looming into view with a tin of tobacco in one hand, a lighter in the other. For once, Jim was glad to see him.

Should he dart into the kitchen, try to get out of the hotel that way? Before Jim could persuade his leaden legs to move, the chef peered up and down the alleyway. He clocked Benny, who didn't change his stance. Then he scanned the rest of the alleyway before fixing his gaze back onto Jim. The look the chef gave Jim was one of complete indifference. As if Benny were a politician holding in his hand nothing more offensive than a campaign leaflet. His eyes were cold and hard, his face totally expressionless.

Taking the lighter into the same hand as the tin, the chef backed carefully into the dark space he had only just emerged from and, without saying a word, he pulled the doors deliberately and firmly closed.

Jim let out the breath he realized he had been holding. With nowhere to go, he raised his hands, keeping his focus on Benny as he fought to stay calm.

"Gray, fucking wake up and come here," Benny bellowed, his gaze flicking past Jim to the men at the end of the alley.

"What's going on, Benny?" Jim said, doing his best to act confused. "Why are you holding a gun on me? You're scaring me."

"Shut up and stand still."

"But I don't understand." Jim could hear another set of heavy steps behind him. "Benny, what's going on? Tell me, please." Jim tried again.

"Shut him up, will you, Gray," Benny said.

Jim dared not take his focus from Benny. He didn't know what Gray was going to do, where he was going to hit him, until Gray landed a heavy blow into his kidneys. Jim's vision clouded, his body doubling up involuntarily with the intensity of the pain. His lungs spluttered as his knees hit wet tarmac.

He glanced up in time to see Benny turn the gun and bring it sharply against the side of his head. The pain was all-consuming. The alleyway swam in front of Jim's eyes, darkness cascading from all corners as his vision blurred inky black. He slumped to the ground, a cold, wet, rough surface against the side of his face the final sensation in his slide into the abyss of unconsciousness.

~ * ~

"Would you mind?" Madison flashed them another red-rimmed smile. It must take countless reapplications a day to maintain that look. A red oil slick. She refocused as an iPad was pushed into her hands. "Customer satisfaction is our primary goal. If you could fill in this questionnaire, we would be enormously grateful." Madison gestured toward the screen. "When you scroll down to the bottom, there's a section for you to add your details. Everyone who completes the form gets entered into a lotto for a weekend stay right here, courtesy of Mr. Valentine himself."

The broad smile with its perfect set of teeth was almost hypnotic, like an advert for toothpaste, or corrective dentistry.

Megan tried to appear enthusiastic. Not only did she never intend to set foot in this place ever again, there was also absolutely no way she was filling in any details on this form. Madison could go whistle.

"Mr. Valentine will be here momentarily." Madison smoothed down the lines of her suit, flashing them another lipstick-laden smile. "I'll fetch some coffee."

Megan glanced at Jolie. She wanted to get going, knew that Jim wanted her away from this place. If she made too great a fuss about not wanting to meet Mr. Valentine, might that draw unwanted attention to herself? She was probably overthinking; they were in a public space after all.

Plus, a coffee before they left wouldn't be the end of the world. "I suppose we have a few minutes."

"Perfect. Take a seat, I'll be over in a second." Madison disappeared into another room.

Megan looked at Jolie, shrugging. They wandered over to a regency-style scroll-ended couch. Megan dumped her case and laid her flowers carefully on top of it. She scrolled through the iPad screen, then pushed it onto the low table standing in front of the couch.

"I'm not filling that in," she said. "Do you want to?"

Jolie sat beside her and shook her head. She picked at the edge of her sleeve, then said, "Megan, I need to talk to you about something."

"I need to talk to you, too, once we're away from here," Megan said, trying and failing to dampen down a smile. "About Jim."

"No, I mean I really need to talk to you about something."

There was a seriousness to Jolie's tone that was unfamiliar to Megan. She was about to ask Jolie about it when Madison returned, bearing a tray. Two delicate cups and saucers, already filled, sat on the tray alongside a jug of cream and a pot containing sugar crystals. There was even a tiny pair of sugar tongs. This place was such a mismatch— part *Brideshead*, part *Brides of Dracula*.

With the tray delivered, Madison glanced around, her gaze lighting on a tall man. The same man she'd met in the bar. Mr. Valentine. Dressed impeccably today in a dark gray suit, with a deep purple tie and matching colored pocket handkerchief, creased in the flat-fold style at right angles to the pocket, his gaze scanning the foyer until his focus alighted on them.

He smiled, straightening his immaculate cuffs as he headed in their direction. Momentarily, Megan wondered if this might be what William would look like in twenty years' time. The mirror-image of Medusa. At least she had the decency to wear her snakes on the outside.

She stood as he approached. Jolie scrambled to her feet.

"No need, ladies. Not on my account. It's lovely to see you again." Hands were shaken, greetings made, seats reclaimed.

"Madison was kind enough to alert me to the fact you need to leave early, and I wanted to double-check that you have enjoyed your stay. We strive to ensure that every person's stay here is memorable." He flashed them both a wide smile.

Megan had to resist the urge to shift away from him. "I can happily confirm that my stay here has definitely been memorable, Mr. Valentine. No doubt about that. It's just that I need to get home. Something's come up, and I need to deal with it."

"What a delightful accent. British, unless I'm very much mistaken."

"That's right."

"I thought I picked it up the other evening. You reside in the States, I presume? The Valentine Retreat would love to offer you a ride to wherever you're going, but I'm not sure we can stretch to a trans-Atlantic trip." He chuckled at his own joke.

"No, don't worry. I've lived in the States for a number of years."

"Well, that's a relief." His gaze shifted to the front entrance. "I'll organize a car. Are you headed to the airport?"

Megan shook her head. "Honestly, there's no need. We'll grab a cab and be on our way." She slid her cup onto its saucer, gathering her belongings as she prepared to stand.

Mr. Valentine didn't seem to hear her. "It won't take a moment. I'll make sure the car is out front for you." He headed for the hotel entrance, placing his mobile to his ear.

Megan sighed. "Come on, Jolie. Looks like we're getting a lift after all." They could get the driver to take them a few blocks, then let them out. Swap the hotel car for a cab. She would be able to talk to Jolie freely, then.

Outside, they descended the hotel's steps and crossed to where Mr. Valentine stood. He still had his phone resting against his ear. His expression brightened when a black minivan emerged from an alley at the far end of the hotel. It joined the flow of traffic inching through town, sliding to a halt outside the hotel seconds later.

"That must be our ride," Jolie said, her voice monotone and flat. They could talk about whatever was worrying Jolie, too, once they swapped to a cab. Megan hitched her flowers against the crook of her arm.

"Pretty flowers," Mr. Valentine said, pocketing his phone to slide open the side door on the black car.

"They are," Megan said. "I couldn't bear to leave them behind."

As the driver jumped out, she glanced down at the blooms, the tightly packed yellow centers radiating out like starbursts into the slides of the purple petals. It wasn't until she looked up again that she clocked Jim and Chris inside the vehicle. Chris appeared to be asleep, his head lolling to one side. Jim had blood on one side of his head, his groggy eyes widening as he saw her.

He shook his head and began to speak as Mr. Valentine said, "Take them—now."

Strong hands grabbed at the back of her arms, propelling her forward into the belly of the vehicle. She landed on her knees, handbag twisted underneath her. She lost her grip on her bag and the flowers. There were two more men inside the vehicle, men she didn't recognize. Jim tried to shout, but as he did one of the men punched him square in the face.

Megan cried out as blood flowed fresh from Jim's nose, his eyes clouding as he lost consciousness. The same man, dressed all in black, reached forward and took a firm hold of her. He had a hand over her mouth before she managed any further noise and wrapped his other arm around her shoulders. His hand held her so hard she began to wonder if she would be able to breathe at all. He squeezed her nostrils together and, try as she might, she was unable to get any air past his firm hold.

She thrashed wildly, but it was no use. The man was too strong, his grip vice-like. Jolie was beside her on the floor of the vehicle, the other man restraining her. The driver tossed both their cases inside, slamming the sliding door closed.

Megan caught a glimpse of Mr. Valentine. He remained on the pavement, a hand raised in farewell, a smile on his face. Her vision clouded then, her eyelids drooping and closing as she ran out of oxygen. Her last sensation was one of movement as the vehicle eased out into the stream of traffic and drove away.

Chapter Thirty

"Jesus wept, Rhonda, are you sure that's what you heard?" Aware he was shouting into his phone, Andy tried to control his voice, only succeeding in deepening his frown. This was exactly what he'd feared. But he hadn't believed Onesta would resort to this, not even in the midst of the man's tight, cold anger.

"Yes, Andy, I heard the whole conversation. Well, Mr. Onesta's part of it, anyway. He asked to speak to Mr. Valentine, and I clearly heard him telling whoever he was speaking to that there was an undercover cop working at The Valentine Retreat. I know I only work in the office, I'm not privy to the ins and outs of the whole thing, but that can't be a healthy situation."

"Jesus wept, Rhonda," he repeated, rubbing at the crevices in his forehead. "If only you knew how unhealthy that could be for this cop. And for Megan if she's with him. I can't believe Onesta would do such a thing. What's he trying to achieve?"

"I have no idea. He had a telephone conversation with Mr. Wiseman shortly beforehand. I don't think it went well. Whatever Mr. Onesta had cooked up for this weekend, whatever Mrs. Wiseman, or rather the ex-Mrs. Wiseman, was supposed to do, I don't think it panned out."

Andy wasn't so sure about that. He thought it had panned out just as that snake had planned, but the addition of Jim Carello to the mix had thrown the scheme off-kilter.

"After the phone conversation, Mr. Onesta was ranting to himself in his office. He kept referring to another woman, saying she hadn't come through with her end of the bargain. That it had been an error of judgement to use her. That he would turn the information over to the authorities and let the courts deal with her."

"Who was he talking about?" Andy didn't think it would take a genius to work out who they were referring to. He was ninety-nine percent sure he knew.

"I don't know. He didn't mention any names. He kept shouting about them all getting what was coming to them. I don't think I've ever heard him sound so vitriolic. He frightened me, Andy. Then he stormed out of here, saying he needed some fresh air."

"For God's sake. Has he any idea what a man like Valentine is likely to do to this guy if he finds out he's a cop? Valentine's only a stone's throw from Mafia, and the stone was thrown by a three-year-old with their arms strapped to their sides." In his frustration he pulled at his beard.

"Listen, I'm still outside the hotel. Don't ask me why, but I am. I'm going in. God knows what I can do, but I can't sit here any longer." He should have acted before this, should have trusted his instincts with more conviction, been braver. "I'm going to get Megan out of there, right now. And the cop, too, if I can find him." Andy glanced around, scanning the area outside the hotel.

"Do you think you should? Why don't you call the cops?"

"I'll do that, but I can't wait for them. I'll go in and say I'm her uncle or something, and that we're supposed to be meeting up. I'll see if she's on the premises and go from there. I should have spoken to them earlier, but I thought everything was okay. Jesus." He popped the catch on his door and was about to push it open when he scanned the hotel steps again. He paused. "No, wait," he said. "I see her. She's coming out of the hotel now, with her suitcase. Oh, thank God, looks like she's leaving, Rhonda. Her friend is with her. No sign of the cop."

Rhonda's voice dropped to barely more than a whisper. "Andy, I gotta go. Mr. Onesta's back, and he looks as mad as a tank of tiger sharks. I'll speak to you soon."

"For sure," Andy said, ending the call and pocketing the phone. He intended to get out of the car, take a walk along the street to be sure Megan left, and perhaps see if the cop was anywhere in the vicinity.

The two women were on the curb. Megan hitched the bunch of purple daisies into the crook of her arm as she lifted her suitcase. Beside her was a smartly dressed man, talking on his cell. Convinced it was Valentine, Andy watched him as he smiled at Megan and her friend. Andy craned his neck to try to see them all more clearly. A black minivan slid along the street and came to a halt, blocking his view of the three of them. The windows of the vehicle were so heavily tinted he couldn't even see into the car, let alone through it.

He tugged at his door handle again, half-stepping from his car to get a better vantage point. The women must have hired a car to take them home. The driver climbed out and made his way around to open the door for them. A few moments later he reappeared, his face a study of concentration as he checked up and down the street, jumped back into the driving seat, and pulled the vehicle back out into the flow of traffic.

Andy allowed his shoulders to relax. With Megan safely away from the hotel, he would call Chief Jackson and lay his cards on the table, suggest they get their guy out of there without further ado.

Valentine held a hand up in farewell. His benevolent expression made Andy's forehead crease. Why would someone like Valentine personally wave off a couple of guests? The niggling was back, in the base of Andy's belly.

Valentine bent, gathering something from the sidewalk. He straightened, holding a fistful of purple daisies. The flowers Megan had brought out with her only moments earlier. He riffled the flowers into some semblance of order in his hand, then headed back up the steps and disappeared into the shadows of the hotel lobby.

Half-in and half-out of his car, Andy froze. What had he just seen? Why would Megan carry those flowers so carefully out of the hotel only to drop them moments before she got into her transport? That didn't make any sense.

Sliding back into his seat, he slotted his car key into the ignition as he checked up and down the street. He pulled his Ford out into the traffic. The black minivan was just about in sight, everything was moving slowly, traffic flow permanently lethargic in this part of town. Andy changed lanes a few times in order to catch up to the black car, but it wasn't hard to keep it in his sights.

He would tail it in case the niggling feeling was on to something.

Chapter Thirty-One
Tuesday Late Morning

Megan woke with a start. She blinked several times in an attempt to fully open her eyes before the pounding headache forced her to close them tight and groan. Eventually, she braved opening them again.

Seated on the floor of the minivan, with her back resting uncomfortably against the side of the vehicle, her body was wedged between that and a pair of dark-clad legs.

She tried to move, lost her balance, and lurched against the plastic cladding of the car. She frowned and looked around, trying to make sense of things.

Jim was opposite her, partially dried blood streaked down one side of his face. A fresh trickle ran from his nose. He fixed his gaze on her, with an expression she couldn't pinpoint. Was it concern?

No, it was more than that; it ran deeper. Whatever it was, it wasn't positive.

He lifted his hands to his nose, wiping the fresh blood onto his sleeve. A cable tie fixed his wrists together. She glanced down. Her own wrists were similarly bound. She wriggled her hands, but the tight plastic tie was completely unyielding and cut into her skin.

She looked at him again, trying to make sense of what she was seeing, trying to understand what was going on. Next to Jim sat Chris, a blank look on his face, his wrists also tied.

Her gaze dropped to the plastic cords looped tightly around both their ankles, trussing their feet together.

Megan shifted until she could see Jolie. Still unconscious, she was slumped against the side of a seat. Swiveling as far as she could manage, she caught sight of the other men sat behind her. They filled the bench seat. Both had dark hair and were wearing dark glasses and suits.

A hazy memory floated into the forefront of her mind. Someone had shoved her and Jolie into the vehicle, and these two men had grabbed them. One had tried to smother her.

Panic rose inside her. Their faces remained impassive as they sat there, swaying slightly as the car rolled over an uneven piece of road. One of them was wearing strong cologne. The scent was thick and heavy.

A wave of nausea hit Megan. Her head was pounding, trepidation clawed at her insides, and that smell seemed inescapable.

"I think I'm going to be sick," she managed to croak, desperately trying to wriggle herself into a better position.

Completely hindered by the tie around her wrists, she fell one way and banged an elbow against the floor. Then she flipped the other way, ending up against one of the suited men.

He looked at her in disgust and shoved her with his knee, inclining his head toward the driver. "Pull over, for fuck's sake. One of them says she's going to hurl, and I don't want it all over my shoes."

"Not here," the driver replied. "Too public, too much traffic. Tell her to hold it. For Christ's sake, can't she use a bag or something?"

Megan put a hand up to her mouth, the other hand travelling with it. It was awkward even to be able to press her fingers to her lips. Fixing her attention to somewhere outside the window, she concentrated on breathing slowly, in and out through her mouth, in an attempt to minimize the smell of the cologne. To try to cut down her burgeoning realization of what was happening, with the accompanying fresh wave of panic prickling up her spine.

Jolie stirred, moaned, and opened her eyes, going through the same process Megan had just experienced. The confusion on her face was quickly replaced by fear. She pulled at her hands, to no avail. The fact they were tied together dawned in her expression, the loose curls of her hair whipping her face as she tried to move.

"What's going on?" she said, her voice barely more than a whisper.

"I don't know." Megan's voice fared little better.

Her throat felt thick with fear, sore from uttering those few words. They had been abducted, that much was clear. She didn't want to speak the words, didn't want to give them the credence which would come with saying them out loud.

What would be the point? They all knew. That much was obvious from the looks on their faces.

"Stop the car, I want to get out. You have to let me get out." The pitch of Jolie's voice escalated. "Let me go."

One of the men huffed with laughter. Megan had no idea if the mirth reached his eyes, which remained hidden behind dark glasses. He didn't reply.

Tears sprang in the corners of Jolie's eyes. She brought both hands up to wipe them away, but they kept coming. Her breathing quickened, her expression wild.

"Let me out, you have to let me out of here. You've got it all wrong. He didn't say anything about this. You've got to tell him. You need to tell him…" She stared at Megan, her nose running now as freely as the tears from her wide, panic-stricken eyes. "I wanted to tell you before, but I couldn't. It's all gone wrong. This is all wrong."

What was Jolie talking about? Megan silently begged her friend for an explanation, but she was spiraling out of control.

The suited man stopped laughing. He lifted his dark glasses, pulling them from his face and folding them slowly and deliberately.

He fixed Jolie with a steel-edged glare. "I have absolutely no idea what you're talking about. But if you don't shut up, I'm going to get my friend to shut you up for me. Do you understand? Stop talking. Nobody's letting anybody out. It's simple."

His voice reminded Megan of gravel pouring through metal.

"Whatever it is, Jolie, tell me later. We'll work this out, I promise. Just try to keep calm." Megan wasn't sure where the words came from. She certainly didn't feel calm.

"I wanted to tell you, right at the beginning, but he said I'd end up in jail if I didn't go through with it. I had no choice, Megan." Jolie buried her face in her hands and wailed.

Megan looked at Jim. He said nothing. A slight shake of his head in her direction, a dipping of his eyebrows like a warning to stay quiet, but he otherwise remained still.

"For fuck's sake, shut her up, Gray. I'm fed up listening to her whining."

The other suited man leant forward, his fingers flexing and tightening around the curls of Jolie's hair.

His movement prompted Jim to speak. "No. Don't," he said. "Leave her alone."

His voice was strong and clear, his confident tone belying the gravity of their situation. Megan soaked up some of the conviction with which he spoke.

"She's just scared, Benny. We're all scared."

"She'll be quiet now," Megan said, willing Jolie to listen. "You'll be quiet, won't you, Jolie? Leave her alone, please. Don't hurt her."

Her voice caught in her throat, hot tears spilling down her cheeks as one suited man gestured to the other to let her go. He settled back and folded his arms.

"I'll be quiet," Jolie said, from behind her hands. "I'll be quiet, I'll be quiet, I'll be quiet…" Repeating the phrase softly, the words came and went through her uneven breathing. She began to sway backward and forward.

"Five minutes, then we'll be there," the driver said.

Five minutes until we're where? Jim's gaze had settled on her again. She searched his face for an explanation, but there wasn't one. Wherever they were five minutes from, Megan very much doubted it would be an improvement on their present situation.

Chapter Thirty-Two
Tuesday Midday

Tailing the black minivan out of the city was easy with the traffic crawling along. Andy could stay well back from the vehicle without fear of losing them. As he drove, he became increasingly convinced he had witnessed an abduction. The whole thing felt wrong. And the minivan wasn't heading anywhere near the area of Jolie and Megan's apartment. It wasn't on the right route for Union Station, the bus depot, or even the airport. It was driving out of town in a completely different direction.

Eventually, the city fell away and it became more of a challenge for Andy to remain undetected. The traffic thinned and sped up but, luckily for Andy, there were other vehicles sticking to the same route. He managed to maintain his position about five cars back. The black minivan wasn't in a hurry. It stuck to every speed restriction, something else which made Andy nervous.

In his experience, most drivers exceeded speed limits at some point or another, when the road ahead became clear, or the piece of freeway was straight, or the driver checked their watch and realized they were running late. Andy reckoned the driver was doing everything to ensure he didn't draw attention to the vehicle.

About ten miles east of the city, the minivan veered off the main highway. A few miles further on another right had it on a narrow, dirt road surrounded by lines of trees.

Andy drove past the opening, craning his neck to see as far down the track as he could without slowing too much. The track continued for a couple of hundred yards, then it disappeared around a bend. On the forecourt of a gas station a short distance up the road, Andy swung his car and crawled back, trying to decide if he should drive down the track or call the cops from where he was.

He indicated and turned. He'd come this far. Might as well go the whole hog. He pulled his cellphone out and dialed, the car's suspension creaking and protesting as it bounced along the track, the potholes challenging the quality of the Ford's chassis.

He slowed the car as the track bent to the left. On both sides rows of young trees stood like foot soldiers, with ranks of mature trees behind them, forming a natural screen. There was no way to see what lay beyond without taking the corner.

Around the bend, the track continued in a similar way, although this section was far better maintained. Perhaps the first stretch had been left deliberately rough to deter casual motorists. He eased past an opening to the right. There was no property name, no mailbox, but Andy glimpsed buildings through the thick foliage. Maybe some kind of a farm? He noticed the black minivan parked in front of buildings, the sunlight able to penetrate the area glinting on a side mirror and reflecting from the windshield.

Andy kept his car moving along the track as his call was finally put through to the right department. "Hello?" he said. "I think I just witnessed an abduction."

~ * ~

This whole thing was Jim's fault, and it was going to get them all killed.

Once he'd regained consciousness for the second time and had shaken off the feeling that something was attempting to split his brain in half, he tried to work out what had gone wrong. He was so sure he hadn't done anything to blow his cover in the hotel. He'd made plenty of other errors, there was no escaping that fact, but nothing which could have led to Valentine finding out the truth.

Well, only one thing.

A thought had flitted through his brain for a moment, in that alleyway. Had Megan told someone? Had it got back to Valentine that way? He hated himself for even allowing it headspace as he stared into the barrel of Benny's gun. Just as quickly, he had dismissed it. They may have only just met, but he trusted Megan. At least, there was no way he didn't desperately want to be able to trust her implicitly.

The horror of being powerless when Megan and her friend were bundled into the vehicle resonated through him. He remembered shouting out, being punched again, everything going black for a while. When he woke she lay slumped on the floor, and he was terrified about what they'd done to her. Hoped to God she was only unconscious.

She looked completely vulnerable. Strands of her hair fell over her face, the knees of her jeans were scuffed and dirty, her hands bound together by the same type of cable-tie which held his own.

He wondered if he would feel better if she had blown his cover.

At least that way she wouldn't be lying unconscious on the floor of a minivan which wasn't heading anywhere good, she would be safe.

Or maybe that was exactly why she was in the car with him. Jim tried to swallow, but his mouth was too dry.

Seeing her slumped on the floor like that had to be as bad as it got, he'd thought. But it wasn't. Because it got worse the moment she regained consciousness. Total incomprehension flashed across her face before her gaze found his. The look she'd given him was more than he could bear. She was struggling to understand what was going on but mixed into that was the fact she knew who he really was. She was intelligent enough to make the connection; her facial expression told him she was aware that what was happening must be something to do with him. At the same time, the way she searched him for reassurance banished any seed of a thought that it could have been she who knowingly alerted Valentine to his real identity.

In the confines of the vehicle, there was no way he could do or say anything to reassure her. He wasn't even sure he could think of anything reassuring to say right now.

When he realized the importance of Valentine's notebook then managed to get photos of some of its pages, he had been so sure he'd done it. Everything was under control. He was on his way to winning the girl of his dreams, and he'd uncovered the proof about the bad guy, single-handedly. He was going to redeem himself and be the toast of the department. As he sent his photos to Chief Jackson, the word "hero" had popped into his head.

He should have known better and stuck to the goddamn plan instead of trying to ace it.

If only he could work out when it had gone wrong.

This had to be about him being a cop, about him being undercover. Not that it explained what Chris was doing here, bolt upright beside him, frozen into position by what Jim could only imagine was unadulterated terror.

Was it possible Valentine didn't know which of them was the cop?

That would explain why Chris was there. If Valentine suspected there was a cop on his patch, the fact they were both there and still alive must be because the identity of the cop was in doubt. That made sense. If Valentine had been certain the cop was Jim, he would be making this journey alone, for sure. Probably in a body bag.

That gave him the tiniest amount of wiggle room. There might be a way out of this. Even the slimmest chance was better than no chance. The knowledge was cold comfort as he looked at the other three. Because it didn't explain why Megan and Jolie were a part of this.

Before they were bundled into the vehicle, Jim thought Benny and the other men were going to take Chris and him somewhere, beat the crap out of them, and leave them for dead. If they were lucky. But with the women there, this whole thing was looking more and more ominous.

Jim shook his head, an unconscious reaction to his thoughts. He tried to hide it, but Megan noticed. She must have, because her eyes filled with tears again.

He had to work out how to deal with this situation. It was one thing to face the danger you placed yourself into. After all, it had been his choice to become a police officer. He'd taken this assignment willingly, agreed to go undercover. It had been his decision to disobey the instructions of his superior officer and to go back into Valentine's office. It should be up to him to face the ramifications of his own actions.

But it was a totally different thing to witness other people being put into danger, with no way to help them. All because of him. All because of his actions. What made it even harder was the fact one of them was the woman he knew he was beginning to care deeply for.

Megan kept looking at him, silently pleading for an explanation, but he couldn't give her one. He just hoped they would have a chance to talk when they reached the end of the road, wherever that might be.

Chapter Thirty-Three

As the vehicle drew to a halt, Megan craned her neck to see where they were. To one side stood what looked like an abandoned farmhouse. Old and dilapidated, with four wide steps up to the front door. A wraparound wooden porch stretched away in both directions, with what remained of a swing seat at one end. The porch floor was rotten in places, a couple of ragged holes clearly visible from where she was sitting.

The weatherboarding to the front of the house might have been painted a creamy color at some point, in the very dim and distant past. Most of the paint was long gone, the odd piece clung here and there like lichen to a rock.

To one side of the farmhouse were outbuildings, barns with gated fronts, painted a dull red. Equally unused and unkempt if the broken weatherboards were anything to go by. If Megan twisted, she could see one final building, set away from the rest. It appeared more substantial than the others and better maintained than the house, weatherboarded in a similar style but painted much more recently with the red stain. Its doors were firmly closed, a large shiny padlock on the latch.

She could see nothing else, no details or clues about what it might be used for except for a large chimney stack protruding from the roof.

The driver killed the engine then climbed out and stretched his back. At the same time Benny stood as best he could in the confines of the vehicle. "Stay put and keep quiet until we tell you to move. Do you understand?"

Megan nodded, pressing her lips together to stop them from quivering in fright. This place didn't strike her as somewhere she wanted to be. It looked like a building from one of those horror movies, where the mad old man with the chainsaws lived. The others were nodding too.

Jim fixed his focus on her. She wished he would say something, but it was clear he wasn't going to whilst those men were within hearing distance.

As the side door of the minivan slid open, Jolie, leaning partially against it, almost fell out. She squealed as she lurched heavily to one side, unable to stop herself with her hands bound together.

The other suited man, the one called Gray, grabbed her arm and pulled at her roughly until she was sitting upright again. He shoved her back against the interior of the car before he and Benny jumped down through the open door. Benny started a low conversation with the driver.

Megan couldn't hear the words, but as Benny adjusted the waistband on his trousers, he pushed his jacket to one side. Underneath he wore a large gun in a shoulder holster. Megan's mouth dropped open. She shouldn't be surprised, she supposed, given what was happening to them. But it was still a shock to see it.

"He's got a gun," Megan whispered. Her eyes filled with tears yet again. This was all too much.

Jolie's head jerked up. "He's got what?" Her expression grew wild again.

Jim leant toward them. "It'll all be okay. Stay strong. We'll sort this out." He sounded confident, but then he tried to smile at them. He failed. He stared through the window instead. His expression made Megan's tears fall even faster. This situation was as bad as she thought it might be.

Back in the open car doorway, Benny's massive presence was enough to draw their attention. "Are you listening?" He didn't wait for a reply. "Do what I tell you and everything stays cool. We're going to go inside the property, get comfortable, chill out for a while. Simple and straightforward. Nothing to worry about. Then we're going to ask you some questions on behalf of our employer."

"Questions about what?" Megan said quietly. "I don't understand."

Benny didn't reply, just stared at her for a moment before his gaze slid away toward Jim and Chris. "Get up," he said. "You two are going first."

He leant into the vehicle, pulling a butterfly knife from a pocket. A flick of his wrist revealed a broad blade, another flick showing how sharp it was, cutting the tie from Jim's ankles in one movement. Then he released Chris's, who flinched as the blade passed millimeters from his skin.

Benny cocked his wrist again, returning the blade to its split-sided housing. His gaze passed over Megan. His expression was to all intents blank, but she was beginning to understand he was in charge of whatever this thing was. She preferred it when his attention wasn't on her, that much she was already sure about.

Jim shuffled obediently to the front of the vinyl seat, his hands held up in front to balance himself as he stood. He inched his way toward the door, taking care not to stand on anyone or trip over anything.

Megan drew her legs up against herself so she was as small as possible. She could almost wrap her bound hands around her knees. Somehow it gave her a crumb of comfort to sit like that, as if someone was holding her.

"Come on, Chris," Jim said, as he climbed from the vehicle.

Chris shook his head and spoke for the first time since the journey began. "No. I don't think I want to. I don't want to go in there. I want to go back. I want to go home."

"Shut up," Jim said sharply. "Shut up, man, and get out. Do as they say." His tone caught everyone up short. Then his voice softened. "Come on, Chris. You can do this."

Chris tried to heave himself out of the seat. Unable to balance himself without the proper use of his hands he fell backward and let out a strangled cry. His lips quivered, and his breath heaved for a moment or two. Shuffling himself to the edge of the seat as Jim had done, he managed to stand more easily this time. He used the door pillar for support as he climbed out.

Benny and Gray pushed them up the steps and onto the creaky, run-down porch. Gray unlocked the large padlock which held the house door secure, latching it back into the catch once the flap of metal was out of the way. He pushed the door, shoving it a couple of times. It seemed unwilling to yield, so Benny put his shoulder to it. This time the door shifted.

It was as if the building itself was trying to reject Benny. When they did get the door open, Megan tried to get a glimpse into the house. The sunshine was bright, and the difference between the intense patterns of light dappling through the trees outside and the dark, dank interior of the property was stark, making it impossible to see anything inside in detail.

The four men disappeared from Megan's line of sight. The driver remained beside the open car door, his focus on the pair of them. His arms were folded, his jacket hitched back behind the holster he wore on his waistband, the visible gun barrel glinting every now and again in the sunlight. A reminder of its presence, if one was needed.

Jolie's eyes were glazed. The shock and fear had gone, replaced now with a blank stare.

"Jolie?" Megan said. Jolie glanced in her direction and focused for a second or two before looking away. "It'll be okay, you'll see."

Jolie began to nod, then stopped, shaking her head instead. "No, it won't. It's never going to be okay." Her eyes filled with tears. "And it's all my fault, Megan. This is my fault."

"What do you mean? How can it be your fault?"

"It's Don Onesta. He must have arranged this because I didn't go through with what they wanted me to do."

"What are you talking about?" Megan said, her eyebrows knitting together. How could this have anything to do with that man? By default, that would mean William was also involved.

"Onesta said he would turn me over to the police if I didn't go through with it. They had evidence of what I did, and he said he'd make sure I went to jail for a long time unless I got you to do what they wanted."

"Got me to do what?" Megan said.

Jolie didn't reply.

"Got me to do what?" she repeated, her gaze fixed on her friend. What on earth had Jolie done?

Jolie's eyes glazed over again. "I didn't want to go to jail, but I don't want this, either. I'm so frightened…" She repeated the phrase, the words lost in her hands as she buried her face.

Megan shuffled across, pressing herself against Jolie, trying to comfort her. Whatever the hell was going on, it was possible her fear of it having to do with Jim's true profession was unfounded. It seemed possible it was something to do with her, instead. With William and his refusal to believe that she wasn't going back to him.

Did the phone call from William on the first night of their stay at The Valentine Retreat have some bearing on all this? She'd been so desperate to ignore his call, to ignore him. From experience she knew he would simply continue to dial her number until she picked up. She'd tried to brush him off, but perhaps she should have listened to him more carefully.

As she sat against the unyielding floor of the minivan, one side of her body hot against Jolie's weeping frame, she tried to remember his exact words.

"Hello, William. What do you want?"

"Megan, honey. Where are you?"

"Out of town. Why?"

She had been careful not to tell him where she was; he had no right to ask. With hindsight, perhaps he was already aware of her weekend plans.

"Out of town? Are you sure?"

"Why does it matter where I am, William?"

"Listen, honey. I want to meet. We need to talk. Before it's too late."

"What do you want to talk about?"

She wished now she'd pressed him on what he meant by "before it's too late." At the time, she'd assumed it was a play to get her attention. She'd thought he might be issuing another one of his under-the-radar threats about the money for Craig's care. She remembered thinking she would need to navigate the conversation carefully.

"We can't go on like this," he said.

"Why not?"

"I want you to come back."

"I can't. You know that."

"I love you. I know we can work out any issues. Megan, we belong together."

"Please, William, you need to respect the fact we're divorced. If you want to meet to discuss the agreement, then feel free to contact my lawyers. They'll set up a date. You know I'm always willing to do that."

"I was so sure you took it. I was sure it meant you still loved me, that you'd come back, given a little time. That you'd realize your mistake."

"You have to believe me; I didn't take anything with me when I moved out. Nothing. I didn't take the Easter egg."

"It doesn't matter. None of it will matter in the long term. I'm sure you'll see that soon enough."

At the time, she'd dismissed the call as just another in a long line of calls from William. Half-expected to hear from her lawyers, wanting to set up a meeting with him. But now? Perhaps she needed to interpret it differently. Maybe his talk about last chances and not mattering in the long term had meant something totally different.

For months, Megan had prayed that William would move on with his life and let her go. It struck her that maybe this was exactly what he was doing. Just not in the way she had envisaged. Her mind floated back to the day she'd confronted William about the other women, the confidence in his words.

"The thing is, Megan, if I wanted out, I could get rid of you like that." He clicked his fingers. "Pouf. You're gone."

Maybe that was what this was. Had her constant refusals to go back to him led to this moment, to him getting rid of her—once and for all? Even in her wildest nightmares, an option as dark as this had never occurred to her.

Her priority was finding out what Jolie was talking about and how it was linked to William. One thing became crystal clear as she sat there. If this was about her and William, she had to get these men to let her speak to him. She would tell him she'd do whatever it took—she'd go back to him if that was what he wanted—anything to ensure he'd let the others go and not hurt anyone.

Benny strode over to the car. "Your turn," he said, leaning into the vehicle and grabbing Jolie by the arm.

As he pulled, her foot caught under her body, halting her forward momentum. She tried to scrabble her feet back around, squealing as Benny lifted and hefted her across the gravelly dirt, manhandling her into the farmhouse.

The driver leant into the car, gesturing for Megan to slide over as well. She had the sudden desire to kick at his face and run for it, but she wouldn't get far. His gun glinted in the sunlight. Her hands were tied. She shoved her way over, using her elbows to prop herself up until her feet touched the ground and he took hold of her under one arm, pulling her upright.

Each step on the rough gravel of the driveway dug into the soft soles of her travel shoes. Although it hardly felt as if she was touching the ground at all, the driver was so strong he half-dragged, half-lifted her across the stony ground. He held onto her arm, shoving her in front of him, up the steps, and into the darkness of the farmhouse.

Chapter Thirty-Four

Andy was halfway through what had been described to him in the gas station's shop as a meat pasty when the cops showed up. Nerves always made Andy hungry. Come to think of it, he wasn't sure there was an emotion which didn't pull at his stomach strings. But this pie was the pits. He threw the rest of it into the trash and brushed the grease from his fingers into his trousers.

The cars were civilian issue, but Andy spotted them coming up the road. They reminded him of a million films where the CIA arrives in a convoy of black SUVs. Except they were minus the SUVs, and no one wore a dark suit. Or an earpiece.

Instead, the lead vehicle—a large Ford F-series in russet red with a rust patch above one of its wheel arches—pulled off the highway and circled back toward him. A late model sedan and smaller Jeep followed in its wake, rolling to a stop in a line.

A tall black man, somewhere past his mid-fifties if Andy had to guess, unfolded himself from the driver's seat of the Ford. "Are you Andy Mossbury?" he said.

Andy nodded.

"I'm Chief Jackson." He stuck out a hand, and Andy gave his own a final wipe before having his fingers crushed in greeting. "Thanks for the info, we'll take it from here. There's no need for you to get yourself any deeper into this thing."

The others began to climb from their vehicles, the passenger door of the Ford disgorging a shorter figure, a square box rather than a rectangle of a man, with sandy hair and a serious expression.

The detective rounded the side of the F-series, holding out a hand for Andy to shake. No prizes for detecting the Irish lilt in his voice as he said, "Detective Killenny. Good to meet you."

"Andy Mossbury."

"This is Jim's usual partner," Jackson said, waving a hand at

Killenny. "Is there anything else you can think of to tell us?"

Andy shook his head. He'd explained what he'd seen, where he'd tailed the minivan to, and the layout of the farm as far as he had been able to see it.

"Two female hostages?" Jackson asked.

"For definite."

"At least two hostage takers."

"A driver, and there had to be at least one other in the back to restrain the women, don't you think?"

"You couldn't be sure how many in total inside the vehicle?"

"I couldn't see into the vehicle at all; the windows were completely tinted out. That doesn't mean there couldn't have been more people inside."

Jackson pulled in a big breath, his expression becoming steely. "Unknown number of hostages," he said to Killenny. A look passed between them.

"That would explain his no-show," Killenny replied.

A little verbal dance around the fact that Jim Carello must also be missing.

Jackson nodded curtly. "And at least two hostage takers, maybe more." The rest of the officers were gathered around him like a crescent moon. "Suit up, people. We've got work to do." Almost as an afterthought, he looked at Andy. "As I say, we are indebted to you, but it's time to leave things to the professionals."

Andy surprised himself by shaking his head. "No, Chief Jackson, if it's all the same to you, I'm going to hang around. I've seen this thing through this far, and I want to know Megan gets out okay. I mean, I've never met the woman, but I feel like I know her. Sounds a bit weird, I know, and I don't mean it in a creepy, stalker way, either..." He stood square on to the chief. "Thing is, I never graduated, but I went through police academy training, same as all your guys." No need to elaborate on the reason he'd never graduated, a badly judged friendship and a DUI enough to stop his career prospects in their tracks. "And I know what the driver looks like, so I can help you if you'll let me?"

He shifted his weight from one foot to the other, holding the chief's gaze until Jackson raised his eyebrows. "Killenny, grab a spare flak jacket, will you? Mr. Mossbury's riding along with us on this one."

~ * ~

"All the doors are locked and the windows are nailed shut, so don't go getting any crazy ideas," Gray said, his tone flat as he lifted his dark glasses from his face for the first time before folding them and putting them into his pocket.

He was probably in his forties, Jim thought. Tall and muscular, with extraordinarily bright gray eyes, so light they were almost silver. As he tucked the glasses away, he lifted his suit jacket away from his side, making it easy for them to see the gun held beneath, strapped to his waistline.

"Take a seat, boys," Gray said in a thick southern drawl. "You go right ahead and get comfortable."

Jim was in what he assumed to be the living room of the property. An old musty couch covered in a dust-laden crochet throw, a wooden rocking chair, and a couple of other easy chairs were scattered around the room. Shelves on one side were still lined with books and personal knick-knacks. There were a couple of prints on the wall. Everything looked as if someone walked out one day and never came back.

"Gray, what the hell's going on?" Jim pleaded with the man. "While it's just us, level with me, please. There's no need to scare the girls, but I want to know. What's all this about?"

"Not for me to say." He crossed his arms. It would seem the conversation was at an end.

Jim took a seat at one end of the couch. Chris chose one of the chairs, mute again, his focus pinned on Gray.

Megan and Jolie were hustled into the room a minute or so later. Megan made a beeline for Jim, stumbling as she caught an edge on the lumpy rug covering part of the floor. He could do nothing to help her as she almost fell, recovering her balance and slotting her body against his. She wedged herself as close to him as their bound wrists would allow. She didn't speak. Her gaze was fixed on their abductors, but he could feel how shallow and rapid her breathing was. She seemed to be doing her best to hang on, same as him. Hanging on to rational behavior by a whisker.

Benny, Gray, and the driver held a low-key conversation at the other end of the room. Jim couldn't hear much, but he did hear snatches. "It'll take a few hours... You go and unlock the barn, Paul, check everything's there... Get it started. Gray, you stay here."

Gray leaned against one side of the stone hearth with mock casualness. There was nothing casual about this situation. He took the revolver from his waistband, holding it in front of himself, his fingers relaxed along the length of its barrel. If only Jim could get a hold of that weapon, this would be over in no time.

The driver and Benny left the room. "What are they doing?" Jim asked. "Why don't we get on with this? What's going to take a few hours?"

"You don't need to know any of that. Just sit tight. We'll get started soon enough."

Nobody said anything for a while. Jim pressed his thigh tightly against Megan, listening to her breath consciously drawn in through her nose and out through her mouth. He held her hands in his, squeezing her fingers every few moments, steadied by the sensation of her squeezing his in return.

Jim had run through this kind of scenario in his head, thinking about what he would do if he were abducted in the line of duty. It happened. Not that often, but it did happen. He'd spent time calculating the odds depending on how many assailants there were, how many weapons they had, and what sort. Whether he could expect backup to be on its way, and where they found themselves being held. There were a million variables.

The one scenario he had never run through his head was the one he now found himself in, where the woman he might be falling in love with was caught up in the abduction too. All his calculations had been about risk to himself, fellow officers, and unknown abductees. But his calculations had all been blown out of the water by Megan being here.

The quiet in the room became absolute. Nobody moved or spoke, like a glitch in the streaming of a film when everything paused, but nobody knew for how long. The only things moving were the dust motes floating in the light brave enough to penetrate the gloomy space.

Megan squeezed his fingers again, but this time she didn't let go. "I think this is all my fault," she whispered.

Chapter Thirty-Five

Jim's face radiated confusion. Megan was aware that he had assumed the abduction was linked to his undercover work, that there could be no other reason. But Jim didn't know what William was capable of. It seemed she might not have appreciated what he was capable of, either.

"How can you think that?" he said, his voice low, his tone incredulous.

"If it is to do with me, I think I can fix it." Jolie sat hunched on the other easy chair. Megan raised her voice to gain her attention. "It's time to tell me, Jolie. All of it. Don't you think?" Her words were strained and tight.

Jolie shook her head, the fingers of one hand picking at the other. Her gaze darted randomly, looking anywhere but at Megan. "I think it's too late."

"No. It's not. We can fix this. Please, tell me what happened."

"Oh God, I was so stupid. I took it on impulse," Jolie said, her eyes filling with tears.

"Took what?" Megan already knew; it was the only thing which made any sense. She asked, to be sure, "Jolie, did *you* take the egg?"

"I was so angry with him for putting you through so much, and it was just sitting there on your dressing table, that final day—the day we went to get your things. I wanted to punish him somehow." She sighed, the misery clear in her voice as she said, "I didn't know there was a security camera in that room. They had me on film."

"Oh, Jolie." Above Megan's dressing table hung the Degas, her favorite painting.

There had been no chance William would allow her to have the painting in her private rooms without full-scale security, but she insisted the camera should have a limited viewpoint: the painting and what stood beneath it—her dressing table.

She hardly used the dresser, anyway, it was more of a surface on which she dumped perfume bottles and trinkets. The serious jewelry was housed in the safe, but the Easter egg never made it that far. She'd taken it off one day, when the last of the gloss had slipped from the relationship and had shoved it amongst everything else on the glass surface. It had remained there ever since. At least, that was where she'd left it.

"But why did William think I had it?" Megan said. She wondered why he hadn't checked the video straight away.

"I think he presumed that you had taken it, Megan." She leant forward, resting her forearms on her knees. "I know you don't want to hear this, but in his own screwed up way, William still loves you. I think he thought that if you had taken the egg, it was because deep down you still loved him and you would recognize it and go back to him. I think that's why he kept phoning you. He hoped that you had taken it and you just needed some time to think things through. And then, when he finally began to accept you weren't going to change your mind, I think he began to look for other explanations. That's when he must have checked the footage."

It didn't surprise Megan that the camera footage would be stored, rather than deleted, along with everything else William collected.

Jolie bit her lip. "I wanted to tell you. I should have given it back to you but..." She hung her head.

"Why didn't you?"

"I didn't have it any longer. Troy borrowed money from a loan shark and needed to pay it back, like *really* needed to pay it back. He was so scared. It was the only thing I could think to do to raise enough cash. Then we broke up anyway..."

Jolie looked utterly miserable. Megan should be angry, she supposed, but she had so many other emotions broiling around inside there was no room left for another. "You still should have told me. We could have worked it out somehow."

Jolie shook her head. "It was too late. Onesta came to see me at work one day, not long after Troy and I split. He said I was looking at time in jail for what I'd done and that he would make sure the time was doubled if I mentioned anything about it to you." She paused, then huffed out a huge breath. "The next day he came to me again and told me what I had to do if I wanted to stay out of jail."

Megan took her hands back from Jim, resting them in her lap. The cold twist was back in her stomach. She didn't speak, waiting instead for Jolie to continue in her own time.

"The trip to The Valentine Retreat?" Jolie said. "I didn't win it in a competition like I said. The whole thing was a set-up. You were supposed to fall for one of the red-braid guys, then I had to let the PI into the suite so he could take pictures." Jolie's cheeks burnt inferno red. "It sounds so cheap when I say it like that." She swallowed.

Jolie was right, it did sound cheap when she said it like that. Megan glanced at Jim. He blinked, his eyes staying closed for a few seconds as if he were trying to erase the image from his mind.

"What if I hadn't gone along with the plan like a lamb to the slaughter?" Megan said, feeling Jim's fingers reach for hers. She pulled her hands away. "What then?"

"Onesta gave me something to put in your drink. He said he'd get his photos one way or another, and if I came away from the weekend without them, I was only headed one place."

Jim swore under his breath, shaking his head. He reached for her hands again. This time she let him take hold of them.

"But I couldn't do it. I couldn't go through with calling the PI, even though I knew you and Jim were…" Jolie swallowed again, unable to finish the sentence. She didn't need to. They all knew what she was alluding to. "I thought we'd go home today and the police would be knocking on my door once Onesta realized what I'd done. Or rather, what I hadn't done. After the last few months, I thought it would be a relief, in a funny way, to face the consequences square on. To leave the lies behind." Jolie rubbed at an eye. "I wouldn't blame you if you never speak to me again, but I need you to know I'm so sorry. I'd do anything to gain your forgiveness, even though I don't deserve it." She looked around, her gaze falling on Gray. "I didn't think any of this would happen…"

"Maybe we can still sort this out," Megan said, eyeing Gray too. "Excuse me? Sir?"

"What do you want?" he said.

"If this has anything to do with William Wiseman or Don Onesta, I think there's been a huge misunderstanding. It's one I'm sure I can sort out. Tell them I'll do whatever it is they want if you let everyone else go."

Onesta wanted photos of her having sex with what should have amounted to a male prostitute. A clear breach of her agreement with William and an easy way to break the contract regarding Craig's care. Did he want photos for that reason alone? So that William could cease payments for her brother's care? Maybe that was what William had meant when he told her it wouldn't matter in the long term.

Or did Onesta intend to use the photos to force her back with William, something to blackmail her with for the rest of her life? Earn himself the maximum in brownie points with his boss by returning her to him like a prize dish, her head on a platter.

Perhaps when he failed to get the photographs he wanted, he'd moved to Plan B. Maybe he wanted to frighten her into going back. That could be what this was.

Either way, the plan had been to screw her over. Well and truly. There was no doubt in her mind that if she'd brought this on the others, even by default, she would do whatever it took to sort it out. The coldness in her stomach expanded its reach as she realized she would give in and go back to William if it came to it. To keep the people in this room safe, she would do that without question.

The man looked at her, his head cocked to one side as he studied her face. He didn't reply. Before she could say anything further, Benny came into the room.

"Hey, Benny, this chick is asking if this whole thing is something to do with some guy called Wiseman. Who the fuck is that?" Gray said.

Megan's hopes faded as Benny shook his head. "This ain't nothing to do with him. Time to tell you all why we *are* here, though."

~ * ~

Jim's shoulders stiffened. Had he hoped this whole thing was some twisted spousal issue with Megan's ex-husband? It was undeniable that he'd give anything to have the responsibility lifted, unlikely though it was. Benny worked for Valentine. This was to do with Valentine, without question.

"I would apologize for the way you have all been brought here," Benny said. "But at least one of you will understand the need for swift action. One of you knows exactly where we're coming from." He focused his attention on Chris then Jim.

Benny's stare weighed heavily. Jim did his best to concentrate on keeping his breathing regular and calm. Sweat prickled under his collar, and he longed to run a hand around his neck to ease the tension. Instead, he was grateful when Megan tightened her fingers against his. It was a subtle touch, but it was there.

"There are a few questions we need the answers to. If all goes according to plan and we discover what we need to know, then you can all go home." Benny's gaze slid back to Chris.

Who was he trying to kid? Jim glanced at Chris. One knee bobbed up and down almost uncontrollably, but he had a livelier edge to his gaze. He was focused on what he was hearing. Did he believe what Benny was saying?

"Most importantly, we need to find out which one of you broke into Mr. Valentine's desk and looked through his private papers. We know you both had the opportunity."

"No." Chris shook his head. "No, it wasn't me. I don't know what you're talking about. I would never—"

Benny held a finger up to his lips. The face behind the hand was ice-cold, and Chris fell silent, his head still as Benny continued, "We're not interested in what you don't know. Telling us what you don't know is of no help to us, or you. As I was saying, we need to know which one of you did it and what you did with the information. Secondly, we want to know which one of you is the *cop*." He spat the word out.

Jim concentrated on a flake of paint on the wall, working to keep his breathing level and even.

"We got a phone call telling us one of you is LAPD, and that you've been undercover at The Valentine Retreat to try to bring Mr. Valentine's business into disrepute. Be assured, Mr. Valentine is less than happy about both things." Benny shifted his stance. "In fact, Mr. Valentine is really pissed about it."

Jim had to fight to keep his reaction under control. Someone had phoned The Valentine Retreat and told them? Who the hell would have done something like that? Who even knew he was there? He discounted members of the department and Megan. The only other person who knew was the PI. But why would he have phoned his recognition of Jim into Chief Jackson one moment only to turn around and blow his cover to the hotel the next? That didn't make much sense.

Benny walked to the window and stared at the scenery, presumably to let his words sink in. "I have a few options for you to consider. Option one. Mr. Police Officer can do the honorable thing and tell us who you are. And if you also peeked in Mr. Valentine's desk, that would be very neat. Then we could let the others go. No harm, no foul."

Benny looked around. He held up his hand, two fingers outstretched as he continued, "Option two. If one of you knows who the cop is, or who snuck into the boss's office, you can tell us, and you can walk out of here." A third finger joined the other two, his thumb squashing down the smallest digit. "Option three. We don't bother with the niceties, and we start hurting people until we find out what we want to know."

He dropped his hand to his side. "Option three is my option of choice. Just in case you were wondering. But Mr. Valentine likes to play fair, so we'll give you a few minutes to think about whether you have the information we need. Let the whole thing percolate." Benny mimed quotation marks around the words, as if they weren't his own. "That's how Mr. Valentine wants it, so that's what will happen. Gray will be right outside the door. You've got five minutes."

Both men left the room, the key turning in the lock with an

audible clunk.

Once the door was closed, Jim was on his feet. He moved quickly and quietly across to one of the windows, checking that it was, as they said, nailed closed. It was. Whoever had wielded the hammer had been no expert, the heads of the large nails bent and rammed into place with little care. However, the glass looked mottled and old, the frames flaky and rotten in places. He pushed at the wooden edges. They gave fractionally, but not enough to pry the glass from the frame. Breaking the glass would be a possibility, but it would make too much noise.

"What the hell are they talking about?" Chris said, his leg still bobbing up and down. "They think one of us is a cop. Why would they think that? I'm not a cop, I'm an actor. And you're not a cop either." Chris's face creased in confusion. "You're not? Are you?"

Chapter Thirty-Six

"Don't be ridiculous. Of course I'm not," Jim said, the lie burning the back of his throat. "This whole thing is completely nuts."

There was no way he was telling Chris the truth. His jiggling leg and fragile expression were enough to tell Jim the moment he did Chris would be shouting for Benny to come back. He wanted out of this place—they all did—and Jim would put money on Chris having believed what Benny had told them about going home. He looked as if he needed to believe that. He wasn't giving any other possibility head space.

The thing was, Jim would be prepared to tell Benny the truth if he thought it would guarantee safety for the rest of them. But everything hinged on that seemingly insignificant word: if.

If he confessed to being the police officer, it would seal his own fate, irreparably. There would be no going home for him. There would be no going anywhere. There was no "if" about that. Nevertheless, if he honestly believed doing that would keep Megan safe, he'd do it in a heartbeat.

The trouble was, none of the abductors had made any effort to hide their identities, nor that of the person behind the whole operation. And if their sole purpose was to find the cop and dispose of him, why were Megan and Jolie even here? The only reason he could think of was the fact they would be the only two people who might miss them and connect them with The Valentine Retreat.

From the window, Jim could see the outbuildings arcing away to one side. At the end, the building which had been locked up tight on their arrival now had its doors flung wide. Pluming from the chimney was a curl of smoke, spreading out and smudging against the blue sky. There must be a fire burning inside. Why would they have lit a fire? Jim scanned the building, looking for a clue as to its purpose. He noticed rings set at intervals across the front to either side of the doors.

A thought crossed his mind, causing him to pull in a sudden

breath. Maybe he was wrong, but he had a horrible idea he knew what the fire was. It was possible the building was a forge of some sort, which would mean they were heating up a furnace.

It made saliva prickle the back of his mouth, and he had to work hard not to retch at the thought, but there was no getting away from it. This abduction had all the hallmarks of a thorough clean up. It was hard to dispose of bodies properly, but it would be more than possible in a hot enough fire.

If any of them wanted to get out of this farmhouse alive, Jim could only see one course of action. He needed to buy them some time while he worked out an escape plan.

"So why do they think one of us is a cop? I don't understand." Chris sounded desperate.

"None of us do," Megan said, shuffling along to the end of the couch closest to the chair in which he sat, leaning toward him. "This is like a bad dream for all of us. You need to hang on a bit longer, and we'll all get out of here, somehow."

Jim would have wrapped his arms around her and kissed her there and then if his hands weren't bound. Fresh from Jolie's revelations and with the knowledge of who the cop was—and that they were all there because of him—Megan was now doing her best to comfort someone else. Had she too identified Chris as the weak link in their dysfunctional chain?

He headed back to her, slotting himself beside her, taking hold of her hands again. He got as close as he could to her ear. "I'm going to get you out of here." His words were barely a whisper.

She nodded.

"Whatever it takes. Do you understand?"

A frown deepened on her brow. "Don't you dare tell them," she said, the words nothing more than puffs of warm air in his ear.

"Whatever it takes," he repeated gently.

Tears formed in the corners of her eyes, diluting the sea-green and making the gold flecks swim. The tears pooled then began to roll down her cheeks. She shook her head, as if dismissing his comment. "We're all going to go home," she said, louder and with a conviction he wasn't sure any of them felt.

Then she smiled at him. It was a glorious sight, like sunshine on a stormy day, and it took his breath away. The smile was replaced with a frown just as quickly.

"We're all going home," she repeated.

Fueled by her smile, Jim said, "There has to be a way out of this. We need to work out what it is."

Megan brought her lips to his and kissed him, a feather's touch against his skin. Her lips quivered as they brushed his. It was exquisite.

"Meeting you is the best thing that's ever happened to me," she said. Then she shrugged. "Mind you, that's not necessarily saying much." The rueful smile which accompanied her follow-up comment made him grin for a moment too.

He didn't have the faintest idea what he would do, but he would get her out. He would get them all out. She brought her hands up, one of them touching the side of his face, her gaze tracing the same path as her fingers. The sensation of them on his skin was almost too much to bear. He was in danger of tearing up, but then he heard the key turn in the door lock. Megan heard it too, her hand dropping from his face as she turned with him to see who would come through the door.

~ * ~

Andy hovered around the edge of the group, aware he was a spare pin in the game, but unwilling to walk away from it. He fiddled with the edge of the bullet-proof vest hidden under his sports jacket. He'd forgotten how damn uncomfortable they were. And hot.

"Let me make sure I've got this straight," Pete Killenny said. "We'll drive in, you and me, in the truck. Pretend like we're on vacation, looking for somewhere to do a bit of casual hunting. Then act all surprised when we come across the property. Meanwhile everyone else will take up position in the surrounding area?"

"That's about the size of it," said Jackson. "I'll go knock on the door, ask for permission to hunt the woods, and see if we get an idea of who's in there. Then we'll make our move."

"I think there's a fair chance Jim's in there with them."

"It's a strong possibility. To be honest, I hope he's in there completely unharmed, so that when I get my hands on him, I can get first shot at busting his balls. He's played fast and loose with this whole damn operation.." Jackson raised his voice. "Is everyone clear about what we're doing? Those of you with radios, keep them close, but keep the noise down. Okay, let's go."

The other officers made final preparations, ribbing one another, psyching themselves up for what was to come.

Andy stood beside Jackson's truck, shifting his weight from one foot to the other. Jackson checked his watch, and the other vehicles began to move out. Finally, Jackson transferred his attention to Andy.

"You've done a great thing, getting us here. Without you, well, at best we'd be looking to recover bodies. At least now we're in with a chance of getting people out alive. Don't feel you have to continue with the bravado for any of our benefit."

Andy took a deep breath, packaging the nerves which had accompanied the zipping up of the flak jacket back into a dark corner of his mind. "I'll come with you. Like I said, I can identify at least one of the abductors. I'll stay in the car, but they're never going to think I could be a cop, are they? I'm great at undercover. I've been unremarkable for twenty-five years. It's been my whole career, after all." He managed a tight smile.

Chief Jackson nodded once before gesturing for them all to climb into the truck.

~ * ~

It was Benny who came back into the room, flanked by Gray.

He stood in front of them, a hand resting on the hilt of his gun, as if he wasn't intimidating enough. Megan tried to swallow, but there was nothing there.

"Has anyone got anything to tell me?" He allowed his gaze to linger on Jim then Chris. "Anyone got anything to tell me about Mr. Valentine's book?" No one moved. Even Chris fell still as they all looked at Benny. "Or the cop?" No one said a word. The big man pursed his lips. "Well, I can't say I'm surprised. I gave you a chance to do it Mr. Valentine's way. But, if you're all playing dumb, we'll just have to ask our questions my way."

His jacket fell back to hide the hilt of his gun as he pointed at Megan. He raised an eyebrow and glanced at Gray. "We'll start with her."

Megan's eyes widened desperately as she looked at Jim. Benny grabbed her arm.

"Let's see what the lady can tell us, shall we?" A strange smile settled on his face. His grip tightened on her skin, tugging her to her feet. She leant away from him, trying to pull herself free from his iron grip.

"Jesus Christ, Benny. You can't be serious." Jim shuffled himself to the front of the sofa, climbing to his feet. "If you need to beat on anyone, take me."

"Who said anything about hitting her?"

"For God's sake, leave her alone. Fucking animal," Jim said, the vitriol in his words unmistakable.

"Touching. The prostitute cares about his Jane. Or is it the cop playing the good guy?" With a shove, Benny released his grip on her arm, sending her tumbling back onto the couch. He gestured to Jim. "You, then."

Her eyes filled with tears again. However strong she had determined to be, she couldn't stop them. "Please don't take him," she whispered.

Benny ignored her. "Move, Jim. We'll go somewhere else for our chat."

Jim twisted, keeping his gaze on her for as long as he could, until Benny shoved him through the door and Gray closed it behind them. The key clicked in the lock again, footsteps receded, then the sounds stopped.

The room was silent for a while. The skin on her arm throbbed, the tie on her wrists having cut into her flesh, but it was certain to be nothing compared to what Jim would be going through. After a while, she couldn't stay still any longer. She pressed an ear to the door, trying to hear what was happening. She didn't want to, but she needed to, needed to know they hadn't taken him away forever. It didn't matter how hard she listened, she couldn't make out any sounds.

"We've got to find a way out of here," she said.

Jolie let out a strangled sob. "What are you talking about?" She held her bound wrists up in front of her. "How the fuck are we supposed to get out? The windows are nailed shut, our hands are tied together, and they've all got *guns*, Megan, or hadn't you noticed?"

She frowned. "Yes, I had noticed. But God only knows what they're doing to Jim. You think they're going to stop with him?" Her focus flicked to Chris, then came back to rest on Jolie and her tortured face. "This isn't your fault, Jolie. This isn't any of our faults. But if we sit here waiting to be rescued or hoping that they're going to let us go…? They're not going to let us go. You must see that."

"I'm supposed to be doing my callback today. I don't think any of you have any idea how important this day was supposed to be in my life. I'm supposed to be getting my part in *Daylight Dreams*. This was going to be my big break." The pitch of Chris's voice accentuated the strain he was feeling. "Instead, I'm here, in some God-forsaken farmhouse that time forgot, being held at gunpoint by people who think I've stolen from Mr. Valentine, who thinks I'm a cop." He laughed. "I don't get it. I don't get why a cosmic cock-up of these proportions has to be happening to me." He stared uncomprehendingly at Megan, then at Jolie. "Do you?" He didn't wait for an answer. "I mean, I bet Bruce Willis never has to deal with shit like this, does he?"

Megan bit her lip. Had the pressure gotten to him? Had Chris completely lost the plot?

"Or The Rock, or Jason fucking Statham, or Aaron Paul for that matter?" He shook his head. "Of course not. I'll tell you one thing. When we get out of this, I'm going to be able to give the best and most goddamn convincing performance anyone has ever seen at an audition. I'm going to blow everyone else away with my hostage portrayal. This whole shitty situation—and I have no frigging idea what any of it has to do with me—

could work to my advantage. Don't you think?" On his feet now, he paced the room, glanced through the windows before looking at the shelves lining one side of the room.

Was he unaware of what was happening to Jim, somewhere else in the building, or was this his way of coping? It was almost as if he had taken on the persona of one of his actor heroes as he scanned the room again. He lifted one of the prints from the wall and shoved it face down on the back of the couch, working at the reverse of the frame with his fingers. Stripping off the binding tape, he lifted the backboard away from the rest of the frame.

Discarding the print, he took hold of the glass. "Aha," he said. "Now we have something sharp, we can cut these ties off."

Footsteps sounded outside the room. There were voices.

"Chris," Megan hissed. "Hide it. They're coming back."

His gaze swung in her direction, his expression fiercely bright for a moment. Then he nodded, gathering up all the pieces and dropping to his knees so he could push it all out of sight under the couch. He crawled backward until he was sitting against Jolie's chair as the key turned in the door. Jolie gripped his shoulder between her fingers as the door swung open.

Chapter Thirty-Seven

Tuesday Early Afternoon

Benny shoved Jim into the room with as much care as if he were a roll of old carpet. With his hands still bound, Jim stumbled and was unable to control his fall, landing first on his knees then pitching onto his face with a grunt. Megan winced, shuffling herself to the front of her seat. She was about to go to him when Benny fixed her with a look any rattlesnake would have been proud of.

"Leave him," he said. Benny's gravelly voice had gained a bottom note of nails. "We'll be back for another one of you in a while. Unless anyone has anything they want to share?" He glanced around. "Anything you've suddenly remembered? Anything to stop yourself ending up like him?"

When no one spoke, Benny kicked at Jim, his foot landing with a dull thud against a thigh. Jim grunted again, rolling onto his side and doing his best to ball himself up.

Once the door was locked and they were alone again, Megan shot over to Jim and managed to help him turn himself around. When he was able to sit upright, he leant himself back against the stone hearth, his breath coming in ragged gasps.

She didn't know which bit of him to look at first. Someone had wiped the worst of the blood from his face, but it still flowed freely from a cut above one eye. An angry welt was forming down one side of his face, his eyes were beginning to swell, and his lip was split. She reached out to touch him, gently on the shoulder first, then the cheek, and had to swallow a sob when she noticed the small red patch—his shaving incident from the previous day—was completely obscured by his injuries.

He sucked in a sharp breath, his eyebrows furrowing. He closed his eyes.

"Look what they did to you." She didn't know what to do, how to help him. Something else crystallized in that moment, though, something unexpected. Seeing him like this ripped her in half; the strength of the emotion ambushing her with unbelievable ferocity. She loved this man. She loved him in a wild, fierce way she'd never experienced before. It was instinctive, almost primal, in its intensity.

"I'm okay," he said. "It looks worse than it is, honest. Cracked a couple of ribs, I think. They've made a bit of a mess of my face. I'll live." He attempted a smile, winced, and frowned instead. "We've got to get out of here, Megan. Get me up."

Chris crawled over, retrieving the glass from the picture frame. He set about holding it, encouraging Jolie to use the edge to cut through her cable tie. She shook her head. "I don't want to make them angry," she whispered.

Chris ledged the glass against the couch for a moment and rested his hands on her knee. "Sweetheart, look what they've done to Jim. Megan's right. They're going to kill us anyway. Cut your tie off so we can at least try to get away. Do you hear me?" He pulled at her hands. "Come on, babe."

At last Jolie nodded. "Okay." She held her wrists out, rubbing the tie up and down against the edge of the glass Chris held between his fingers. She whimpered as she did it.

Megan supported Jim as best she could as he struggled to his feet. He stumbled and gasped as he stood, then pushed his way over to the window. With Jolie's wrists free, Megan took her turn against the piece of glass. It was more difficult than it looked and she needed to press the plastic hard to cut it. With every slide the plastic bit and the glass sliced at her skin, but she kept going until she was free. Taking hold of the glass, she allowed Chris his turn. The edge of the sharp, brittle glass against her fingers was equally painful, tiny lacerations forming on her skin, blood pricking from multiple sources and building into blobs which slid down her hands.

"Keep your tie in your hand," Chris said. "When they come back, make it look like they're still done up."

He grabbed the glass from her, cutting Jim's hands free whilst he stared through the window. Megan joined him.

"What is it?" she said.

The room they occupied took up the whole end of one side of the building, allowing them a view out front as well as toward the back of the property. An extra vehicle had drawn to a stop on the rough gravel of the driveway. A dirty-red Ford F-Series. Two guys climbed out, one of them looked to be in his late fifties. He was tall, his hair salt-and-pepper gray. The other was shorter, stockier, and younger, with sandy hair.

"Oh my god," she breathed, panic spiking again. Were they more of Valentine's people? Yet another man was in the back of the truck.

Jim took hold of her arm, hissing in her ear, "That's my boss and my partner. Go sit down, pretend you're still tied up. One of them will be back to keep us quiet any second. Go!"

Megan spun away, getting the others to sit down. Jim stayed at the window, three fingers held up tight against the glass, four fingers on the other hand pressed to his chest.

~ * ~

While Chief Jackson and Pete climbed out of the truck, Andy stayed put, winding down his window so he could hear what was happening.

The Oscar went to Jackson, without a doubt. Andy watched him hitching up his jeans, stretching his back out as if they'd been travelling for hours. Andy guessed the chief was using the opportunity to have a good look around. As he released his hands from the small of his back, he indicated something to Pete, who focused his attention on one of the windows facing the driveway. Andy could make out a shadowy figure standing behind the glass. Unless he was very much mistaken, it was Jim Carello.

Jackson ambled toward the porch. Before his foot landed on the bottom step, the front door opened just widely enough to allow a bulky, suited man to exit.

"Hi there, friend," Jackson said, his New Orleans twang on full whack. "How're you doing? Lovely old place you've got here."

"What do you want? You're on private property." The man spoke sharply, his voice deep and husky, friendliness dialed down to zero.

The guy couldn't have looked more out of place, stood outside the decrepit property in his sharp suit and city shoes. He wasn't the driver of the minivan, Andy was sure of that. He ran a hand across his forehead, scanning the driveway, feigning lack of interest.

"Well, the thing is, friend," Jackson gestured toward Pete, then waved his hand briefly in Andy's direction. "My buddies and me, we're itching to get on our orange vests and get us some hunting, and we thought this woodland looked ideal. We didn't even think there was anything back here but more trees, did we?" He grinned at Pete, who grinned back, shaking his head. "But once we saw your property, well, the only neighborly thing to do is to ask permission."

Jackson stood his ground, keeping his smile fixed in place.

"Listen, *friend*," the suited man said, his tone still icy. His meaty

197

hand pulled the door closed and he took a couple of steps forward, pressing home his intimidating height advantage from the top of the porch. He crossed his arms. "I'd rather you headed on out of here, if it's all the same. This was my father-in-law's place. He upped and died so we're trying to sort it all out, you know?"

Jackson backed away, smile still in place. "No problem, sir, sorry for your loss. No harm in asking, though, is there?"

"No harm at all. But as I say, we'd rather you took your truck and headed on out of here."

"We'll get out of your hair, no sweat. What are y'all burning in your building over there?" The question sounded innocent enough, but the chief wasn't making idle chat.

The guy looked at him sharply, then shrugged. "Just getting rid of some trash."

The conversation clearly at an end, Jackson and Pete climbed back into the truck. Jackson slammed his door shut.

"I don't recognize that guy," Andy said. "So that makes at least two abductors."

"There are three," Pete said. "Jim was signaling from the window—three perps, four hostages. Must be the two women, Jim, and someone else."

Jackson shoved the vehicle into reverse, his concentration fixed on the rear-view mirror as he turned the truck. "'Just getting rid of some trash.' The lying piece of scum. They've got a goddamn furnace lit in that building. Radio the others, Pete. We need to move, and fast."

With Jackson's foot hard on the gas, the truck shot away from the property. Turning the corner, they hammered partway down the uneven stretch of the track, everyone bouncing around in their seats. He spun the vehicle off road, ploughing it between two groups of saplings.

Andy slid from the vehicle, unsure what to do, waiting as the chief and Pete equipped themselves with weapons.

"Let's go, Pete," Jackson said. "Andy, stay in the truck or head back to the gas station but stay the hell out of our way. I don't need any dead weight on this, you hear me?"

Andy nodded as Jackson's face fixed into a hard, determined expression. Jackson broke into a lope as he headed up the track, shoulder to shoulder with Killenny.

"Let's get our boy back," Jackson said.

~ * ~

Jim was right. Moments after Megan hit the couch, squeezing the cable tie back around her wrist as best she could, the door to the room flung open. Gray fumbled to secure the door, brandishing his gun at them. He waved it at Jim.

"Get the fuck away from the window right now. Sit down with the others. Nobody makes a goddamn sound."

He took a long metal tube from his pocket and began to twist it onto the end of his gun. Was that a silencer? It had to be. His actions reminded her of scenes from secret-agent dramas on TV. Spy films. Or something from a gangster movie. Except that it wasn't. This was real. This was happening right in front of her. This was happening *to* her. She looked wildly at Jim, her heart rate spiraling. Was this it? Was he going to shoot them all, right here, right now?

Sitting awkwardly beside her, pretending his arms were still tied, Jim pressed his face right up against her ear and whispered, "Be ready."

Gray finished twisting. He held the gun out in front of himself and glanced at the four of them, his breathing quick and shallow. "Nobody fucking move," he said.

Nobody did. Megan wanted to keep her focus on anything other than the gun, its barrel shaking up and down as Gray twitched and shifted. Try as she might, she couldn't drag her gaze onto anything else.

A minute or so later, a muffled voice called from outside the door. "Gray, they've gone. Keep them quiet. We're going to make sure there's no one else lurking around out there."

"For fuck's sake hurry up. We need to get on with this thing and get the hell out of here."

"Grow a pair, Gray. Just keep them quiet."

Gray eyed them all, one by one. A bead of sweat formed on one side of his temple. It stayed there for a while, then it trickled down the side of his face. He wiped it away with his sleeve, huffed, and shook his head. He advanced toward them, a rapid movement bringing him right in front of them. The burnished metal gun barrel was now so close to her that Megan could see every detail of it. Every ounce of her screamed to look away, to close her eyes, but she couldn't.

Gray turned the gun, twisting the silencer barrel again, as if to make sure it was properly attached. He clicked something and the clip holding the bullets slid out into his palm. His gaze dropped. In that moment, Jim propelled himself off the couch, moving with sudden speed and power toward the man.

He hit Gray full on, knocking him backward and sending him off balance. Jim let out a stifled yelp, whether from the effort or from pain she couldn't tell, but he kept pushing until the man lost his balance completely, falling back against the stone hearth. Gray hit his head on something on the way down, losing his grip on the gun and the clip of bullets. He wasn't unconscious, he was still moving, but he was clearly stunned.

Jim landed on top of him, then scrabbled to one side, grabbing the gun. He hit Gray on the side of the head, hard, with the butt of the gun. Gray stopped moving.

Megan flung her cable tie away and darted forward, shoving at the unconscious man's shoulder until she located the clip. She handed it to Jim.

"Window," he said, through gritted teeth.

The pain was clear to see on his face, but he kept moving, picking up a wooden stool en route. He hurled it through the window to the rear of the property, grunting with the effort, and shards of glass exploded in all directions. The noise was intense, and it shook the other two into action. Megan snatched the musty crochet throw from the back of the couch on her way to the window.

Once the worst of the glass shards had been knocked from the window's edges with the gun, she folded up the throw and shoved it over the lower edge of the window frame. Jolie went through first, followed by Chris. Jim pushed at Megan.

"Go," he hissed, and she climbed through the space, her thin-soled shoes crunching on the broken glass outside.

Her arm caught on a shard still in the frame. There was blood. Was it her blood? She turned to help Jim through.

As he climbed, he said in sharp tone, "Run. Different directions, into the trees. Keep low, don't run straight, zigzag about. Find somewhere to hide. The cops are on their way. Run and hide. Go."

Chris and Jolie took off like startled rabbits. Megan was slower to react. He shoved at her arm. "Go. Hide. I'll find you."

Chapter Thirty-Eight

Megan ran, zigzagging her way across the open ground, sprinting for the line of trees. Chris was up ahead, pelting headlong into the cover of the wood. There was shouting, but by then she had lost sight of the others, lost sight of Jim.

She sprinted on into the trees, the soft green leaves of the young saplings slapping against her face as she moved. Holding up one arm then the other to shield herself, she kept going, doing her best to dodge from side-to-side as Jim had told her. All the while she searched for somewhere to hide. Something whistled past her smacking through the leaves to her left. She kept moving, forcing her legs to pump faster and faster.

Trying to ignore the shouting and sounds of gunshots, then the ghoulish noise when someone screamed in pain, she kept running. Who screamed? Please, God, not Jim. Or Jolie. Or Chris. Tears streamed down her face, clouding her vision. She wiped her arm across her face, which only made it worse. A momentary confusion. Why couldn't she see where she was going? She wiped again, this time using the other arm, and it came away streaked with red. Blood. She'd covered her eyes in her own blood. She dashed away the blood then pushed on through the trees.

How far should she go? Maybe she should keep going until she found another property, or a road, or something. The ground grew soft under her feet. The trees were mature, taller and with broader trunks. Stopping behind one of them for a second, she tried to catch her breath. Could she hear something else? Was there movement?

Sucking in a breath and holding it, she crouched down. What had she heard? Was it something other than the beating of her own heart? Listening again, she couldn't be sure. Maybe it had been a twig snapping. Was someone chasing her down?

Her breathing came again, more like a sob now. She peered

around the trunk of the tree. Everything was green or brown, the leaves rippling in the air. It was impossible to be sure she was alone, she couldn't even tell where the farmhouse was any longer. Starting to run again, her legs were uncooperative and wooden. She couldn't go much further.

Without warning, the ground began to drop away, a stream or a watercourse of some kind glittering at the bottom of a steep incline. Leaves underfoot and loose stones had her slipping down the first part of the slope, then she lost her footing completely and slid the rest of the way.

At the bottom, what remained of a huge fallen tree lay at right-angles to her descent. Unable to control her speed or avoid it, the impact knocked what was left of the air from her lungs with a jolt. Her knees buckled and she hit the ground, her senses filling with the smell of leaf mold and the damp odor of moss. Could she hide behind the trunk? Would it be enough to conceal her if those men came looking?

Grabbing at the trunk to try and pull herself up, she came away with handfuls of loose, rotten bark. Insects scuttled and fell from where she disturbed them.

Moving on hands and knees through the sodden undergrowth, she scrabbled around the end of the trunk, the center of which had long since rotted out. Inside. Get inside.

Balled up against the decaying interior of the tree, she buried her face against her knees and hugged her arms to herself, the fingers of one hand wrapped around a stick she'd found as she shuffled across the ground. A makeshift weapon, of sorts. She altered her grip, tightening it.

She would come out swinging, even if there was no point. It was dark in there, but she squeezed her eyes closed anyway, tried to shut out the thought of those men finding her, of what might be happening if they found the others. Of what they would do to him if they found Jim. The thought was too terrible, a sob escaping before she could suppress it. *Quiet.* She needed to be quiet.

Powerless and terrified, Megan could do nothing except stay hidden for as long as she could, and pray it was Jim who found her.

~ * ~

Andy followed Chief Jackson and Pete Killenny back up the track toward the farmhouse. He knew he shouldn't, and he didn't want to get in the way. But he couldn't walk away, not now.

For a fleeting moment, he saw a glimpse of what his life might have been like if he had graduated from the academy. If he hadn't crashed out in disgrace. He meant that literally, as well as figuratively. A whisky chaser-fueled evening playing pool with friends six months before graduation had ended with him wrapping his car around a streetlight. He'd been too dazed—or hammered—to run away before the real cops showed up and booked him. He remembered what shame tasted like. It was sharp and metallic, blood mixed with bourbon.

In an alternative version of life, it might have been him standing beside Chief Jackson, instead of someone like Killenny. It could have been him eying a disheveled PI who was behaving like a wannabe action man, him indulging the fantasies of an inept civilian while weighing the options for taking action that would mean something, maybe even save lives. That's what Andy had thrown away.

As he did his best to keep parallel with the cops, a part of him hoped it might be possible that his taking action—rather than watching other people doing it—could perhaps be a part of his life after all.

Staying far enough back to remain hidden from their view, he watched from the edge of the track as the officers made their way resolutely toward the farmhouse and outbuildings. They signaled to one another; no one said a word as they worked their way around until everyone was in position. Then Jackson broke cover and sprinted up the porch steps, Killenny in close formation behind him. Killenny took the front door, kicking it open, standing back as Jackson went in.

"Police. LAPD. Hands where we can see them."

Andy heard the phrase repeated as officers entered the outbuildings. He crept closer. There was shouting. Someone yelled, "We've got one," from inside the farmhouse. Andy made his way across the roughly graveled driveway, only to dive behind the black minivan as rapid gunfire echoed from the rear of the property.

Someone was screaming. It lasted for a while, then it stopped. Andy wasn't sure what was worse: the screaming or the silence that followed. He could no longer see what was going on. The action seemed to have moved inside the buildings. Peering inside, Andy checked the interior of the minivan. There were a couple of small suitcases in the back, a shoulder bag and some phones scattered over the passenger area. On the driver's side, the keys still hung from the ignition.

Andy opened the door, pulling out the keys and pocketing them. He pushed the door, confused when the click of the closing door seemed to come from behind him. He turned and came face-to-face with the barrel of a revolver.

"Give me those keys," a gravelly voice said from behind the gun. "Now."

Refocusing on the guy holding the weapon, Andy inched away, pulling the keys from his pocket as he did so. "These ones?" He jangled the keys, edging further away, his gaze fixed on the man. The same man who had come to the door minutes ago. The man who thought it okay to snatch two women from the side of the street, in broad daylight. Anger welled inside him, years of frustration crystallizing in a single moment.

"No, I don't think so," Andy said, twisting and throwing the keys as hard as he could into a low set of bushes.

As he broke into a run away from both the keys and the gun, the realization dawned that his sudden burst of heroism might have been hugely shortsighted. The thought gained traction as he faltered, the rows of saplings he was headed for too far away. Even Usain Bolt couldn't make that distance in time, and Andy's fitness levels fell woefully short of that of a world-class sprinter.

What the hell had he been thinking? He should have dove behind the vehicle instead. Jesus wept, he didn't want to die, not like this. He hadn't even phoned his wife yet.

How much did being shot hurt? How long did it take to die? The revolver was sizeable. Big bullets. Would that make it quicker? His feet pounded gravel, every step taking him closer to cover. Not daring to look back, a different thought surfaced. Rather than being a target, perhaps the gun had already been holstered and he had been forgotten whilst that guy searched for the keys instead. His heart leapt in his chest. That had to be it because he wasn't dead yet. Thank God. He was going to make it.

Andy hardly noticed the noise, like the popping of a cork, because at the same time something impacted right between his shoulder blades, taking him clean off his feet. Ending up face down in the dirt, the sting of gravel was nothing compared to the other pain. It was all he could do to drag in a breath, with what might as well be a rhino sitting on his back.

There were footsteps, coming closer. Jesus wept, was he going to get another bullet, this time in the head? Andy sucked in what oxygen he could, doing his best to play dead. Not too big of an ask, with the way his spine screamed. Another thought surfaced, through the pain, that the vest must have taken the worst of the impact. He could still feel his fingers and toes.

Should he play dead, hope the guy really had lost interest in him this time? There was no way he would get very far if he tried to stand; he knew that much. His vision was limited to the patch of ground to his left, couldn't see what was happening behind him, but he didn't dare move his head. The heavy footsteps continued to crunch closer.

Without warning, everything went quiet. The footsteps stopped. Unable to tell how close the kidnapper was, Andy closed his eyes and held his breath. Was this it? Maybe his number was up for real this time.

Playing the hero had never really had the chance of being in his repertoire, and now it looked like it never would. Instead of a bullet, Andy heard another voice.

"LAPD. Stay right where you are. Drop your weapon and keep your hands where I can see them. Do it right now."

Andy twisted his head to see who was speaking. The guy with the gun swiveled too. "Fuck. It *was* you."

Staying on the ground, he inched his way around to get a better view. The relief at no longer being anybody's primary focus flooded his system, giving him enough impetus to get himself up onto an elbow. From that position he could see that the cop holding a gun on his assailant was Jim Carello. A very bruised and battered Jim Carello, but him, nonetheless. Jim continued to hold his gun steady, taking a step or two forward.

"Drop the gun, Benny. There's no way out of this. There are officers everywhere, and we've got the other two. Give it up while you still have the choice."

Benny's eyes narrowed. The level of determination on Jim's face was clear for anyone to see, like ice and fire in equal measure.

"If your finger so much as twitches on that trigger, I *will* shoot you—you know that, right?" Jim said.

Eventually, Benny let out a long breath, releasing his grip on his gun, the barrel spinning toward the ground. He held the other hand up at the same time and the gun slipped onto the ground.

"Now kick it this way. Gently." Jim kept his gaze fixed on Benny, taking a few more steps toward him until he could back swipe the weapon behind himself, well out of reach.

Once the gun was out of play, Jim glanced at Andy for the first time. "Are you shot?" he said.

"Yes. I mean, no, he shot me but I'm wearing a vest. I'm with Chief Jackson."

"Are you with the department?"

"No, I'm a PI..."

"Can you stand?"

"Yup." Andy heaved himself from the ground, wincing as he straightened. "Jesus, that hurts."

"Get behind me," Jim said. He looked as though he might keel over at any second. In Andy's opinion, the guy should be propped up in a hospital bed, not holding a gun on his own abductor.

"Know how to use a gun?" Jim asked.

"It's been a while, but yeah," Andy said.

"Good. Pick that one up and keep it pointed at this lump of shit.

If he moves, you have my permission to shoot him."

Benny started to laugh, his focus snaking from Jim to Andy and back again. "You have no idea what you've done, do you? Mr. Valentine isn't likely to forget this in a hurry. He'll make sure you pay for this." He faked a step forward and Jim held his gun up higher.

"You think? Anthony Valentine's going to jail, just like you, you piece of trash. Not an inch closer, Benny. If you come any nearer, I'm going to shoot you. In fact, on second thought, please do come closer. Please give me an excuse to get rid of a world-class piece of scum." Jim tightened his finger on the trigger. Andy glanced at him, not convinced he mightn't pull the trigger anyway.

"Jim, are you okay?" Jackson rounded the corner, flanked by a couple of officers.

Relief flooded through Andy. He handed his gun to one of the officers, while Chief Jackson set about cuffing Benny's hands. He wasn't particularly careful about it.

Benny winced as Jackson racked his arms up behind him. "We've got the other two, the one with silver eyes was in the house, the other was out back. Someone already popped him."

"I know. I had no choice," Jim said. All of a sudden, he sounded exhausted. He stumbled to one side, and Andy put an arm under his for support. "Where's Megan?"

"We haven't found the other hostages, yet. The boys are searching for them now," Jackson said.

"What do you mean, you haven't found them yet? Oh, Jesus Christ. Megan..." Jim placed a hand on his ribs as he pushed off from Andy's arm, shoving the gun he was carrying into the waistband of his trousers. He disappeared around the side of the farmhouse, moving as fast as his injuries would allow.

Chapter Thirty-Nine

They had already found Chris. As Jim rounded the back of the farmhouse, he was being led toward the wraparound porch by one of the officers. Disheveled and shocked, his face was streaked with dirt. The officer held him firmly by the shoulders, talking to him in quiet, reassuring tones.

"Are you okay?" Jim called as he made his way past him. "Which way did Megan go?"

Chris shrugged. "I didn't see her. I'm sorry."

Jim headed for the trees. He wanted to be able to run faster, but it was so hard to breathe. Every step sent knives through his body. He desperately needed to stop, to lie down and rest, but he couldn't stop until he found Megan.

Sirens echoing in the trees heralded the arrival of the uniforms and paramedics. He could let them search for her. Get some medical attention for the pain in his chest which intensified with every step. He didn't stop. Jim pushed on around the back of the property. He passed the driver's body, an officer's jacket thrown over its upper half to hide the face.

Jim's shot hadn't been a clean one. It had been enough to take the driver down, but he'd made a lot of noise before the end. He'd clawed at the ground as he writhed around. Each mark in the loose soil was like an arrow pointing toward his body, screaming "you killed me" loud and clear. His hands and shoes were covered in dirt. Jim closed his eyes for a second.

He'd had no choice. The driver was firing wildly into the woods, trying to hit Jolie, Megan, or Chris as they ran away. Jim ordered him to stop shooting, but instead the driver squeezed off at least three rounds in Jim's direction. He repeated his order to stop, and again was ignored, so he'd had no choice but to take the shot. He did his best to make it clean but hadn't succeeded. Enough to take the man down, it had stopped him from loosing off any more bullets. Even so, the sight of a dead body never got any easier. At least he couldn't see the face.

Jim took as deep a breath as his damaged ribs would allow. He had no idea which direction to try, so he just kept moving toward the trees, calling her name and scanning as much of the area as he could for suitable hiding places. On either side were other officers approaching the search in a far more organized and thorough way, one of them liaising on a radio.

"Jim, are you okay?" Someone shouted at him. He held a hand up in acknowledgement, pressing his other arm more tightly around his chest. He did his best to ignore the burning pain, gritting his teeth and scanning the area again.

On the edge of the tree line further to the right he could see Killenny checking the thicker brush at the edge of the woods. Abruptly he stopped, then crouched. Seconds later he stood again. "I've got someone," he shouted. "I need paramedics. *Now.*"

A cry went up for the paramedic team. Jim couldn't see who it was, the undergrowth too thick and Killenny was kneeling between him and the prone figure. Jim veered toward them.

"Who...?" He didn't get the rest of the words out.

He didn't think he could bear to hear the answer. It took interminable seconds before he was close enough to see the blonde hair. It was Jolie. Her eyes were wide, her mouth trying to form words. She saw Jim and lifted her head. Jim couldn't hear what she was saying, so he drew in closer. But there weren't any words. Instead, spots of bloodied spittle specked her face, her eyes glazing over and then closing. One of the bullets from the driver's gun had found its mark.

"Entry wound at the back," Killenny said quietly. He lifted one of his hands, coated in Jolie's blood. Then, more loudly, he began to talk to her, telling her it was going to be all right, the paramedics were on their way so she just needed to hang in there.

"Stay with us, Jolie. Pete, I've got to find Megan," Jim said, his throat tight with the effort of keeping his voice calm.

"Jim, wait, you're in no state—"

Not waiting for his partner to finish his sentence, Jim wrapped his arm around his ribs again and focused on the sea of tree trunks. The leaves and the mottled, dappled light playing through from above made it look like everything was moving. How would he ever find her in this? What if she was shot too? Lying somewhere all alone, bleeding out. What if he didn't find her in time? He ran again.

Had he made the right decision? Back in the farmhouse, when Gray started to look nervous and double-checked the silencer, he'd primed himself. This could be their only chance. When Gray slipped the clip out of the revolver, Jim had realized in that split-second that he wouldn't get a better opportunity. If he'd waited for Jackson and the rest to storm the place, Gray would probably have shot them where they sat before anyone could get to them. So he'd gone for it. His ribs gave way as he pushed Gray, but by then his adrenalin was pumping so hard he kept going.

Once they were outside, he remained hidden against the back of the building, trying to get his breath, trying not to throw up from the pain. Megan and the other two ran across the grass toward the trees. There was no way he could run with them, no way he could move quickly enough. So he stayed, waiting for Benny and the driver to act when they heard the smashing of the window.

But now he had to find Megan. He needed to find her, and he needed her to be okay. If there was any possibility his decision and his instruction had caused her injury... Stop thinking, he told himself. *Just find her.*

He was moving so slowly now. Every step forced through quicksand. Every shout of her name ending in a spasm of coughing. Eventually, the ground began to slope away. There was a stream or something at the bottom, and a large fallen tree at right-angles to the slope. Jim struggled to stay on his feet as he slipped his way down the bank, still calling her name as best he could.

At the bottom of the slope, he called again, his gaze raking the area for signs of movement. And then he saw her. She peered tentatively from the end of the trunk, her fingers wrapping around the rotting wood. She crawled out, dropping the piece of wood she was holding and pushing hair from her eyes as she looked at him.

He slid the rest of the way down the bank, standing awkwardly then limping toward her, his gaze darting across her as he checked for injury.

"Are you okay?" he whispered. He tried to make his voice louder. "Are you okay?" he repeated.

She took a couple of steps toward him, inching her way across the leaf-littered ground. Her feet were bare, covered in dirt. She moved slowly at first, hesitantly. Then her pace quickened, her face a mask, the only emotion showing in her eyes.

It took him forever to take each step. He couldn't seem to get enough air into his lungs. She reached him, stopping short as she noticed his arm clutched across his chest.

"Are you all right?" she said.

"I'm fine," he replied, the words nothing more than a croak. He would have grinned if he had the strength. He held her at arm's length. There was blood all over her face and her arm, and on her shirt. Was she shot too?

"Are you shot?"

"No." She looked confused, then glanced down at herself. "No, it's a cut, that's all. I'm okay, Jim." She put her arms around his neck, and he hugged her as tightly as he could. She was alive and that was all that mattered. "Are you really okay?" she said. "What happened? Are the others all right?"

He tried to speak, but his voice whispered away, like the rustling of the leaves which surrounded them. "You're safe." His legs turned to jelly as he spoke. He couldn't stop himself from lurching to one side and sliding down onto one knee. "You're safe."

Her face clouded, and she tried to grab at him, tried to hold him up. But he couldn't keep himself upright any longer. As he slumped to the ground the damp seeped through his shirt, the leaf litter soft beneath him. The dappled sunlight played on his face and it was comforting, familiar and warm. When she fell to her knees beside him and took hold of his hand, that was good too.

The exhaustion was overwhelming, he needed to lie here for a few moments, just until he got his breath back. She was safe, that was all that mattered. He closed his eyes. It was comfortable on the leafy ground, much more comfortable than it looked. A memory surfaced of a feather bed, a floaty, soft, feather bed. Maybe he was floating, he wasn't sure anymore. Wasn't sure if he could hear her voice, or whether it was the call of a bird, soaring high above them…

"Jim. Jim? Jim, wake up. Jim, what's wrong? Oh my god, oh my god, no."

He was floating now, no question. Megan's voice—he was sure it was her voice even though it was so far away—sounded full of concern. There was nothing to worry about any longer. No matter how hard he tried to tell her it was okay, the words were like quicksilver, slipping from his mind before he could say them. It was of no consequence; nothing mattered so long as she was all right.

He let out a slow breath and gave in to ultimate softness. Then her voice floated one way as he floated the other, and everything spiraled into a quiet darkness.

Chapter Forty
Wednesday Morning

Megan bit at the edge of her fingernail as she stood in the hospital lobby. Her other hand rested on the bandage covering the stitches they put into her arm in the emergency room the day before.

With everything that happened in the woods, she'd forgotten about the cut until one of the paramedics took hold of her by the wrist, examining her wound. However hard she insisted that it was nothing, that she could care less about a stupid cut, the paramedic wouldn't leave it be. Back at the ambulance, he cleaned and dressed it. He made it clear she needed to get to the hospital all the same to get a tetanus shot and have it treated properly. He didn't seem to understand she didn't care anymore about herself. That it didn't matter. Nothing much mattered without Jim.

She couldn't find a way to vocalize what it had done to her, watching the other paramedics working on him as he lay at the bottom of that leaf-strewn slope. Seeing his fellow police officers standing around with a universal look on their faces, their collective pain clear in their expressions, was one of the worst experiences of her life.

Far worse than the abduction. Far worse than anything she'd gone through with William. Her utter inability to help Jim left her drained. She was empty. A husk of a person with everything seeping away from her into the cold, dank leaf litter beneath her feet, as she watched them fighting to stop Jim seeping away from them all.

That was yesterday. Today, she was back at the hospital. She took her fingers away from her lips, running them through her hair as she moved her weight from one leg to the other, her attention fixed on the information board.

A nurse walked past her, then paused. "Can I help you? Are you lost?"

"I hope not," Megan said. "I'm about to find out, I think."

The nurse looked confused, then smiled. "Well, be sure to ask someone if you need directions." She carried on her way with a nod. Megan took a big breath, then headed for the elevators.

A few seconds in the elevator, and a lot longer spent walking along seemingly never-ending corridors, brought Megan to the place she needed to be. She knocked on the door.

"Come in." The voice was weak, but it was his. She pushed her way in.

Jim lay on the bed, the upper portion set at a steep angle so he was all but sitting upright. His eyes were closed, one lid swollen a deep purple. A dressing covered the forehead above the other eye, strips of tape held the skin below his lower lip together, welts of bruising were already forming all over his upper body. A tube protruded from one side of his chest, taped securely into place. He was breathing calmly, but each breath was quick and shallow.

He opened his eyes as the door sucked back into place. Confusion filled his face; he was struggling to focus. "Megan?"

To hear his voice, weaker than it should be but still deep and resonant, had more of an effect on her than she could have imagined.

"Yes, it's me. How are you feeling?" She dumped her bag by the bed and took hold of his hand.

His fingers squeezed hers ferociously. She wrapped her other hand over the top, soaking up the warmth. The day before, standing in the woods, Megan hadn't been sure she'd ever feel warm again.

He gave her a lopsided smile, then touched his split lip with his free hand, his eyebrows furrowing again. "I've been worse."

Megan smiled. She didn't believe him. He was a mess.

"I've never minded a bit of pain; it reminds me I'm still alive." He tried to laugh, but he couldn't, not properly. He huffed a bit, then looked at her and shook his head, his brow furrowing again.

"Have they given you enough pain medication? Do you want me to tell them you're uncomfortable?"

"No. I'm good. They've given me enough to send a horse into orbit. It's not that." He closed his eyes for a few moments, then said, "I imagine you've come to say goodbye."

"What? Why?" Her nerves kicked in.

"It was all my fault, the whole thing. I can't think why you'd want to do anything but get the hell away from me." He stared at the ceiling. "I'll never forgive myself for what happened. And I'm so sorry about Jolie." He pulled his hand away from hers, resting it on top of the bedsheet instead.

Megan's eyes filled with tears again. She'd lost count of how many times she'd cried since they broke the news the previous afternoon that Jolie had suffered a catastrophic gunshot wound and never made it through the surgery.

"I didn't get to tell her I forgave her. Even though she didn't need my forgiveness, I know she wanted me to say it." She brushed the tears away. "I wish I had. She was such an amazing person."

A thousand images of Jolie ran through her mind's eye. There was so much about her friend that was good and positive and wonderful. No way was she going to allow her to be remembered forever for one silly mistake.

"I knew something was worrying her, but I was so wrapped up in my own problems, I never pushed her to find out. Maybe things would have turned out differently if I had."

He tilted his head to look at her. "None of this is remotely your fault. It sits squarely at my door, Megan, and you know it."

She took hold of his hand again. "No. It doesn't. They didn't know the cop was you, did they? So you didn't give yourself away." She allowed a tiny smile to creep onto her face. "Well, only to me."

"Don't let me off the hook that easily," he said. "You don't know all of it. I told you and Chief Jackson I was going to quit the job at The Valentine Retreat and get out. It didn't work out that way."

The smile faded from her lips. "What do you mean?"

"I intended to quit the hotel and leave. Then I saw Valentine writing information into a notebook. I thought if I could get my hands on it, I could get myself back on track with Jackson. I wanted to do it all: keep you safe, get the proof, and get out." He paused, his face a hotbed of shifting emotions. "It all went wrong. I nearly cost you your life. And Jolie…" He shook his head. "That's on me. That's what you need to understand."

Should she blame him? Did she want to? Would it take away some of her own guilt? After all, if it hadn't been for Megan's screwed-up relationship with William, Jolie wouldn't have got herself into this mess in the first place. They would never even have gone to The Valentine Retreat. None of this would ever have happened.

Before she could say any of that, Jim began to wheeze—gently to begin with and then more loudly and uncontrollably, a look of panic fleeting across his face as he reached for the oxygen mask. Holding it over his nose and mouth, his breathing settled, although his expression didn't. Finally, desolation replaced the panic, the skin that wasn't battered and bruised taking on an unnaturally pale hue.

If she'd never gone to The Valentine Retreat, she would never have met Jim, either. For a moment, Megan imagined herself inhabiting a parallel universe, one where she still lived under William's control, but Jolie was alive and well. As for Jim? She tried to picture him with someone else, anyone else. She couldn't. Her thoughts skimmed around the edges of a life having never met him, never knowing him. It was too difficult to think about. She shook her head, shaking away more tears which threatened to form.

Trying to focus instead on what Jim said about how his actions had caused the abduction, she said, "There's something I don't understand." She hadn't slept a great deal the night before, perhaps unsurprisingly. She wasn't sure she'd ever sleep very soundly again, and whilst she lay in the dark, pieces of the day had floated back in a mismatched way. "He said they got a phone call to tell them about an undercover police officer. Do you remember?"

Jim nodded, pulling the mask away from his face. "I remember thinking that made no sense. Wondering who would be in a position to tip Valentine off and why."

"That's what I mean. If they were tipped off, it can't have been your fault, can it?"

He hooked the mask back onto its stand, staring at the ceiling again. "I appreciate what you're doing, Megan, really I do. But at the end of the day, I lost Jolie. I almost lost you." He paused. "The ins and outs of it will come into the light in time, I'm sure, but it won't take away from how badly I feel about it. Nothing will."

She touched the side of his face, tracing a finger over the place where his shaving wound was obscured by bruising. He looked at her again. She preferred it when he was looking at her, she decided.

A knock on the door heralded the arrival of a nurse. Megan retracted her hand.

"How are you doing, Jim, are you comfortable?" The nurse smiled a brief greeting before switching her full attention to her patient. She ran a professional eye over him, checked his notes, took some readings.

"I'm doing well, thanks."

"Good." After checking the fob watch pinned to her chest and noting a couple of things on his chart, she slotted the file back at the end of the bed and tilted her head toward Jim. "You've got a strong one here." She breezed out of the room, the door closing behind her.

Aware of Jim's attention on her, his gaze unwavering, she stayed still. A thought overwhelmed her. *Have I? Have I got him?*

Another knock was accompanied by a big brick of a man in the doorway holding a brown paper bag.

"Ah, here he is. Brought you some grapes, Jim. Do you even like them? It occurred to me on my way up here I wasn't sure, but I know how much the nurses frown on bourbon for the inmates." He raised his eyebrows as he set the paper bag on the end of the bed. "I think I'll bring a bottle next time, though. Looks like you need it. How's the form, Jim, how're you doing?"

"Thanks, Pete. I'm okay."

"Really? You look like shite." He grinned.

Jim gave him a weak smile in return. "Megan, this is my partner, Pete Killenny. Complete with all his blarney charm. At least, that's what he calls it."

The guy wasn't any taller than she was, but his handshake was like iron. She recognized him from outside the farmhouse the previous day.

"Good to meet you properly, Megan, to be sure. I've heard a lot about you, in a round-about way. Mostly from the chief, actually… Listen, sorry to talk shop, but I need a quick word with the man here, if you don't mind? Got to keep him in the loop."

"Of course, no problem. I'll go and grab a drink. Can I get anyone else something?" Both men shook their heads. "I'll be back shortly."

"Good," Jim said.

Pete slotted himself into a chair, pulling the bag of grapes within reach. He tugged a couple from their stalks.

"I love grapes," he said, popping them into his mouth. "Haven't had any for ages. You want one?"

"No. What's going on?" Jim said, his attention totally fixed on Pete.

As Megan left the room, she heard Pete say, "We got him."

Desperate to know what was going on, she wanted to stand outside the door and listen in. Presumably he was talking about Mr. Valentine. But there was a stream of people heading up and down the corridor. She couldn't stand outside the room, eavesdropping. Instead she went and got coffee from the machine at the end of the corridor. It was foul. Industrially bitter, and almost impossible to hold in a thin disposable cup.

Doing her best to sip the liquid even though it was disgusting and too hot, she wondered how long to wait before going back to Jim's room. And once she was back there, how should she approach things? How should she handle the guilt Jim felt? Could she layer it onto her own grief at losing Jolie? She had no real idea how to cope with everything she would have to deal with in the fall-out from Onesta's manipulation of Jolie. Or of how she could best try to move forward with

Jim in her life. Because she wanted him in her life, she knew that much. That was bright and clear, even if everything else was muddy and spoiled.

The drink scorched the roof of her mouth, and it was burning her fingers through the thin cardboard. She dumped it into the bin, taking a drink from the water fountain instead. Heading back along the corridor, she noticed a man checking room numbers against a scrap of paper. He sported a scruffy beard; in fact, his whole appearance was straight out of a tumble dryer. He looked up as she approached, did a double-take and seemed momentarily flustered by her presence.

"Megan… I mean Mrs. Wise—Miss Leadbetter?" he said.

It was Megan's turn to be confused. "Yes?"

"I was looking for Jim Carello's room, but it's you I really wanted to talk to. I thought you might be here." He cleared his throat, as if embarrassed by his presumption.

"I'm sorry, do I know you?"

"Listen, I'm just going to come right out and say it; I'm not going to try to sugarcoat it. I'm the PI hired to tail you at The Valentine Retreat. The name's Andy Mossbury."

This was the man who had followed her around, making notes on her life. This was the man prepared to come into her bedroom and take photographs of her with Jim. He stuck out a hand, then realized the piece of paper was still lodged between his thumb and fingers, so shuffled it into a pocket and tried again. Megan was so taken aback, she shook it.

"I was sorry to hear about your friend. I'm so sorry for your loss."

The tears threatened her again. To stop them, she snatched her hand away from him and allowed anger to take a leading role. "I don't understand why you think I would want to talk to you."

"I wouldn't normally intrude, especially like this. I totally get that you probably don't want to have anything to do with me." He shrugged. "I wouldn't want anything to do with me, to be honest, if the shoe was on the other foot."

She crossed her arms. The last thing she wanted was to talk to this man, what she wanted was to get back to Jim. At some point she would have to face everything this man embodied about her past, that was inescapable. Just not right now.

But it appeared no one had given Andy Mossbury that memo. He stood his ground and said, "I don't want to be indelicate, but I wonder if you've taken any calls from Mr. Wiseman in the last twelve hours?"

Chapter Forty-One

Megan hadn't taken any calls from anyone in the last twelve hours. She'd switched her phone to mute once she heard the news about Jolie. She pulled it from a pocket. Ten missed calls from William. Two voicemails. That was a record.

"It appears I've missed a few calls. Why?" she said.

"You have to understand that in my line of work the things I'm asked to do don't always sit happily, and this whole deal at The Valentine Retreat was one of them. I know what you went through prior to your divorce, and when Don Onesta called me in on this I... well, I was offered a lot of money to do it, much more than my normal rates, and..." He cleared his throat again.

"You've followed me before?"

He shifted from one foot to the other. "Yes. Prior to your divorce. Mr. Wiseman wanted—"

"You don't need to elaborate. I can imagine what he wanted."

"Anyway, I'm here because after what happened yesterday, I decided to phone Mr. Wiseman personally. Normally everything is done through Onesta's office, you see. But I needed to talk to the organ grinder, not the monkey, for once."

Megan couldn't help the corners of her mouth twitching at his description. "Why?"

"Because it was important he knew exactly what happened. I didn't want the facts manipulated and dipped in honey by Onesta. Thing is, I told Onesta in confidence that I recognized Jim. I needed to clarify my position, in light of Jim being a cop and all." He sighed, his eyebrows meeting above the bridge of his nose. He ran a hand across his rough beard. "Well, when things went base over apex, I had to do something. I figured Mr. Wiseman should be in possession of all the facts, not just Onesta's version. His secretary overheard a phone call he made to the hotel, you see. They owe you big time for what they've put you through.

I told Wiseman as much." He ran a hand down his shirt, doing his best to flatten the creases. "Nearly messed myself during the phone call, don't mind telling you, but I think I got the message across."

Megan stared at the man. "Are you telling me that Don Onesta's responsible for what happened to us? He's the reason Jim is in here, and Jolie is…" She couldn't complete the sentence.

He patted at her arm, his sudden proximity a surprise. "The police know too. Of course," he continued to speak as if he were attempting to jolly things along. "I told them everything. They'll sort it out, I have no doubt. Don't envy them the paperwork attached to this mess, though."

She raised her eyebrows but stayed quiet.

He cleared his throat. "Anyway, I'll let you get on. You have my deepest condolences about your friend, and…" He glanced at the phone she still held in her hand. "You've got some voicemails from Mr. Wiseman?"

"Yes."

"I suggest it might be to your advantage to listen to them."

Andy's focus shifted as he patted a pocket then pulled out his own mobile. "Got it on silent. Wondered what was buzzing." He glanced at it. "Message from the wife. We've been going through a bit of a rough patch, not spending enough time together, you know the sort of thing. So I phoned her yesterday after I phoned Mr. Wiseman—I was on a roll, I can tell you—invited her out on a date. Sounds a bit lame, but we're going to pretend we've just met, see where it goes. Try to put all the shit behind us, you know?" A surprisingly broad grin reached all the way to his eyes, which twinkled as he read a text. "Looks like we're going bowling."

"I hope you have a great time," she said. "If you don't mind?" She gestured toward Jim's door.

"Of course." He stepped to one side. "I hope it all works out for you."

"You too," she said, brushing past him and pressing her phone to an ear as she dialed her voicemail.

By the time she'd listened to both of William's messages, the PI was long gone, and Megan was at the far end of the corridor, staring through a window. She hardly dared believe what she'd just heard. It sounded like William's voice, but it was difficult to compute the level of emotion with which he spoke or what he said. On autopilot, she dialed his number; she had to check he meant it. Almost immediately the call was answered.

"Megan, thank God. I've been calling and calling. I left

messages. Did you get them?"

"I've just picked them up."

"Honey, are you okay? Did they hurt you?"

"I'm fine."

"Thank God. I can't even imagine… I'm so sorry about Jolie. I know how much she meant to you."

"Yeah." It was difficult to speak, her throat tightening against the word.

"I'm in shock about the whole thing."

"You and me both." She studied the traffic passing on the street below the window.

"In all honesty, when the PI rang I almost hung up on him, thought he was drunk. I couldn't believe what he was saying to me. I trusted Don, left all the day-to-day menial stuff to him. I never in a million years thought him capable of something like this."

"But you believed the PI?"

"I may have left the minutiae to Don, but I know exactly who Andy Mossbury is. He's worked for me for years, on and off. Yes, I believed him, plus the secretary backed his version of events. I will make sure Don Onesta faces the full force of the law, without question."

"It was nothing to do with you?"

She had to ask, needed to make him understand how deeply her fear ran. The loaded silence was answer enough, she supposed, then he said, "If you only knew how that makes me feel, that you believe me capable of something so…so heinous. You might consider me to be all sorts of a bastard, but that?"

Momentarily transported back to that farmhouse, she pressed her fingers against trembling lips to gain control. Then she said, "They were going to shoot us all, Bill." She hadn't used that name in years, but he sounded more like the man she'd married than he had in years too. Regret was something she'd forgotten he was capable of.

"I can't even begin to imagine…" His voice cracked as his words faltered.

"Did you mean it?"

"What?"

"The things you promised in the messages."

His sigh was audible. "I always mean what I say. You of all people should know that."

"I suppose." He'd been penitent in the messages, almost unrecognizable in a display of weakness Megan didn't think she'd ever experienced from him in person. Never in her wildest dreams had she imagined him promising to destroy the agreement she had signed.

"The PI said it was about time I took it on the chin and let you get on with your life. He's wasted behind a long-lens camera, should have been a councilor or something. Are you absolutely sure we can't work it out?"

"One-hundred percent."

"It's just, I knew how much you loved that necklace from the moment I gave it to you. When you stopped wearing it, I should have realized things weren't right."

Things were already very wrong by then, but she didn't say anything.

He continued, "When it disappeared, I hoped it meant you weren't completely through with me. I always thought if I gave you some time… That you'd see sense and come home. They never meant anything to me, you know."

"Who?"

"The other women. I meant what I said about loving you. It's only ever been you."

Megan frowned. It was only ever about being in control, was what he should have said. And that wasn't love. "So why go with them? I don't understand."

"The first time was after a business dinner. We'd just signed a big investor, ended up in a club to celebrate. I was bombed, and she told me she wasn't wearing any—"

"I don't want the details, William, I want the why."

"The truth is it was so easy. A few drinks here, a dinner there, sometimes the promise of a gift, some stupid gold bracelet, or a pair of earrings. I guess some of them knew who I was. Maybe that made a difference. Maybe they were looking to replace you. Once I started, I couldn't seem to stop. I suppose it was a power trip, Megan. There. I said it. Bottom line? I never thought you'd find out. How dumb am I?"

"Thank you for telling me, I appreciate your honesty." She tipped her chin toward the daylight, closing her eyes as the sun beat its way through a rogue cloud and bathed her face. "How does the rest of it work?"

"I instructed my lawyers to shred the only copy of the document today, if that's what you mean."

"We're really done?"

"Yeah, we're really done." His voice was loaded with regret.

Feeling sorry for William wasn't an emotion Megan thought she would experience. "I know you hoped I would change my mind, but I was never going to. It's time for us both to start fresh. You know it, same as I do." There was one remaining hurdle. "Can I ask one thing of you, though?"

"Check your deposit account," he said. "It should be more than enough for your brother's lifetime."

As the tones sounded denoting William had ended the call, Megan slumped against the wall. Accessing her bank details had her knees buckling, there was enough money in her account for everything Craig could ever need, plus some. There were more zeros than she dared count. It might be small change as far as William was concerned, but it meant more to her than he would ever know. Or perhaps he did understand, deep down.

Either way there was nothing she could do to stop a loud sob escaping her lips, the tears which had been building cascading unchecked. Freedom, sadness, regret, and joy bubbled in equal measure as she took a moment to gain control then headed back to Jim's room, her shoulders more relaxed than they had been in a very long time.

Pete stood in the doorway, his focus on Jim. "Catch you later," he said. "At least I'll know where to find you for a couple of days, won't I?" He turned. "I'll leave you to it. Good to meet you Megan. Any time you want the skinny on that man in there, call me. I know all his secrets." He winked at her.

"Thanks. See you again," she said.

"No doubt. Look after him," he said. "God knows he needs plenty help with that."

"Grape?" Jim said, propping the bag onto the bedside cabinet as she took her place again on the chair. His brows furrowed as he shuffled to get comfortable, then he fixed her with an intense expression. "Pete had news on the tip-off, about how they knew there was a cop. He said I shouldn't tell you about it until they know all the facts." He raised his shoulders in a gentle shrug. "He knows I will, though."

She allowed him free rein with the information, making no mention of her meeting with the PI in the corridor outside, or about her conversation with William. All that could wait. The relief on Jim's face was palpable, and Megan wanted him to enjoy it. He smiled at her, the emotion behind it plain to see.

Afterward she sat quietly while he rested. She ached to tell him how his smile—even his lop-sided, injured smile—completely overwhelmed her, physically and emotionally. How much it made her desperate to block out the rest of the world, stick metaphorical fingers in her ears, close her eyes and ignore everything except the way he made her feel.

But now that it seemed she might truly be inching back to a normal life, ignoring that life and its everyday pressures would also be completely unrealistic. It would be perpetuating the engineered way in which they met. The attraction was intense, there was no doubt about that, but was it real? Or was it more of a reaction to circumstances? To the bottled-up environment in which they had found themselves at the hotel and the terror of the farmhouse.

Megan's thoughts meandered back to her conversation with the PI. It gave her an idea.

"I was wondering," she said. "We met under such weird circumstances. I think we should make sure we still feel the same about one another when life is back to normal."

He frowned. Was he thinking the same as her, was he too struggling to remember what normal was?

"Anyway, I was thinking. Can we start this thing again, right from the beginning? Pretend we're meeting for the first time, right now. Pretend I've come into this room by mistake or something? Then we can decide if it's what we both want, once we know what we're getting into. Is that something you would consider?"

He studied her face for a moment. The focus of his attention like the sunbathing her skin as it broke through cloud cover.

"Hi, I'm Jim," he said, holding out a hand for her to shake. "Are you from around here?" The look in his eyes made her cheeks warm.

"No, but I'm thinking of moving to the area."

"Sounds good. What's your name?"

"Megan."

"Pretty name," he said, a grin forming. "You've got amazing eyes, by the way."

"Thanks." The heat in her cheeks racked up a notch.

"What do you do?"

"I'm into art. Buying and selling, that sort of thing." She gave him a rueful smile.

He laughed, then wheezed, then looked sheepish. "I'm not sure I'm pulling this off totally authentically, sorry."

She trailed her fingers down the side of his face, allowing them to linger against his skin for a moment or two. "Nor am I." She wanted to lean forward and kiss him. This man was amazing. Tears prickled the edges of her vision, and she blinked them away. "Do you work in the area?" she said, removing her hand and forcing herself back into role.

"Yeah. I'm a detective with the LAPD. Listen, once I get out of here, how about I show you around the neighborhood? I know a great little diner that does the best pancakes…"

Epilogue
Some Months Later

"Did you find him yet?" Anthony spoke quickly, enunciating his words into the smuggled mobile phone.

He glanced around, irritated when the person he had risked a week in solitary to call responded with lukewarm enthusiasm. Anthony perched on some staging, flanked by a loyal group of fellow inmates. Each one of them faced a different direction, their demeanor outwardly relaxed but inwardly taut, like hyenas keeping watch for lions.

He had a sneaking suspicion Pierce was being purposefully inept in his search for Jim Carello. After all, how hard could it be to find a fucking cop? He might have moved on from his position in the LAPD, but he hadn't dropped from the face of the planet.

He pressed again. "Are you trying to tell me you still haven't located them?" Anthony was well aware that Pierce wouldn't appreciate his acidic tone, but he wasn't the one rotting in jail.

"I'll find him, it's not that. It's the rest of it which concerns me."

Pierce had been enjoying a sabbatical in Europe, seeing the sights, savoring the cuisine, separating troublesome bodies from their souls for anyone with enough cold hard cash to make it worth his while. Perhaps sabbatical was the wrong term; perhaps busman's holiday would be nearer the mark.

Either way, he'd been away when Anthony's kingdom crumbled around his ears. Maybe the entire fiasco with the cop would never have happened if Pierce had been in town, but there was nothing to be gained from regrets like that. Now he was back stateside, and despite his lackadaisical replies, there was no one else Anthony would trust with this job. Pierce would come through for him, would see things his way eventually. Anthony was sure of that. In the meantime, he needed to do his best to remain patient. Having his autonomy removed was easily the hardest thing about being locked up.

"When you do manage to locate them, you let me know where they are, in the normal way. Then I'll tell you what I've decided."

"Sure I will." Pierce had his own ideas about what dealing with Carello should entail, and it didn't entirely match up with Anthony's plan. It relied more heavily on accuracy with a long-range rifle, and that wasn't going to cut it as far as Anthony was concerned. He wouldn't take things into his own hands, though, Anthony trusted him on that.

"Fire on the line, boss," hissed one of the hyenas from somewhere behind Anthony.

"I've got to go."

"Stay strong. Nothing's forever," Pierce said. "I'm working on getting you out."

"Work faster," he said, screwing his eyes tightly closed for a second. "This place is a shit-hole."

Anthony ended the call, handing the phone to another hyena who vanished it inside his prison jumpsuit, sauntering away as he did so.

The rest of the protective circle evaporated as the approaching prison guard said, "What are you doing, Valentine?"

"Officer Monroe, please call me Anthony," he said. He held a hand up, checking his nails, then did the same with the other, making it clear he held nothing in either one. "We're all friends here, after all."

Officer Monroe snorted, shifting the belt on his uniform trousers. "Yeah, right. Whatever, Valentine. You boys need to get your butts inside now, anyway. Rec time is over."

"Whatever you say, Officer," Anthony said, tilting his face to get a last touch from the bright sunshine, glancing at the other prison officers in their towers, each with a hand on a rifle. If Jim Carello thought he was going to sit quietly, rotting in this hellhole for the next twenty years whilst he got on with his life? Well, he was very much mistaken. He narrowed his eyes against the deep blue sky, before he sauntered back toward the prison block. "Whatever you say…"

Acknowledgements

Where to begin with my acknowledgments? I have so many people to thank for making *The Valentine Retreat* the book it is today.

Without doubt I must thank the team at Champagne Book Group—especially my wonderful editor, Lisa Bambrick, for her boundless patience whilst coping with my dodgy editing skills and endless daft questions.

Here in the UK, I need to thank Cornerstones' editor Ellie Leese for her immeasurable input (and her similar patience with my endless daft questions).

I must also thank my Romantic Novelists' Association NWS reader—who to this day remains anonymous—for giving me the belief that this novel had "legs", even in its fledgling form.

Thanks too goes to members of my local writing group—Hanne, Anne and Caroline—who provided invaluable feedback as well as more than a few bright ideas whilst we monopolized a window table of our favorite coffee shop in Salisbury.

Special mention must go to my bestie, Tanya Gibbins, who has read everything I have ever written and is endlessly supportive and positive. Always my go-to sounding board whenever I have an idea, I would not have made it this far without her.

Now, this might sound counter-intuitive, but I also want to thank my family for keeping their noses out. For giving me space. For allowing me the time I needed to sit and type, and delete, and type, and stare at the ceiling, and type, and make a mug of tea, and type some more. For never questioning my determination or my purpose (well, only a few times) and allowing me to reach for my goal. Chris and Charlotte, I love you very much.

The funny thing is how the solitary occupation of writing becomes a total team effort by the time a novel is completed. The journey from first crazy thought to final edit requires support in many forms—and I thank every single person who has given me that. *The Valentine Retreat* is for all of you.

About the Author

Laura Leeson lives in the UK, a stone's throw from Salisbury Cathedral and the ancient site of Stonehenge, surrounded by the rolling green landscape of Wiltshire. A far cry from downtown Los Angeles, but she has always loved everything about the States. Time spent in California twenty years ago sealed the deal and is why her character, Megan, finds herself living on that side of the pond.

Whilst writing, Laura enjoys slotting interesting characters into challenging relationships and tricky circumstances, mostly to see what might happen. She likes to find out if she can blow more than the bl**dy doors off.

In real life, she can usually be found trying (and failing) to do three things at once, and she always, always forgets why she went upstairs.

Laura loves to hear from her readers. You can find and connect with her at the links below.

Website/Blog: www.laurarleeson.home.blog
Facebook: www.facebook.com/LauraRLeeson
Goodreads: www.goodreads.com/Laura_R_Leeson
Instagram: www.instagram.com/Laura_R_Leeson
Pinterest: www.pinterest.co.uk/RachelBarnett07
Twitter: www.twitter.com/Laura_R_Leeson

Thank you for taking the time to read *The Valentine Retreat*. If you enjoyed the story, please tell your friends and leave a review. Reviews support authors and ensure they continue to bring readers books to love and enjoy.

~~~

Now, turn the page for *Retribution*, book 1 in the thrilling and dangerous Donaghey Brothers series by Wendy Million.

AN UNDERCOVER FBI AGENT
TWO DANGEROUS BROTHERS
A DEADLY CHOICE

TURN THE PAGE
FOR A LOOK INSIDE!

Chapter One

The phone in my front pocket vibrates. Checking it is the only thing I want to do right now. I shift in the metal chair and keep my hands clasped on top of the aluminum conference table that has seen better days.

The warehouse is deserted except for the six of us. It's a weird setup, but I learned a long time ago the right questions to ask and the ones to avoid. At least there's a table. This is a negotiation, not a confrontation. The table is important.

My heart thumps a violent rhythm in my chest, but I've gotten used to that too. The erratic heartbeat is my tell, and I'm thankful the people I work with can't hear it, even when it pounds in my ears. I've been well-trained for this double life, at least on the outside.

"Look," I let impatience seep into my voice. "Carys is going to be pissed when she finds out you guys are screwing her over." My first indication this meeting wouldn't be lucrative should have been the lack of heat in the building. It's so cold that each time I speak, I wonder if I'll see my breath. Teddy is too cheap to pay the prices we need to make this deal worthwhile.

"Next time, she comes to the meeting herself or we'll be taking care of business in a different way." The metal of Teddy's gun twinkles at me as he flips his suit jacket with false casualness.

I give him a mild glance and suppress my eye roll. Guys who have this burning desire to whip out their gun as a substitute for their dick piss me off. *You got a gun. Good for you. I have four.* The one up the sleeve of my leather jacket would nail him between the eyes before he even unholstered his archaic piece of crap. It's no wonder he's searching for an arms deal.

"I have a feeling she's not going to want to do any business with you after this stunt." I keep my features neutral. This is a wasted opportunity, and frustration eats at me. "Call me when you're serious about working with us. Maybe she'll still be interested." I nod to the two men who came with me, and they mirror my movements, ready to follow my lead.

"What's she paying you, Kim? I'll double it." Teddy readjusts himself under the table.

As I amble toward the exit, my throat fills with unease. My brain should be engaged in this conversation, but I can't stop thinking about the message on my phone. I call over my shoulder, "You couldn't afford me, Teddy. I'm above your pay grade."

"You got balls of steel." He chuckles when I keep walking. The warehouse is large and has too many of his steel products lying around which doesn't absorb his voice. His voice echoes, drawing my attention even when I'd prefer to ignore him. I'm not sure what he wants with Carys, but I doubt it has anything to do with guns.

Pausing before the exit, I shake my head, half turning back to him, flanked by Carys's two burly men. "I'd take a pussy made of diamonds over balls of steel any day."

Teddy's grin fades, and his chair screeches across the concrete when he stands. The two men with him are like shadows. "You want diamonds? I can arrange that."

"Forget you know my number." I push the emergency exit door, and it pops open. "Unless you have money for the deal."

The door slams behind my last man as we head to our black SUV waiting in the deserted gravel parking lot. The sky is blue-black, and the snow on the ground is melting, creating puddles in the potholes. Spring is on the way, but it isn't here yet. At some point, we'll get another blast of winter.

"What a waste of time." I pull out the phone in my pocket as it vibrates again.

"That Carys?" Jay raises his dark eyebrows as he opens the rear passenger door for me. His close-cropped brown hair is ruffed by a sudden breeze.

"Could be." I duck down, folding my almost six-foot frame into the car, but I don't take the phone out. Why am I being contacted? The FBI programmed the phone with a unique vibration for agency texts. When it went off in the meeting, I worried someone would notice my reaction. Creating suspicion in any of the people I work with could get me killed—shot dead without hesitation.

Dead.

The car jerks forward, and Jay mumbles an apology as I focus on my hands, turning them over.

Dead.

My pocket vibrates again, and this time when I look down at my hands, they're covered in blood.

"Kim?" He tries to catch my gaze in the mirror. "Carys is going to be ticked."

My head snaps up, and I tuck my hands under my thighs, sliding along the black leather, and release a dark chuckle. "I told Carys I didn't think there was any way Teddy was buying from us. He hasn't got enough money, and no use for guns." Carys making me the point person for the deal was a step in the right direction. So, I didn't argue too much.

"He's got lots of use for you." Jay meets my gaze.

"He wouldn't be able to handle me." I ease back into the seat and stare out the window as Chicago zooms by. The skyline is one of the things I love about this city, and dusk brings it to life, the lights dancing across the lake's surface.

"You ever work for a man before?" Jay checks his mirrors.

The new guy beside him, whose name I can't remember, pipes up, "She's too much of a ballbuster to work for a man."

Jay gives him an annoyed look. "Carys will shoot you herself for chirping Kim like that."

"I'm perfectly capable of shooting him," I say, my tone mild. The cityscape outside the window rushes by. I can't stop thinking about my phone, but it's too risky to take it out right now. "Yeah, I've worked for some men. I try to avoid it. They're too preoccupied with their balls."

The new guy laughs, and Jay gives him another sideways glance.

"I can see why." He isn't getting Jay's silent message. Over the seat, he's scanning my dark ponytail secured near the top of my head down to my Lululemon pants. "What are you, anyway? You're like, exotic or something. I can't put my finger on it."

Giving him a cold stare, I say, "Your fingers don't belong anywhere near me." Compared to me and Jay, this kid is as pale as a ghost.

"You're getting fired, man." Jay shakes his head and adjusts his hands on the steering wheel as we merge into heavier traffic. "If you keep talking, you're going to end up in concrete shoes at the bottom of Lake Michigan."

The only bit of color in his face disappears. At least the new guy has the good sense to take Jay's comment seriously. He's probably in his early twenties, a kid looking to make a quick buck. Everything about him reminds me of someone I don't want to remember but can never forget.

"That's not a real thing." His voice quivers.

"They're all real things," Jay says. "You don't mess around

with these people, Paul. The stereotypes, the rumors, the shit you see on TV—most of it is taken from someone's real life."

Ah, a name. Not that I'll need to remember it after the conversation we're having.

The car glides to a stop in front of my four-story brown brick apartment building. The trees lining the street are mature, hanging over the sidewalk and road. The streetlights work, and the front door has a security guard. Not that I need one of those. I chose this neighborhood on purpose. It's not too run-down, but it's not new and shiny either. Carys has offered to let me live with her outside the city. I can't, though. While it might make aspects of the job easier, it would make others infinitely harder.

"I didn't mean anything by my comments." Paul's voice is uncertain.

He isn't as big as Jay and, standing up, he and I are about the same height. I'm maybe ten years older than him, but that gap is massive right now. I've been on this job with Carys for almost a year, but in some ways, it's my whole life.

"You're not cut out for this, Paul. Quit before someone kills you." I'm half out the door when I turn to Jay and say, "Tell Carys I have some personal business. I'll be back in a few days."

"Your brother?" His brown eyes are full of sympathy.

"Yeah." I give a curt nod. "Anniversary of his death."

"I'll let her know."

I slam the door behind me and enter the building, waving to the security guard at the desk. In the elevator, I put my hand over the phone in my pocket. How much time will I have?

At my door, I slide the key in the lock. My steady hands belie my racing heart as I slip inside. I flip all the locks in place and tug the phone from my pocket.

It's been almost six months.

Airport. Two hours.

Glancing at the current time and when the text was sent, I'm pretty sure I can make it. It's going to be tight. Opening the entryway closet, I grab the prepacked bag and then undo the locks on the door.

I disappear into the night.

Chapter Two

Malik likes meeting at the same hotel, same room, every time. It's a mid-level chain in a mid-sized city. Everything about the meeting is constructed so I don't have the run-in we dread. Being undercover and seeing someone from either version of our lives is one of the few things that makes people like me wake up in the middle of the night, covered in sweat, making sure there isn't a bullet lodged in our brain.

When I slip into the hotel room, the scent of stale cigarettes hits my nose. The rooms need to be renovated, but I never question Malik's desire to meet here. This is his area of expertise, not mine. He stops pacing when the door clicks shut behind me. His dark face and eyes soothe my unease.

He scans me from head to toe, assessing. "I wasn't sure you'd be able to make it."

"Your message didn't come at the best time. Carys let me take another meeting today. It was a waste of time though."

"Like the last one," he says, finishing my thought.

I shrug. "It'll come. She's giving me more and more authority."

"So that explains why you're dressed like a ninja supermodel." His smile is half-hearted. "What have you got for me?"

Twisting, I swing my black bag forward until I can dig into the pocket for the latest USB drive. It's full of whatever documents I've managed to get off devices in the office, screenshots of texts and emails, anything that might have a shred of evidence to build a case against Carys. I hold the device between my fingers, flipping it over and over.

With a sigh, I drop it into Malik's open palm. He doesn't say anything. I'm sure he knows. Carys is the kind of woman I like, and gathering information on her doesn't sit well with me. She's not a bad person, but sometimes she does bad things.

"I have some...news," Malik hesitates.

I glance up, trying to catch his attention, but he's not looking at me anymore. "Something I won't like."

"Maybe you will."

"Malik, seriously, you've been my handler for a few years." I let out a huff. "The way you started this conversation tells me I'm not going to be happy. Are they pulling me?"

"Yes." Malik sighs, his shoulders dropping. "Probably."

"I'm getting somewhere. It takes time." I've never been pulled off an assignment before, and it stings more than I expect. Time, that's what I need. She trusts me.

"It's not what you're assuming." He sits on the edge of the double bed. The white duvet cover is too pristine, too pure compared to the rest of the dingy room.

I sit next to him, and he takes my dusty brown hand in his two darker ones. My body relaxes as though it's releasing a giant breath. I've been holding myself in for weeks. Being on high alert is exhausting. Here, with him, I can be me, Kimi. Out there, I'm Kim and keeping my lies straight is like walking a tightrope. One wrong move, and I'm falling to my death.

With a side glance, I appreciate the familiarity of him, his broad shoulders, muscular biceps, and angular, open face. From the first time I arrived at a hotel room to find he replaced my previous handler, we've had an easy, steady relationship.

"For what it's worth, I asked them to keep you on this assignment. You might stay. It depends on whether you're picked or whether we can slot you in easily."

"Picked? Malik, you know I hate riddles. Out with it."

"Are you familiar with the Donaghey family?"

I frown, ticking through the operations I've been part of the last few years. "No," I admit. Something about the name is just out of my grasp. The name spins around my consciousness searching for the last time I heard it.

"Hmm. That's probably good. We couldn't find any direct employment connections even though you grew up outside Boston. You consistently use Kim which makes it easier compared to other undercover agents."

A name close to my own keeps me grounded. Some people need to divorce their normal selves. For me, weaving details is easier than inventing them, then remembering my inventions.

"What about the Donaghey family?" I remove my hand from Malik's to rub his thigh in slow circles.

"Brothers. Mafia in Boston. The head of the organization, Eamon Donaghey, their father, was murdered."

Now my brain latches onto what I saw on TV a while ago in Carys's office. She knew the brothers and liked them. Or she liked one of them. My eyes narrow, trying to remember what she said. Her wording was precise, as though there was more to the story. At the time, I wondered if I should pry, but it hadn't been information I needed for either job.

"The organization is fracturing. Lorcan and Finn are on the cusp of an all-out war."

"And?" How well would Carys know these men? Sometimes connections between people are stronger than they appear.

"The younger brother, Lorcan, has been low-key looking for a female bodyguard to add to his staff."

I freeze and remove my hand from Malik's leg. "They want to undo months of work on my part to make me a *bodyguard*? Are you kidding me? I'm practically the second in command with Carys. This is ridiculous. Off the top of my head, there are at least ten FBI women who could do this."

"Any of those women read, write, and speak Irish Gaelic?" He cocks an eyebrow.

I frown. "They only communicate in Irish?"

Malik's shrug is almost imperceptible while his dark eyes search my face. "Our mole says most top-secret communication happens in Irish Gaelic—emails, verbal conversations, text messages."

Shit. I can see why they'd want to move me. My father, after my older half-brother was killed, developed an obsession with Irish Gaelic. It was all he spoke until his death. I had to learn it.

"So, I guess that answers the *why me* part." I sigh and stand up, crossing to the mini-bar and plucking out a couple of bottles. I pour Malik a whiskey in a coffee cup and pass it to him and then pour one for myself. "Am I getting an introduction? Is there a plan?"

"You're not mad? You're okay with being close to home?" Malik eyes me while he takes a sip of his whiskey.

"I'm not thrilled." I put my own glass to my lips and breathe in the sharp aroma.

"You might be able to slip away and see your mom."

Tension radiates through me at the mention of my mother. On the wall is a painting of a lone boat in the middle of stormy seas. Each time we're in this room, it catches my eye. Something about it reminds me of my mother, or maybe it's me. She's all I have left.

"A plan?" I prompt again.

"We think Carys knows them."

I laugh, the tension easing out of me. The whiskey burns my throat when I take a sip. "Carys knows everyone. But she's not going to broker an introduction. Why would she hand me over or even consider giving me up?"

Malik grins and takes a long drink. "*How* do they know each other?"

"An arms deal makes sense." The conversation with Carys about the brothers refuses to resurface from the caverns of my memory.

"And yet, that's not it. Or at least we don't think so. What's near and dear to the heart of your beloved Carys?"

His tone is teasing, but it still pisses me off. I hate when he pokes my weaknesses like it's a game.

"Kids with cancer," I mumble. Carys funnels a lot of her money into charities which aim to treat or support childhood cancers. Her brother died from a brain tumor when they were in high school. A few months ago, we got drunk and traded dead brother stories. Well, she got drunk. I pretended to be drunk.

"Lorcan also has a soft spot for cancer patients." Malik tips back the rest of his drink and stares into the coffee cup. "There's a cancer fundraiser coming up in Boston, on the cusp of being big, not there yet. We've asked them to highlight children's cancers and breast cancer—that's how his mother died. Lorcan has confirmed he'll attend."

"So, I only have to convince Carys? Fly from Chicago to Boston on a whim?" That's a tall order without raising suspicion.

"Not quite. We've arranged for her to get an invitation. You need to give her a gentle nudge. If Lorcan and Finn do escalate into a full-on war, it'll be ripe for arms deals."

"If she doesn't take the bait?"

"I have no doubt you can be persuasive." He puts his empty glass on the TV stand. "We'll figure out a way to broker a meeting another way if you can't make it work. We have a substantial file on the father but not on the two sons." He nods to the duffle bag in the corner of the room. "I brought some information so you're not going in blind."

"The assignment goal? An arrest? War?" I stare into what's left of my drink, swirling it around.

"No, no war. We want to avoid that. Civilian causalities would be out of control. Both brothers are prone to escalation. An arrest is best if you can get the right information but otherwise, try to keep the situation stable. We'll tackle whatever information you acquire."

"You'll stay my contact?" I glance up at him, worry eating at me. He knows and understands me better than anyone else at the bureau. His replacement would never be good enough.

"I will." Malik smiles.

I move to him, sliding my glass onto the table beside his. "Did you want another?" My voice dips low.

We're almost the same height, and the way I've lingered with my fingertips on the table means we're inches apart. His gaze flicks from my eyes to my lips and back again.

"I'll never say no to you." His tone matches mine.

I shift closer, my chest grazing his. "In case I die tomorrow, I'm going to live for today."

His lips lift into a half smile. "Have I ever told you how much I love your motto?"

"A few times." I take in his dark features under my lashes, enjoying the hunger I see. "What are you waiting for?" I murmur. "Make me feel alive."

It's the only invitation he needs before his lips dip to capture mine. His hand tugs the elastic out of my hair, releasing my long, dark strands. I sigh, pressing my body tight to his, the parts of him that have come to life brushing against mine. We may only do this dance every few months, but I know each step by heart.

Familiar. Easy. Safe.

All the things I usually hate.

Chapter Three

Hot pink. It's not a color I would choose, but it goes well with the darker coloring I inherited from my father. Carys insisted on buying my dress for this function. Convincing her to come was the least of my worries. I had more trouble talking her out of the ridiculous wardrobe choices for me.

"So, Native Barbie, are you enjoying the spectacle?" Carys clutches her champagne flute in her manicured hands.

I give her a sideways glance as I sip from my own glass. "Only *you* could get away with that."

There's a lot of lily-white in me, too, courtesy of my mother. People who need to classify me think I look odd, difficult to pinpoint. My focus skims around the high-ceiling ballroom and catches on the crystal chandelier that lends the majority of the light to where we're standing. I let the fingers of my free hand graze the gun attached to my thigh. For an event that was supposed to be small, it seems to have grown much bigger in the weeks since I met with Malik. Women and men in expensive dresses and tuxes mill around us, chatting in loud voices before wandering off.

"You go write your soul cleansing check yet?"

Carys laughs. "And only *you* could get away with that." Her amber eyes soften when she gazes at me. "How's your dad?"

Still dead.

"Same as always." I give a slight shrug. "The anniversary of Chad's death is hard." Not a lie. At least the emotions aren't, but the details of his death are different for every job. The date, the place, the method of murder are fabrications.

"Well, I hope you and your dad can work out your issues someday. Family is important."

Family. The word echoes around my brain, bumping into memories I keep buried.

Carys flags a waiter to deposit her empty glass and takes another. She signals to me, but I shake my head. "First you insisted on a dress you could move in, and now you won't drink with me. I swear you think someone's lurking around every corner waiting to kill you."

I laugh with her, even though it's not outside the realm of possibility. "You like that I'm prepared."

Carys sighs. "It's true." Her hand nudges a piece of her blonde hair back into its intricate braid. "I'm starting to think Lorcan's not coming. I should have called him and scheduled a meeting. You're right about the territory being ripe for deals if the two of them explode."

"Is it wise to pick a side?"

"Hmm. My side is probably obvious. At least this way it might appear like a genuine coincidence. The charities we support are here, and we happened to run into each other."

I'm about to ask Carys why her side would be clear when I catch sight of a blondish-brown head coming through the open doors of the ballroom. He's dressed in a dark blue suit and a pink tie, not a tux like many of the men. Two men flank him, as tall and broad as the man in the middle, but their suits don't scream money. I tip my head in his direction. "Who's that?"

Carys glances over her shoulder, and her lips curve into a smile. "Speak of the devil."

"Lorcan?" It's him. Malik had photos. They didn't do Lorcan justice. In the flesh, the man is the kind of dangerous, rugged handsome which makes others glance in his direction without realizing they've done it.

"In the flesh," she says as though she can read my mind.

"Have you ever?" I force my focus to Carys. She's fifteen years older than me, which makes her ten years older than Lorcan. Time has been good to her. Well, that and she has a dermatologist and cosmetic surgeon on call.

Carys shakes her head, but her attention lingers on Lorcan. "Being a woman in this business, you have to be careful who you get into bed with—remember that, Kim. A man will get you killed."

"Not all men." My mind strays to Malik.

Carys stares at me before nodding at the bar. "It seems Lorcan's been waylaid by one of the organizers before he got to the bar. I know what he drinks."

She orders three whiskeys and then sashays to where he is talking to a petite blonde who is giddy with nerves or attraction. Either is possible. He is bigger and more intimidating in person. Above his head there might as well be a flashing neon sign that reads *danger*. Tension circulates in the air, surrounding him, enveloping us.

"Lorcan," Carys drawls, allowing her southern accent to pop

out. Her hips sway in a manner she reserves for those she trusts. No one takes a woman seriously in this business if they seem too womanly.

His head whips up at the sound of her voice, and a grin splits his face. He sidesteps the over-eager woman to embrace Carys. "I didn't realize you'd be here. It's been an age."

"A delightful coincidence." She flicks her attention to the other woman before focusing on Lorcan. With a slight bow of deference to Carys, the event organizer wanders off, hands clasped.

While he and Carys chat, I take in his features: the goatee, the slight dimple in his right cheek when he almost smiles, and his hazel eyes which are alight with surprised amusement.

"Who is this bright spot of loveliness behind you?" He nods at me. He searches my face, appraising, but his gaze never travels my body in an assessing way.

"This is Kim." Carys gestures with her hand flung wide. "She's the best at what she does."

As an introduction, I couldn't have hoped for better. The grin on my face is genuine while she slings an arm around my waist in a motherly fashion.

"What's that?" His voice carries a hint of an accent that isn't Bostonian. Of course, I know from the file his parents sent him and his brother to boarding school in Ireland.

"Everything." Carys beams at me.

"That's quite a compliment." Lorcan takes a drink and tilts it in my direction. "What do you think of that?"

"It's not much of an exaggeration."

He chuckles and again his gaze roves over my face as though he's trying to piece me together. My hot pink dress is garnering little attention from him. Should I be pleased or offended?

"You got any mates? I'm looking for someone like you."

Carys tightens her grip on me and sips her whiskey. "She's taken. Keep your mitts off her."

He raises his glass, eyeing me over the top. "People who can be bought aren't for me, Carys. You know that."

She scoffs. "Not true, Lorcan. I *do* know you. I've played this all wrong. I should have told you she was thinking about leaving my organization."

"I *am* terribly unhappy." My gaze connects with Lorcan's, and I offer a mischievous smile.

An answering smile spreads across his face. "That so? Now, Carys, you need to treat *your everything* woman a touch better before someone swoops in and sweeps her away."

"As long as you aren't *the someone*, Lorcan." She glances at me. "I appreciate the effort, but I'm afraid once he's on the hunt, he can't be deterred."

"You make me sound terrible." Amusement pours out of him.

"I used to like you," Carys says. "Finn, on the other hand..."

"...is an acquired taste." Lorcan's grin fades. "One I've gone off recently."

She glances at me and then back to Lorcan. I've seen that look on her face before. She's trying to figure out the best approach.

"Sorry to hear that," I murmur, surprised by the sudden chill in the air.

His lips quirk up. "You wouldn't be sorry if you knew him." He empties his whiskey. "It's been a pleasure, ladies. Thank you for the drink. You know me well, Carys." With a nod to his men, Lorcan drifts into the crowd, leaving me and Carys to finish our drinks on our own.

"Shit." She sighs and taps her glass with a fingernail. "I should have left Finn out of it."

"Can't ask him if he wants a deal without letting him know there's a deal to be done."

"Their organization buys arms, just not from me." Carys purses her lips. "It should be me. It'd be a good time to slip in there. Maybe we can still salvage it later."

"Are you doing that or..."

"If you get a chance to ask, fine by me. Plant a seed, see if it grows."

Lorcan breezes through the crowd with his two burly security guards trailing behind him. He's a small fish in an arms world. Carys does much bigger, more ethically comprised deals than this. She hasn't let me near those yet. If I get out of here tonight with what I want, I'll never see them. I'm going to need to work fast to recapture his attention. His late arrival means there are two hours until this event finishes, and he's cut our conversation short.

"I'll see what I can do."

"You're not one to be charmed," Carys draws out the words, and I think she must be watching Lorcan like me.

I smirk and raise my eyebrows. "Is there a but?"

A smile plays on her lips. "No, I suppose there isn't."

"You've got nothing to worry about," I say. "If I can get him to consider a deal, I will. And, if not, it's been a pleasant evening. We haven't been to an event like this in a while." I knock back the rest of my whiskey and wiggle my glass at her. "Another?"

"No, I have people I want to connect with. Tonight is bigger than I expected."

"I'll be at the bar."

Carys and I move in opposite directions as she heads off to make or solidify her contacts. I sidle up to the bar and place my empty glass to the side. This end of the bar is for standing, but farther down, there are a number of stools with people perched on them, chatting away to each other. The ballroom is vast and airy, though the perfume and cologne circulating are enough to cause an asthma attack. Above the bar, pendulum lights are set low to match the rest of the mood lighting. Most of the charitable events I've attended with Carys have been dimly lit. It must seem too intrusive to ask for money with the brightness turned to full.

I'm waiting for the bartender, wondering how I can slip myself into conversation with Lorcan when a shoulder brushes mine.

"Be a shame for someone as talented as you to be unhappy with your employer," a deep voice says in my ear. His lilting accent is a sound I could get used to. It calls me back to the hours my father spent devouring anything Irish.

He's so close, Lorcan's hazel eyes are piercing in their intensity. The musky scent of his cologne floods my senses, and I'm glad for my training. Cool. Unaffected. "How do you know I'm talented?"

"Carys isn't one for bigging people up who don't deserve it." He turns away to signal the bartender with a finger. "Two whiskeys."

In this business, men are everywhere. But there's something in the curve of his shoulders, the slant of his jaw under the goatee, which makes him familiar. Part of his appeal has nothing to do with appearance and everything to do with the way he carries himself. Confidence seeps out of him, oozing over everything he touches.

The bartender passes the two glasses to us, and I pick mine up with my fingertips, swishing it around, letting the ice clink against the sides.

His back is against the bar railing, and his elbows are on the wood, so he can stare out across the wide expanse of the room. When he shifts toward me, his gaze connects with mine over the rim of his glass. "When are you heading home?"

"Tomorrow afternoon. Carys offered to show me some sites around Boston."

One side of his mouth twitches as though he's holding in his amusement. "Sounds grand."

"Does it?" I avoid looking at him directly, keeping my back to the room.

"Not quite as grand as coming round to mine for a meeting."

"What would we be meeting about?" I peer into my glass, hope rising in me.

"See if one of us can make the other an offer they can't refuse."

"I get offers all the time. I refuse them all." Our little game of cat and mouse amuses me, but I keep my features smooth.

"You never had one from me."

Somehow, I've managed to finish another drink. "I guess we'll see what you've got then. I'm a tough nut to crack."

He places his finished drink onto the bar. "I'm counting on it. Tell Carys to call me."

When I turn around, he and his men are gone.

Out Now!

What's next on your reading list?

Champagne Book Group promises to bring to readers fiction at its finest.

Discover your next
fine read!
http://www.champagnebooks.com/

We are delighted to invite you to receive exclusive rewards. Join our Facebook group for VIP savings, bonus content, early access to new ideas we've cooked up, learn about special events for our readers, and sneak peeks at our fabulous titles.

Join now.
https://www.facebook.com/groups/ChampagneBookClub/

Printed in Great Britain
by Amazon

82052393R00140